Outside, in the deserted alley, she turned to him. Surprised, he gazed down at her, waiting to hear what she wanted to say.

Instead, she pulled him down and kissed him.

There was no hesitation on the sensual movement of her lips on his. The first touch ignited a fire. He tugged her close, body to body, and kissed her back.

Emotions—desire, certainly, but something stronger—flared. He lost track of time, forgot where they were, because everything about her filled up his entire world. He wanted to push her up against the wall and make love to her right then, right there.

When they finally broke apart, each was breathing hard.

"I want you," she said, her forehead resting against his chest.

"I want you too," he replied.

Karen Whiddon started weaving fanciful tales for her younger brothers at the age of eleven. Amid the gorgeous Catskill Mountains, then the majestic Rocky Mountains, she fueled her imagination with the natural beauty surrounding her. Karen now lives in North Texas, writes full-time and volunteers for a boxer dog rescue. She shares her life with her hero of a husband and four to five dogs, depending on if she is fostering. You can email Karen at kwhiddon1@aol.com. Fans can also check out her website, karenwhiddon.com.

Books By Karen Whiddon

Harlequin Nocturne

The Pack Series

Wolf Whisperer
The Wolf Princess
The Wolf Prince
Lone Wolf
The Lost Wolf's Destiny
The Wolf Siren
Shades of the Wolf
Billionaire Wolf
A Hunter Under the Mistletoe (with Addison Fox)
Her Guardian Shifter
The Texas Shifter's Mate

Visit the Author Profile page
at Harlequin.com for more titles.

THE TEXAS SHIFTER'S MATE

KAREN WHIDDON

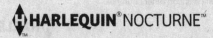

Printed in U.S.A.

Recycling programs
for this product may
not exist in your area.

978-1-335-62946-3

The Texas Shifter's Mate

Printed in U.S.A.

Dear Reader,

I've always, always, always wanted to write a mermaid book. Timing or whatever never worked out and I'm pleased to have been finally able to write my mermaid heroine—and a handsome, wolf shape-shifter hero.

For this story, I returned to Galveston, Texas, a location I've visited many times over the years since my husband's sister lives there. There's a lot of history on this island, and it seemed the perfect place to set a story like this. Creating The Shadow Agency was fun, too, and I'd hoped to write more books featuring this paranormal investigative agency, but it wasn't meant to be.

I hope you enjoy this story. Love, missing women, crazed evil scientists and the ocean—what more can anyone ask for!

Happy reading!

Karen Whiddon

Dedicated to animal rescuers everywhere.

Those who work in the trenches, saving lives, fostering, transporting, evaluating, doing home visits for potential adopters and showing animals love so they can find their forever homes.

I salute you!

Chapter 1

The heavy oak door, scarred and weathered, looked like it had been salvaged from an ancient medieval castle. Above, a simple sign. No words, just a rusted iron bar from which hung two chain links, each half of what had once been whole. There were no lanterns, not even a streetlight to illuminate the shadows. The entrance sat near the end of a dead-end alley, innocuous enough that no soul, human or otherwise, would give it a second glance. Unless of course, one knew what lay inside. No humans ever would.

Shayla Dover had learned of Broken Chains, the bar behind the battered door, from her friend Maddie Kinslow, who happened to be a Shape-shifter. They'd met at a spin class. Maddie had known right away that Shayla wasn't human, and hadn't batted even an eyelash when Shayla had revealed her true nature. Of course, during her first visit with Maddie to Broken Chains, Shayla had learned being a

Mermaid in human form wasn't even the most uncommon of the numerous paranormal beings frequenting the bar.

Broken Chains accepted everyone. The only criteria—no human could ever enter. Vampires, Shape-shifters of all types, as well as Mermaids, Spirits and Wraiths mingled free of judgments, vendettas or complaints. A live band played most nights, rotating groups with enough different genres of music to suit all tastes. The small dance floor stayed crowded, and snagging a table became a matter of luck and skill.

Alcohol was sold, as well as specialty beverages that suited each particular kind of clientele. One sign boasted that Broken Chains carried twenty-seven varieties of blood, especially popular among the Vampire crowd.

Shayla loved the place. For the first time since making the choice to live on land, she felt she had found a spot where she belonged as much as she did under the sea.

While she'd known Houston and areas south of there had to be teeming with non-humans, she hadn't given much thought to the sheer variety of species. In Broken Chains, she'd met numerous Shape-shifters, Vampires and even a Merfolk or two. From Maddie, Shayla had learned how many different kinds of Shape-shifters there actually were. The Wolves, along with their governing body, the Pack, were the most numerous. But there were Lions and Leopards and Bears, even Dragons! Of course, some considered the Merfolk a kind of Shape-shifter, since they could change their beautiful, shimmering fish tail into human legs. None of that mattered once inside Broken Chains. Everyone was welcome.

Tonight, Shayla and Maddie were meeting for drinks after Maddie got off work. Maddie worked as a police dispatcher for Galveston PD and hated her job.

Shayla was self-employed, doing well running an in-

ternet business she'd founded specializing in rare artifacts found under the sea. Though she occasionally loved
to scour the ocean floor, her family also gladly kept her
supplied with inventory. The market for collectors, until
now untapped, seemed limitless. Due to the priceless nature of her inventory, she only needed one or two big sales
per quarter to be prosperous. Most times she did much
better than that. She loved being an entrepreneur, loved
the treasure-hunting aspect of her work and enjoyed the
income her job provided.

Still, despite her success, she found herself often at
loose ends. She'd begun thinking about what other type
of business she might start. Maybe something that Maddie
could help out with, something that would get her friend
away from her stressful dispatcher job.

Shayla arrived a few minutes early, rapping three times
on the door and waiting, before repeating the sequence
with two extra beats tagged on to the end.

The door opened, just as it always did, and Shayla sauntered inside. Instantly, she felt a sense of peace. Funny
thing to consider a bar her home away from home, but
she did.

The band tonight—one of Shayla's favorites—played
a slow bluesy song, a melody that made Shayla want to
twirl and sway. Maybe later, she'd dance. Glancing around
the already crowded bar, she grinned to see Maddie had
snagged a table. Maddie stood, waving to get her attention.
Waving back, Shayla hurried over, happy she'd spent the
time to turn her long black hair into a thick braid.

"Glad you made it early," Maddie said, grinning. Her
curly red hair hung loose around her shoulders. "I've been
here an hour, circling like a hawk on a hunt, until I got
this table."

"I can't believe it's already so crowded." Shayla glanced

around as she pulled out a chair to sit. "It's a Tuesday night. Look at all the tourists in their beachwear. I feel overdressed."

"Pffft." Maddie snorted. "You live to wear those cute little dresses and your heels. Heck, if I had a figure like you, I'd wear them, too."

"A figure like mine?" Shayla eyed her friend's lush curves. "I'm a toothpick. You're the one with the figure. I can barely fill out my B cup."

"I'd rather be skinny." Maddie shrugged. "But isn't that the way of things? We always want what we don't have."

"Maybe." Shayla didn't believe in wasting time pining for things she couldn't have. And truth be told, she considered herself lucky. Just like her mom, she could eat whatever she wanted and never gain weight. She'd also learned long ago never ever to say that to another woman.

"The place is full of Vampires," Maddie grumbled. "Who knew they enjoyed vacationing at the coast?"

Shayla had to grin at the Shifter's disgruntled tone. While they generally got along, Vamps and Shifters had a natural reserve with each other. This despite the fact that Maddie and her were also best friends with Carmen, who happened to be a Vampire. Shayla enjoyed pointing out to each of them that they were the poster children for each giving the other species a fair chance.

"Speaking of Vamps…" Shayla glanced at her watch. "Where's Carmen? She should have been here by now."

"I know." Maddie glanced around. "She's lucky we saved her a chair. It'll be completely full in another hour. This place is becoming more and more popular. Used to be I knew everyone in here. Now, it's about half and half."

"More strangers, more potential new friends. It's all good." Shayla signaled at Johnny, her favorite bartender. He nodded and a minute later brought her a glass of white wine, a nice chardonnay, her usual. Maddie already had her beer, a dark one this time.

The band announced they were taking a break and left the stage. While she'd enjoyed the music, Shayla was glad since this would give her and Maddie an opportunity to talk without having to shout.

"How's things at the job?" Shayla asked. Maddie always had great stories about the drama going on both inside her emergency communication call center and in the outside world. Shayla loved hearing these, since her own work was so solitary.

"I don't know how much longer I can take it there." Maddie's usually ready smile vanished. "With the tourism season upon us, crimes are skyrocketing. They're demanding we work more hours to cover the personnel shortages. All of us are exhausted and miserable and crabby. I almost didn't get off work in time to make it here. One of my coworkers had to cover the last hour for me."

"That sounds rough," Shayla commiserated, even though she had no real frame of reference.

"Oh, it's only just starting. First, we have spring break, which is next week. And then, you know how things are once summer arrives. The island is packed." Shaking her head, Maddie took a slug of beer. "They know I take night classes at Texas A&M Galveston. I can't miss those, but my supervisor told me the job has to come first. I don't think they can force me to work mandatory overtime, but who knows." She sighed. "I've already paid for this semester, so if I don't attend class, I forfeit the fees. I'm working on redoing my resume so I can see what other employment might be available."

This was the first time her friend had mentioned leaving her job. "I could maybe give you some part-time work," Shayla offered. "But it wouldn't pay as much. And it'd be extremely part-time. I don't have a lot extra that I can't do myself. In fact, I was thinking of finding something else to help occupy my time."

Maddie tilted her head, smiling once again. "You're so sweet for offering. Actually, I might take you up on it if they drive me insane enough. Who knows, maybe I can cobble together several part-time jobs and make it work."

"Maybe we can start our own business," Shayla mused. "If you could do anything, what kind of work would you like to do?"

"Private detective work." Maddie didn't even hesitate. "You know my father owned a PI agency. I worked there from the moment I could walk. I hated that Mom sold it after Dad died."

At that moment, Derek, the bass guitarist, and Rory, the lead singer, came over to chat. Their band played Broken Chains several times a month, and the two men continually asked Shayla and Maddie out, alternating which man asked whom. Both women found them amusing, but had no desire to mess up the fun dynamic they currently enjoyed with the band.

The drummer, Waylan, wandered over, reminding the others it was nearly time to get back onstage. Shayla and Maddie shared amused looks as Rory and Derek took their leave, promising to stop back before the evening ended.

"Hey," Maddie said, motioning to Shayla that she should lean in closer. "Don't look now, but the man right behind you has been eating you up with his eyes. Messy, dark blond hair, silver-blue eyes and a body to die for." She sighed. "He's drop-dead gorgeous, so you'd better hope he comes over."

Feigning interest, Shayla nodded, though she didn't turn around. Instead, she took a sip of wine and focused on the band, who were now getting ready to play another song.

* * *

The two women sitting at the table right behind his bar stool were both stunning. When he swiveled around to face the band, they were right there in his line of vision, their beauty a welcome diversion from his dark thoughts. Zach couldn't keep from staring despite his preoccupation with finding Nantha. One of the women's auras revealed her to be Shifter, and he'd bet the other, the slender gorgeous dark-eyed one with long, jet-black hair, was Mermaid. He'd spent enough time with his younger stepsister, Nantha, and her pretty Mermaid friends to recognize that certain glow in their aura.

Pretty didn't even begin to describe this woman. Heart-shaped face, high cheekbones and lithe, graceful movements combined to make her breathtakingly gorgeous. Her long-lashed, emerald eyes spoke of Asian heritage, and the curve of her lush lips revealed her sensuality.

There wasn't a single man in the bar who hadn't noticed her or her redheaded friend. They were both stunning and sexy, in opposite ways.

Any other time, Zach might have approached the table with a flirtatious smile, offering to buy her a drink in exchange for a dance. However, now that he'd agreed to an engagement arranged by his stepfather, his flirting days were over. He could only fervently pray that his fiancée, a Mermaid he hadn't yet met, resembled this one.

Right now though, he had more urgent and pressing business on his mind. Nantha had gone missing and he needed to find her. He'd come to Broken Chains with the intention of asking every Merfolk in the place if they'd seen her.

Might as well start now. He turned, locking gazes with the raven-haired Mermaid. Hounds, he felt the impact of her beauty like a punch in the gut. Even by Mermaid standards, she was gorgeous. Her eyes were the deep green of a stormy sea, framed in long, jet-black lashes. The pout of her lush lips had him longing to claim them with his. Damn. Summoning up all his willpower, he pushed the jolt of attraction aside and stood. Both women eyed him as he took the couple of steps necessary to bring him to their table.

Of course right at that moment, the band started playing again.

"Excuse me," he said loudly, wishing the music could have held off a few more minutes. "Have either of you seen this woman?" He passed the redhead a picture of Nantha, one of his favorite ones of his younger stepsister. He well remembered the day that snapshot had been taken. Nantha had been about to return home after a visit. She'd stood in knee-deep water, filled with the joy the touch of the sea seemed to give its people. The full moon reflected on the calm night sea colored everything with a silver tranquility. She looked young, carefree and happy.

The red-haired Shifter shook her head, handing the photo to her friend.

The Mermaid's long-lashed eyes widened as she accepted the photograph. She inhaled sharply, her gaze rushing from Nantha's image to his. Of course, she immediately recognized that Nantha was Mer. "She's lovely," she finally said, raising her voice to be heard over the music. She passed it back. "But I'm sorry, I haven't seen her. When was she in here last?"

"She hasn't been here. She's too young." He swallowed, trying to contain his disappointment. Of course it wouldn't be that easy. It never was. "Her name is Nantha. She's my sister, and she's missing."

The two women exchanged glances. The red-haired Shifter looked Zach up and down. "What happened to her?" she asked. "How do you know she's missing? She might just be taking a long swim or something."

The Mermaid nodded. "We have been known to disappear under the sea for extended periods of time. I'm guessing, though, that you have more reasons that make you think something has happened to her?"

"I do." He didn't elaborate. Instead, he dragged his gaze away from the attractive pair and began scanning the bar for other Merfolk he could ask.

"I'm Maddie," the Shifter woman said. "And this is my friend Shayla. We'll do our best to help, but I need more information. Such as where and when? What exactly happened to give you reason to be concerned? I work as a police dispatcher, and details are always helpful."

"She has a point," Shayla agreed, noting his hesitation. "I get that you'd planned on walking around asking everyone in here if they'd seen her, but if you really want help finding your sister, we'll need a few details."

Briefly, he considered. She was right, about giving out more information. "She's actually my stepsister," he said. "My mother married her father, Ion. They come on land for weekend visits." Which wasn't at all unusual. Lots of Merfolk enjoyed experiencing life out of the water for short periods of time. Of course, Shayla already would know that.

"So she disappeared here, on Galveston Island?"

"Yes. She and her father were about to return home to the sea, and she went out for a walk. She always loves to walk the edge of Stewart Beach. The far end, near the rocks. Right around sunset, when the crowds thin out." He swallowed hard. "She had a habit of doing this every time before she and Ion went back under the sea. But this time, she didn't come back."

Shayla nodded. "I see. That area is particularly beautiful."

"And dangerous," the redhead interjected. "Especially when the tide comes in."

"Not for a Mermaid." Both Zach and Shayla spoke at the same time. He caught himself exchanging a quick look of recognition with her. He might be Pack, but he'd spent enough time around his sister and stepfather to know more than usual about the Merfolk.

"Zach Cantrell," he said, introducing himself. "Nice to meet you, Shayla and Maddie. Now, if you'll excuse me, I've got to show her picture around and see if anyone might have seen her. It's a long shot, but right now it's all I have."

"Wait, hold on." Maddie pinned him with a fierce stare. "You still haven't given us any usable information."

"Like what?"

"Like, did she have any enemies? Anyone you can think of who might have wanted to do her harm?"

Shayla made a groan of protest.

"Sorry," Maddie said, sounding anything but. "This is necessary. Most people are abducted by someone they know." Waving her hand, she included Zach in her gesture. "This could really help. We need to get all the facts."

To his amazement, he realized she'd taken out a pad of paper and a pen and had begun jotting down notes.

Shayla saw him looking at her friend's paper and shrugged. "She works as a police dispatcher. She's good. If you really want her to help find your sister, give her as much information as you can."

Shifting his weight from foot to foot, he cleared his throat. While he really hadn't planned on having extended conversations with anyone, he figured this actually might be helpful.

"Pull up a chair," Maddie ordered without looking up. "Start at the beginning."

Not sure whether to allow himself to feel hopeful, he

gave in and sat. Some of his dejection must have shown, because to his shock, Shayla reached out and placed her small hand over his.

This simple act of comfort made his throat tighten, even though he had to restrain himself from jerking his hand away. The gesture seemed too intimate somehow, though no doubt this feeling was extremely one-sided, due to the depth of his attraction to her.

When she finally moved, he could breathe again. Aware he couldn't show his relief, he looked anywhere but at her. Despite that, he couldn't help but be far too conscious of her every movement, the way she shifted slightly in her chair, her graceful movement as she reached for her wineglass and took a small sip.

He cleared his throat. "There's not a lot to tell. Nothing unusual happened that weekend. Nantha and her father Ion came ashore Friday afternoon for a weekend visit. As usual, they came ashore on the private beach near my mother's house. I met them at our meeting place, a rocky cove that's roped off and marked as dangerous to humans."

"Which kept it mostly free from both locals and tourists alike," Shayla added. "Most humans are pretty good about obeying the signs."

He nodded. Though it had only been two days, that evening would forever be impressed in his memory. Like always, Ion and Nantha had swum up to the rocks with the sea caressing them. They'd poked their heads up out of the choppy waves, waiting for Zach to give them the all-clear signal before they climbed up on the rocks and changed their form. Sparking lights surrounded them as they did, reflecting on the water like a thousand fireflies. Though the light show was identical to what happened when Zach shape-shifted into Wolf, the combination of water and lights never failed to mesmerize him.

Fifteen years ago, when Zach's mother had announced she was marrying a Merman with a young Mermaid daughter, Zach had been skeptical. But even at ten years old, Zach had seen his mother's grief over his father's passing become a kind of stoic acceptance. She'd been lonely and sad, and she'd directed all her energy into raising her young son. Then she'd met Ion, and her entire world changed.

Zach had recognized the happiness that made her glow when she'd gone someplace with Ion. The fact that she'd actually introduced him to Zach told him the relationship had grown serious. When Ion had wanted to ask her to marry him, he'd asked Zach's permission first. In all the years since, they'd all become a tight-knit, loving family.

Which had now been ripped apart. He swallowed.

"Are you okay?" Shayla asked, making him realize he'd gone silent.

"Sorry. I'm worried about my sister. This isn't at all like her."

"How did a Shifter like you come to have a Mermaid for a sister?" Maddie asked, clearly recognizing his aura.

"My mother, who's also a Shifter, married her father. He's Mer. Nantha was very young."

"What happened to her mother?" This from Shayla.

He forced himself to meet her gaze. When he did, again the flare of attraction zinged through him. "She died shortly after Nantha was born."

"When exactly did your sister vanish?" Maddie asked, pen poised. "How long has she been missing?"

"Sunday. Two days ago."

"She'll be needing to get back to the water soon," Shayla added. "Especially if she spent the weekend on land. One week is about as long as we can go. But I imagine you already know that, right?"

He nodded. "That's one of our main concerns. Though Ion says it's ten days."

Lips pursed, which somehow made her look even sexier, Shayla considered. Finally, she shrugged. "That's pushing it, but he's right. I've made it that long. It wasn't pretty—I got sick. But once I was back in the water, I was fine."

"What have you done so far attempting to locate her?" Maddie asked. "Did you check with the Pack Protectors? I think they might help in a case like this, since she's related by marriage."

Momentarily startled, he stared. Even though he knew she could tell by his aura that he was a Shifter, he hadn't told her what kind of animal he became. While he was Wolf, and definitely part of the Pack, he could just as well have been another species entirely.

However, if this helped with finding his sister, he saw no problem with breaking a few rules. "Yes, I've already enlisted the help of the Pack Protectors. They promised to let me know if they heard anything about a missing Mermaid." He grimaced. "I have to say, they didn't seem really concerned."

"They've probably got more pressing Pack business," Maddie said, her tone commiserating. "But at least you got the word out with them."

"True. I really wish there was some sort of investigative agency where supernatural beings could turn to for help, besides the Pack Protectors." He took a deep breath, willing himself to sound calm rather than desperate. "I've done all I could think of on land. And since I'm not a Merman, I have to believe my stepfather is conducting a thorough search under the water. I'm trying really hard not to think about the horrible things that might have happened to a naïve and sweet young woman like my sister. I just wish I could hire someone to look for her. Someone who could travel under the sea."

Shayla went very still. She and Maddie exchanged a glance.

The two women exchanged another glance.

"That might be possible," Shayla began, her voice low and serious.

"It just might," Maddie agreed, looking at him. "But Shayla and I were just talking about starting up our own private investigative agency. It's been a lifelong dream of mine." When she paused, Shayla took over.

"Maddie's family used to run one. She got her feet wet, so to speak, working for her father. Maybe you could be our first customer." She grimaced. "I guess it depends how desperate you are. While she knows her way around the business, I have zero experience. But I'm Mer, and can search underwater."

Looking into her emerald green eyes, he didn't even hesitate. "Yes. I'm in. Find my sister."

Shayla shook her head. "Don't you even want to know what we charge?"

Though he wanted to say he didn't care what it cost, as long as they were successful, he knew better. "I'm sure it will be reasonable. Just get me the details as soon as possible. Of course, I'll also pay any expenses incurred in the search." He couldn't believe his luck. Having another Mermaid hunt for his sister beneath the sea, and a Shifter who could help with the on-land search, was more than he'd hoped for. He glanced at his watch, jiggling his leg in impatience. "The sooner you can get started on finding her, the better."

"We'll need you to sign a contract," Shayla said smoothly. "We'll need to get that document drawn up. Can you meet us back here tomorrow night around eight?"

"Definitely." He pushed to his feet. "Finally, I feel like I'm doing something constructive. I'll see you ladies tomorrow." Bracing himself, he looked at Shayla first and held out his hand.

When she took it, an electric shock rushed from his fingers up his arm. Her eyes widened, letting him know she likely felt it, too. The way she jerked her hand free confirmed it. So it wasn't just one-sided. Interesting.

Curious to see what would happen, he turned to Maddie; they also shook. Nothing happened. Absolutely nothing. He wasn't sure whether to be relieved or worried.

"Until we have the paperwork signed, please consider this a handshake agreement," he said. "That way, you can get to work immediately."

"We will," Shayla replied. "We'll do our best to find her."

"Thank you." He felt like a bit of the weight had been lifted from his shoulders. Even if they were totally inexperienced, having a Mermaid assisting was huge. At least he was no longer searching alone. "I appreciate your help more than you know."

"Do you mind leaving the photo with us?" Shayla asked. "We can show it around. I assume you have another copy?"

"I can print one." He handed it over. "I'll see you tomorrow night." He left the bar, feeling more hopeful than he had since Sunday night.

Chapter 2

Shayla watched him go, her fingers and arm still tingling. Damned if there wasn't something about that man. "Now we've done it," she told Maddie. "We've got to make this work. That man is pinning his last hope on us."

"And rightly so." Maddie's confidence made Shayla smile. "I'm a damn good police dispatcher, though I'm ready to do something else. A paranormal private investigation agency would be perfect, especially since I grew up with one, even though my family dealt with humans. I know the ins and outs of human law enforcement in this city. Plus, I have contacts. All of that's got to count for something, right?"

Shayla nodded. "It's interesting that I just said I wouldn't mind finding something else to occupy my time. I'll need to do some research. I know next to nothing about private investigators. We need to look into rates so we know what to charge. Do we need to get licensed?"

"Only if we plan on working with humans." Maddie grinned. "Since we don't, I think we'll be okay without one."

"True." Shayla grinned back. "We're also going to need a name. Something catchy."

"I've got that covered. I already know what we'll call ourselves," Maddie said. "Perfect for a paranormal private investigation firm." She gave a dramatic pause.

Crossing her arms, Shayla waited her out.

Finally, Maddie made her pronouncement. "We'll call ourselves the Shadow Agency. Since so many of us operate in the Shadows."

"I like that," a sultry voice said. Carmen Vargas had come up to their table unnoticed. It was one of the more unnerving skills Vampires had. She pulled out a seat and smiled at them. "Especially since Shadows are a huge part of my life. Even more so than yours." With her blond, spiky short hair and bright blue eyes, Carmen looked like anything but the Vampire she was. "So what exactly are you two up to now?"

Maddie told her. "And we already have our first client."

"I want in." Carmen leaned forward, her long silver earrings catching and reflecting the dim light. "Who better to work in the Shadows than a Vamp?"

Shayla considered her. "What about your job?" Carmen worked nights as a government researcher and scientist.

"It won't be a problem. I set my own hours. I'd love to help you two get this business off the ground."

Maddie nodded. "We just came up with the idea a few minutes ago. But if Shayla agrees, I think the three of us would make great partners."

"Yes." Shayla's answer came immediately. "Let's talk specifics."

Over the next several hours, with Maddie taking notes,

they hammered out all the details they could think of for their new business, the Shadow Agency. Since they wouldn't be dealing with humans at all, they decided not to incorporate or worry about insurance. Shifters, Merfolk and Vampires weren't the type to sue if something went wrong—they'd just get even.

"We need to decide on rates," Maddie said next. "Since we'll be splitting the payment three ways."

"Not necessarily," Shayla said. "I think the initial fee should go to the company. Each of us will be paid by the company depending on how much work we put in to each case. For example, this missing Mermaid. If I do a lot of underwater investigating, then I would bill the Shadow Agency for my time. Ditto on any time either of you devote to it. All of our payments come from the company rather than the client."

"That makes sense." Carmen flashed her white teeth in a smile. "I think this calls for another round of drinks." She signaled Johnny, who dipped his head in acknowledgment.

"I think we need to get busy," Maddie started to protest. "Time matters when someone has been abducted."

"True," Carmen agreed. "But Shayla can't exactly jump into the ocean right now, so it's going to have to wait until morning."

Maddie looked from one to the other. "One more drink," she finally agreed. "And then I want to go home and get started on the computer at least. I'll start calling my contacts in the morning."

"What are you drinking?" Shayla asked. Broken Chains kept a wide variety of exotic blood for its Vampire clientele, along with usual bar beverages, both alcoholic and non.

"This is European Farmer," Carmen said, draining her wineglass. "First time I've tried it. Pretty good, too."

Shayla shuddered. "I'll just stick with my wine," she told her friends.

"Me, too." Maddie raised her nearly empty glass. "Beer is better than blood, at least for me."

"I beg to differ." When she took another sip, Carmen deliberately flashed her fangs. As she'd known it would, this made the other two laugh.

Though Maddie had to be at work the next morning, the three of them ended up staying until last call. Shayla had switched from alcohol to seawater, though Maddie had continued to drink beer. She claimed her Shifter metabolism gave her a higher tolerance. This seemed true, since in all the time Shayla had known her, she'd never seen Maddie even tipsy.

Carmen stood, drawing several men's eyes. Tall and slender, her vivid good looks matched her personality. No one, upon first meeting her, ever suspected her to be a Vampire. She delighted in this and exploited it whenever she could.

"I'll walk you two out," Carmen said, showing her teeth. Due to the obscure location of Broken Chains, they had to walk through some sketchy areas of Galveston before they could even catch sight of a cab. And Shayla refused to set foot on the bus. Something about going around the island driven by a complete stranger while packed into a bus with other total strangers made her entire body feel out of tune. Plus, the buses stopped running at eleven thirty. Since tourist season had started, there would be tons of cabs the closer they got to Broadway.

Shayla and Maddie nodded. Carmen knew how much they appreciated her help. More than once they'd been accosted by a human male with bad intent. Though Shayla had taken to carrying a pistol with her, using it would draw more attention than she wanted to deal with. Ditto with Maddie shape-shifting into a Wolf.

Carmen, on the other hand, had no objection to getting a little fresh blood if she had to. Self-defense, she called it. She never took enough to mortally wound anyone, just to weaken them. She'd explained to her friends that not everyone bitten by her would automatically become a Vampire. She had to consciously choose that path, releasing an enzyme when she bit. So far, she'd never made another Vampire. She claimed she wasn't sure if she ever would.

Which explained why there weren't a lot more Vampires running around Houston and areas south of there.

Of the three of them, naturally Carmen felt most at home with the dark alleys and empty warehouses. She glided through the shadows, making Shayla realize her friend was a perfect fit for the Shadow Agency. They each had their own set of skills to bring to the table.

Maddie strode along confidently, too. Only Shayla felt off. Not exactly in the moment, somehow. She was conscious of the distant pull of the harbor and the need to soon slip into the water. Land was fun, but it never would be her true home.

Despite the late hour, the other two women were still energized with excitement. Maddie wanted to get started searching immediately and Shayla agreed with her. Carmen, on the other hand, seemed more focused on getting their business up and running. There were, after all, a hundred things that needed to be done. Flyers and business cards made and printed. A mission statement written. Rates and fees for various services agreed upon. She and Maddie chatted back and forth, assigned each other numerous tasks, though Maddie clearly was itching to leave and get busy. Shayla listened, still feeling a bit detached. She wanted to focus on the case at hand first, even though, of the three of them, she had more spare time. Carmen and Maddie, each with their jobs and other activities, would have to parcel out slots of time for this new venture. Maddie also let them know she'd decided to wait before quitting her job, at least until she could be certain her salary would be enough. She had bills to pay.

Since both Shayla and Carmen could set their own hours, neither would be impacted as severely as Maddie if the Shadow Agency failed.

"But it won't," Carmen declared, her sultry voice ringing with certainty. "Because we've found a niche with a need. As long as we provide good customer service and fulfill that need, we're a shoo-in for success."

Shayla nodded, still lost in her thoughts. Maddie noticed.

"You're awfully quiet." She elbowed Shayla in the side. "What's wrong?"

"I can't stop thinking about that poor missing Mermaid," Shayla admitted. "Nantha. She's young. The young ones are often overconfident and reckless. I have a feeling that there's a lot more to this story than Zach realizes."

"Or maybe more than he's letting on," Maddie interjected.

"No, that wouldn't make sense," Shayla argued. "His number one priority is finding his sister. Why would he hide anything, especially if it might be helpful?"

"True," Carmen said thoughtfully. "I admire the way you're so focused on this case."

"She's also pretty focused on him," Maddie pointed out.

Carmen's brows rose. "Really?" she drawled. "I'm guessing he must be easy on the eyes then. So tell me, Shayla. Was he sexy?"

Maddie laughed. Shayla blushed. "Maybe," she allowed. "He's Shifter. I'd definitely call him hot. Tall, dark blond hair cut short in one of those deliberately messy styles and light gray eyes. Rugged features, which match his muscles." She stopped when she realized both her friends were staring at her.

"What?" she asked, her face heating. "You asked if he was sexy. I was just describing him for you."

The other two women broke out laughing.

"If *you* think he's sexy, then he must be to die for," Carmen teased. "You hardly even notice when I try to put some really gorgeous Vampire men in front of you."

"Same here," Maddie interjected. "I've made it a habit to have a few of my unattached Shifter friends stop by our table over the last few months, and you didn't react to any of them."

Shayla's blush had become an outright burn. "Well, maybe that's because this one is different," she said, flustered.

"Is he now?" In true Carmen fashion, the Vamp wasn't going to let this go. "Interesting. Very interesting indeed."

"I agree." Maddie and Carmen exchanged looks. "Sounds like that's settled then," Maddie said. She seemed so satisfied. If she'd been a feline Shifter she would have purred.

Confused, Shayla glanced from one to the other. Her two best friends appeared to find this massively amusing, whatever *this* might be. Finally, she just had to ask.

"What's settled?"

"You called dibs!" Both Maddie and Carmen spoke at once, grinning from ear to ear. "Finally. We're so happy for you. It's about time." They high-fived.

Shayla opened her mouth to protest and then closed it. She could tell the more she spoke, the deeper a hole she'd dig. Let them think what they wanted. Zach Cantrell was attractive. She was female, so of course she'd noticed. End of story. Her friends knew better than anyone that she had no intentions of getting involved with a man right now. Not for a long, long time, if ever. Her fiancé had died and she never wanted to feel that kind of pain again.

Later that night, once she'd let herself into her house, she went out on the back deck, the side that overlooked the water. The sounds of the waves lapping up against the shore always comforted her and tonight was no exception.

When she'd first made the impulsive, heartbroken decision to abandon the sea for land, she'd gone upstate, to a small town between Houston and Dallas. The town sat near a large, freshwater lake. She hadn't realized lakes wouldn't work the same as the sea, and it had taken her becoming seriously ill for her to understand she'd need to live close to the ocean. So she'd moved to Galveston Island. She'd rented for six months, just long enough to see if she liked it. She did.

Her business procuring and selling rare artifacts found on the ocean floor made more than enough money for her to purchase a single-family home right on the water—a steal at less than a million dollars. From her house, she could not only see the water, but swim in it from her own small, private beach. This brought her peace and no shortage of happiness. And since the house came with a small boat slip, whenever she needed to go under the sea, she simply took the boat out and anchored it before letting her tail grow back.

Perfect solution. She'd truly come to love Galveston Island, even though in the spring and summer it became crowded with tourists. For her, it was the perfect compromise between her new life on land and her old one under the sea.

Maddie lived on the island too, though farther inland, close to The Strand. She shared a small apartment with another woman, also a Shifter. As for Carmen, when anyone asked where she resided, she simply answered in a warning tone that they didn't really want to know. Shayla assumed that meant a cemetery crypt, but who knew? These days, the Vamps had gotten away from their traditional dwellings. It could be entirely possible that Carmen might have a luxury house or condo near the bay. She had that well-groomed look that money brought.

The next morning, after her breakfast of kippers and eggs, Shayla went out in her boat. Her body had already begun to let her know she'd stayed away from her natural habitat too long, and, even though Zach Cantrell hadn't signed a contract yet, she planned to do some investigating while she was under the water. While she didn't know Ion or his missing daughter, Nantha—just like on land, the Merfolk had numerous cities with thousands of residents—she could still ask around. The news that a Mermaid had gone missing would travel like a tidal wave among her people. For all she knew, it might already have.

The weather couldn't have been more perfect. Overcast and slightly chilly, the steady mist that fell ensured she'd have privacy on her swim. She motored past Stewart Park, the beach where most of the tourists swam in the late spring and early summer. Since it was late March, a few weeks after spring break, she knew the beach would be mostly deserted, and it was.

She moored her boat about two hundred yards out, in the area where she'd once seen someone conducting a scuba diving class. Dropping her anchor, she slipped out of her raincoat and shirt, leaving only her bikini top. Brightly colored swimsuit tops had become popular among Mermaids, especially since so many of them enjoyed spending time appearing human. With the sea calling her, she slipped over the edge of the boat, beginning the change from legs to tail as soon as her skin hit the icy water.

The first shock of the cold had her sucking in her breath, but then as she slipped under the waves, her Mermaid nature took over, joyfully reuniting with her still-beloved sea. In her grief after losing her fiancé Richard, she'd had to forgive the very nature of the thing that was part of her essence. The marriage had been arranged, true, but the two of them had hit it off immediately, minutes into their first meeting. Sometimes, she'd thought, you meet someone and you just *know*. They'd both felt that way.

The wedding would unite two separate kingdoms. The celebrations had started immediately. Though they'd met several times in the weeks that followed, they hadn't yet gotten around to discussing where they would live. Even though she'd known she'd have to move to his kingdom where he would someday rule, she'd been so blinded by love that it hadn't mattered.

The wedding plans had gone into full gear. It would be an elaborate ceremony with dignitaries attending from seas all over the world. Her dress had been chosen and fitted, the sea anemones ordered and the invitations mailed out.

And then everything had changed in the flip of a fin. Richard had been out celebrating with his friends. He'd been drinking, and was clearly inebriated when he'd run into the massive great white shark in an isolated area.

Shayla often hoped the substantial amount of alcohol meant he hadn't suffered as much pain.

The shark had later been hunted down and killed, far too late.

The kingdoms had also been stunned. His family went into mourning. Her family did, as well. As for Shayla, her grief turned into rage. She'd gone crazy, acting out, hurting the ones who'd only sought to comfort her. At least

as long as she filled herself with fury, she had no room
for the pain.

But once this had burned through her, she felt hollow
and empty. She became a shadow of her former self, taking comfort in the gray numbness, glad she couldn't seem
to remember how to think, how to feel.

She'd sworn off the sea and tried to turn her back on
the ocean. Coming ashore on South Padre Island, she'd
headed north, inland, hoping to put as much distance between herself and the water as she could. She'd even managed to convince herself the tales of a Mermaid needing
to be around water were old wives' tales without a single
kernel of truth in them.

Now she knew better. She needed the sea as much as
she needed air to breathe when she was in her human form.

For its part, the ocean recognized her, too. Just like the
land, the sea was a living, breathing organism, and as such,
the instant she touched its surface, Shayla became an integral part of it. Joy flooded through her, joy and wonder
and a tiny bit of aching grief that she pushed away.

Time to swim. She dove under. As usual, a few minutes
passed before her eyes adjusted to the murky depths, but
as she swam away from land, gradually going deeper, the
entire seascape changed.

Use of sonar by humans to discover shipwrecks had
made life more difficult for the Merfolk to keep their cities hidden. But in the deeper parts of the ocean, there were
mountains and valleys, just as there were on land, and it
was in those valleys where their civilizations had grown.
In all of the history of humans, there had only been a few
documented instances of them being able to travel so deep,
though they'd started using unmanned probes, which Merfolk had taken to destroying if one came too close.

Shayla would have to swim for at least an hour to reach

her former home. She'd have to assume that Ion and Nantha had come from the same city, as it was closest to the Gulf coastline of the southern United States and Mexico. Though there were several other possibilities, most farther south, though she knew of at least one settlement northeast near Florida.

In her search for the missing Mermaid, her family's home seemed like the perfect place to start.

During the long swim, several sea creatures came to say hello. Fish of all kinds, small schools of striped bass, winter flounders, shad and drums, and so many others she stopped trying to identify them. Dolphins, a huge eel and then some sharks, including one ancient great white shark that she carefully avoided. Most times the sharks left Merfolk alone, as they recognized them as fish too large to be taken without a fight. In Richard's instance, he'd cut himself on some coral. Drunk, disoriented and bleeding, he'd been easy prey for a huge shark.

Pain knifed through her. No. She wouldn't think of this. Not today. Again, she focused on her surroundings and kinder, gentler creatures. A small group of lined seahorses swam up and gently kissed her before swimming away in search of food. Several species of whale that usually swam just a bit farther south of here surrounded her, vocalizing in the deep peaceful tones of their kind. The sound resonated, echoing off the ocean itself, filling Shayla with peace, easing the last lingering remnants of her grief.

This would always be her true home. On land, she occasionally managed to forget how much she loved the underwater world. Once here, she wondered how she ever stayed away.

Finally, she reached the outskirts of her home, a city known among her people as Coral. She swam under a natural rock archway, and as usual, the first glimpse of Coral had her heart skipping a beat.

The city glowed softly, appearing as if it had been constructed from the most precious essence of oysters, the pearl. Muted white, intermingled with bright flashes of color from the live coral gardens, from a distance her home had a mysterious, ancient air. She could only imagine what the humans would make of it if they happened to send an undetected probe close enough to photograph it.

The nearer she drew, the more the place vibrated with life. Fish as bright as the deep-water coral swam up to greet her, escorting her around the protective shield and into one of several unmarked entrances.

Inside, the city teemed with life. Merfolk, as graceful as the fish, swam in the streets, going about their daily lives. Noticing her, several greeted her and waved, others shouted hello, the sound traveling as waves through the water, tickling her skin. This made her smile. These days, sometimes she could come home and forget about her past pain.

She went directly to her parents' house, a large free-form structure made of cobalt glass and green coral, shot through with swirling silver accents. Like all of the buildings here in Coral, the shape and color complemented the sea that surrounded them. Her family's home was larger than the others, due to their royal status. Only the palace, where her brother now resided as king, was bigger and more ornate.

Shayla swam to the door, opening it and going inside without even knocking. Now that her parents were retired from ruling, they occupied their time with various other activities, sometimes together, more often separate. It was fifty-fifty whether she'd even find them at home.

Inside, she headed directly for the kitchen. When her

mother saw her, she cried out and swam to give Shayla a hug. "You just barely caught me," she said. "I was about to leave for afternoon class."

On alternate days, her mother, Blythe, taught young Merfolk the art of preparing fish. Chef Blythe, the kids called her. After acting as a wise queen for several decades, Blythe had been glad to rid herself of her crown and scepter. Most days, she preferred a more casual style, unless she was teaching a cooking class. She wore her long, inky hair up in a tightly wound bun these days.

"Will you be here later today?" Blythe asked, releasing her.

Though Shayla knew her mom would be disappointed, she told her she couldn't stay too long. "I'm actually working," she said.

"On finding artifacts?" Blythe waved her hand in the general direction of the study. "I'm pretty sure your father has several in there waiting for you to pick up."

"I'll grab them before I head back," Shayla said. "I'm actually looking for a missing Mermaid."

"What?" For a second, Queen Blythe returned. Her mother straightened, lifting her chin and fixing Shayla with a no-nonsense stare. "Explain."

As succinctly as possible, Shayla did. When she'd finished, Blythe frowned. "And you say her father's name is Ion? The name sounds familiar, though I can't place it."

"If you do, or if you hear any information about Nantha, will you give me a call?" Shayla asked.

"I sure will." Blythe returned her attention to what she'd been doing when Shayla arrived—packing cooking supplies into a tote. "Right now, though, I've got to run."

"Where's Dad?" Shayla asked. "Please tell me he's not up at the castle pestering Merc again."

"He's not. Your brother banned him." Blythe smiled,

since they both knew such a ban wasn't really possible. A sitting king couldn't forbid a former ruler from visiting the castle. Nor would he really want to. "Since your father had so much difficulty with retirement, he's gone back to fishing a lot. I tried to get him to volunteer at guppy school, but he refused. Whatever. At least he seems happy."

"As long as he continues to look for inventory for me, that's awesome," Shayla said, even though no one had asked her permission. "He finds the best stuff."

"You know he and your brother are in a competition to see who can find the most valuable artifact, don't you?"

Intrigued, Shayla sat on one of the bar stools. Made of coral and glass, they perfectly complemented the stone countertop. "That's actually pretty awesome," she said.

"It's good for you, isn't it?" Blythe hefted her tote and squared her shoulders. "Who knew humans would pay so dearly for such things?" She smiled, hugging Shayla once more, quickly this time. "I'm sorry I can't stay and visit, but you're welcome to come with me and watch the class."

"I would," Shayla said. "But I'd planned on going around and seeing if anyone near here has ever heard of Nantha. I wish I'd thought to ask where her family lived. I figure they're probably from this city, but I have no idea which part." And since there were thousands of Merfolk living in Coral, she'd need to narrow it down quite a bit."

"Nantha is an uncommon name," Blythe mused thoughtfully. "I'll ask around, too, and let you know if I hear anything."

"That'd be great."

"When will you be back?" Blythe asked as she swam toward the front door with Shayla right behind her. Despite being a retired queen, and underwater renowned chef, she'd kept her slender figure. Sometimes when she and Shayla went out together, they were mistaken for sisters.

Not a hint of gray touched Blythe's dark hair, and her face still appeared free of lines or wrinkles. Shayla hoped she'd be as fortunate when she became her mother's age.

"I'm not sure," Shayla admitted. "But since I plan to aggressively work this case, I imagine it will be sooner rather than later."

Blythe cocked her head, studying her daughter. "You look happy," she mused. "Happier than you've been in a long time. I think this new business venture might be agreeing with you."

Immediately, Shayla thought of Zach. Her entire body heated. Glad her mother couldn't see, she nodded. "I think so, too."

With a wave, Blythe swam off. Shayla wandered around the house for a moment, peeking into the study to see what her father had found, before she left to go canvass the part of town closest to her parents' home. She figured it couldn't hurt, though she knew she'd do better once she learned where exactly in Coral Ion and his daughter lived.

Chapter 3

For the next two hours, Shayla traveled up and down the busy streets, wearing her long, dark hair up in a tight bun in hopes of disguising herself. She hoped no one would stop her, wanting to talk about Richard's death or asking her where she'd been. The harder she made it to recognize her, the better her ability to move about freely.

She wasn't sure, but maybe so much time had passed that people didn't recognize her. No one even gave her a second look as she made her rounds, stopping into cafés and bakeries, shops and drugstores, asking everyone she met if they'd heard anything about a missing Mermaid called Nantha. If anyone who recognized her was surprised to see Princess Shayla, back home in Coral, they didn't show it. She was greeted with enthusiasm from everyone, and by now it seemed they felt enough time had passed that they no longer offered her their condolences. Maybe they believed the reminder would only make her sad. Since she tried not to think about Richard or the void he'd left in her life, she felt relieved.

As for Nantha, no one had heard anything, nor did the name sound familiar. Which meant Zach's stepsister hadn't been connected in any way to the royal family, close or extended. That left three other quadrants of the city yet to be explored. This search could take several days, as Coral was a good size.

Shayla made a mental note to use the photo of the girl she'd gotten from Zach and make up some laminated posters to place around town. That and prepare a list of questions to ask him once he'd signed the contract, starting with exactly where the missing Mermaid had lived and where she'd gone to school, and if she'd had a job. Shayla needed to speak with her friends, find out if Nantha had a serious boyfriend or if she'd had any man or girlfriend trouble.

Though she wanted to speak to her father before heading back to Galveston, she had no way of knowing where exactly in the vast ocean he'd decided to go fishing. Briefly, she entertained the idea of visiting the castle and saying hello to her brother, but with all the court protocol, she decided to skip it this time.

Which meant this trip had accomplished nothing. Mentally chastising herself, Shayla got ready for the long swim home. She stopped by her parents' house once more to pick up the three artifacts her father had found. Bundling them into her backpack, she swam away. Though she hadn't had any success, she'd been operating on very little information. At least now, she felt better prepared for the meeting tonight at Broken Chains. Once Zach had signed the contract and answered her questions, she'd be better able to spring into action and help find his stepsister.

All the way home, she kept an eye out for great white sharks. Luckily, she didn't encounter any. Though usually the vivid sea life relaxed her, she felt uneasy. Uncomfortable in her own skin, especially her Mermaid tail. The relative quietness of her swim home did little to distract her from thinking about Zach. Though she'd never admit it to her friends—heck, she could barely admit it to herself—something about him drew her. Mostly his raw sexual appeal. After all, it had been years since she'd opened her body to a man.

When she finally reached her boat again, Shayla pushed off her exhaustion, and she swam close. Reaching up, she grabbed hold of the back step and pulled only her upper body out of the water. Shoulders and neck, nothing more. A quick look around to ensure there weren't any witnesses, and she initiated the change from fish tail to human legs keeping that part of herself hidden beneath the waves. Sometimes this could be painful, especially after a long swim like she'd had today.

At least the exercise helped her nerves. Though her legs were weak, she wobbled up her pier after securing her boat, glad her neighbors paid little attention to her.

Once she got inside her house, she took a hot shower and prepared herself a meal. Though normally she relished the quietness of living alone, tonight she felt restless, even lonely. She didn't like that. She hadn't felt that way in a long time.

To keep herself busy, she decided to clean up the things her father had found for her so she could list them on her website for sale. They were really great artifacts. One of them, a remarkably intact little treasure chest most likely from a sunken ship, contained ancient gold coins and an assortment of brightly colored gemstones. She'd most likely sell them separately, though she might offer them up together and see if she had any takers.

This alone would fetch a pretty penny. The other two

things—excellent finds on their own—would also sell quickly. Good, because she had a hunch she'd have to finance the Shadow Agency until it got up and running. Which might actually be a while. Though Zach, as her first client, would help pay some of the expenses, his bill wouldn't be enough to support them for too long.

Zach. She thought of his tall, powerful body. Muscular and rugged, everything about him seemed the opposite of Mermen, who were, as a general rule, trim and slender. Zach wore his masculinity like a cloak, and his confidence beckoned to her. Zach! There he was again, intruding into her peaceful afternoon. This first case felt more like helping a friend than a job, despite the fact that she'd never met Zach before. Except tonight they'd be signing a contract and money would change hands. How much, Shayla had no idea. Maddie would be handling the amount of their fee, promising it would be reasonable and in keeping with what other people charged.

Since no one knew, Maddie had promised to research what kind of rates private investigation firms charged and type up a handy guide for each of them. Carmen had said something about finding them office space, which could become really interesting since no one even knew where Carmen lived or how her taste ran in buildings. Shayla had to wonder what kind of space the Vampire would consider normal for a business such as theirs.

Of the three, only Shayla had begun the physical investigative part of things. Maddie had scoured the internet and reached out to her contacts, while Carmen had asked questions down near the waterfront. Of course, Shayla was the only one able to explore under the sea. Once the contract had been signed, she'd also go to the Neptune Pod, which was the Merfolk equivalent of the Shifter Pack Protectors. She had no doubt Nantha's father would have already started the process of beginning an investigation, but it couldn't hurt to let them know someone else was actively searching, as well. Especially a royal princess.

Though worry still made his chest tight, at least now Zach felt a renewed sense of hope. Running into the two women at Broken Chains had been the luckiest thing to happen to him in years. As one day turned into two without word from his sister, desperation had set in. Now, just because he'd made an impulsive decision to stop in the bar for a drink, he'd have help. He definitely didn't mind paying for assistance, because with Ion gone under the sea and his mother an emotional wreck, he'd never felt so alone and powerless.

Especially since he couldn't shake the feeling of guilt. He'd promised Nantha he'd look after her while she was on land. And somehow, he'd let her down. He had no idea what might have happened to her.

A thousand scenarios, each more horrible than the last, drifted through his head at night when he closed his eyes and attempted to sleep. Truthfully, he watched way too many crime dramas on TV. The story lines filled his head with dark and disastrous possibilities, things that wouldn't even have occurred to him if he hadn't seen the programs and realized what awful acts humans were capable of. He hoped nothing like that had happened to his sister.

Instead, he kept busy searching. The Monday after she'd disappeared, he'd called in sick to work. Tuesday, the same thing. Wednesday, he showed up, if only to put in to take the rest of the week off as personal vacation days. At the last moment, he'd changed that to taking a two-week long vacation. No one could argue since Zach hadn't taken any actual time off in close to three years.

Because sleeping brought nightmares, he fueled himself with caffeine and tried to stay awake as much as possible. He'd even done a quick shape-shift into his Wolf self in order to search the area around his mother's house by scent. Despite the incredible ability of his Wolf nose, he'd turned up nothing.

Every waking moment since Sunday night, he'd spent searching or thinking about where Nantha could be. He longed for a clue, a hint, anyone catching a glimpse of a tall, willowy blonde with bright blue eyes. He'd done a thorough search of the western area of Galveston Island, close to where she'd disappeared. After that, he'd haunted all the touristy areas, including the beaches, before moving on to other residential neighborhoods.

Despite this, he'd turned up nothing. Absolutely, freaking, nothing. He wished he could have taken the extra step of filing a missing person report with the human police, but Merfolk didn't have human identity. He'd spoken with the Pack Protectors instead, even though they worked with Shifters rather than Mermaids. They'd treated him kindly, if dismissively, but at least they knew to be looking for her. It hadn't helped his state of mind when the Protector taking the report had suggested slyly that maybe his sister had run off with her boyfriend, needing to escape her overprotective brother.

Zach had tamped down his rage at the smirking man. The man didn't know his sister. If he did, he'd never have made such a comment. Nantha might be mischievous, but she adored her family. She'd never do something so irresponsible. If she'd had a boyfriend she'd wanted to run off with, she would have told them all before she waved goodbye. Clearly, her life was in danger, no matter what the Protector believed.

After the sting of that encounter, Zach still didn't regret reaching out to the Pack Protectors. This wasn't about him. He couldn't let injured pride come between him and a chance to rescue Nantha. He'd simply asked to speak to someone else. However, something the second Pack Protector said when taking Zach's information worried him. "Another one?" he'd asked, before appearing to catch himself. After that, despite Zach's repeated attempts to get him to elaborate, he'd refused.

Another one. Had other Mermaids recently gone missing? If so, why? These were the kind of questions that kept him up at night. Maybe Shayla would know. He'd ask her later that evening when they signed the contract.

The Shadow Agency. He liked the name. And even though he knew only one of the woman had any experience whatsoever with private investigation, he knew they'd all give the search everything they had. And he couldn't ask for more than that.

So now he had help, which eased his panic somewhat. He wanted to let his mother know too, hoping it would help her, as well. But it would have seemed odd to tell her that he'd enlisted the assistance of two women he'd met in a bar, so he didn't. Not yet. His shape-shifting mom, June, had gone out hunting as Wolf every night since Nantha had disappeared, hoping to catch a hint of her scent. That was all she knew to do; that and stay close to home in case Nantha returned of her own volition.

Despite how ridiculous it might sound, Zach allowed himself to feel the first bit of hope he'd had since Sunday night. The knowledge that he'd hired a Mermaid and another Shifter to help him search for Nantha made him feel more proactive. He definitely could use another pair of eyes and ears under the sea, because he had no way to know what was going on there unless Ion told him. And truthfully, Nantha's father seemed too devastated by his daughter's disappearance to be of much use. Since Zach loved his stepfather as deeply as if he were biological, the older man's pain had become Zach's, as well.

It was a giant cluster of worry and fear. He didn't see things improving until Nantha was found, which had better be soon.

In the middle of all this, he couldn't stop thinking about Shayla. Even worried about his stepsister, the image of the gorgeous Mermaid haunted him.

Zach would never forget how Ion had reacted when Nantha had vanished. At first, the older Merman had clearly thought she was playing a joke on him. Nantha had a mischievous streak and frequently liked to tease both her father and Zach. She'd gone for her usual walk, just as she always did before returning to the sea.

But as the search turned into hours and the daylight disappeared, they'd all begun to realize that something was very wrong. They'd driven to Stewart Beach, leaving June at home in case Nantha showed up. Zach and Ion had walked the sand, asking anyone they encountered if they'd seen a woman alone. No one had.

Finally, as the sun dipped below the horizon, Zach quietly had to admit defeat. He'd suggested they return home, just in case Nantha showed up there. Of course, they both knew she hadn't as June hadn't called.

Though he'd agreed, Ion had stumbled on the walk back to the car. When he got inside, Zach saw the older man had gone ashen. When they pulled up to the house, Zach had gone around to help Ion out. Again, Ion swayed and nearly fell.

Watching from the front door, June had rushed over to support and reassure her husband. Zach stepped back, glad she at least had a distraction. Soon enough, she'd realize what both he and Ion already had.

Nantha was missing. Something, somewhere, somehow, had gone very wrong. Despite that they'd turned up nothing—no sign of a struggle, no blood, no witnesses—she'd disappeared. Zach's best guess was that she'd been taken. The one thing that gave him solace was the fact that none of Nantha's personal belongings had floated up to the surface.

Later, when none of them wanted to make eye contact with the others and silence made the air feel heavy enough to choke on since no one knew what to say, each grappled internally with their own panic. While no one had the slightest idea what might have happened, they all knew their beloved Nantha was in danger. But where? And how? This not knowing, not having a clue, made it all worse somehow.

Finally, Ion had said goodbye. He'd gone home, diving into the ocean, determined to find his daughter if she was there. June had taken to her bed, her earlier hysterics becoming a sort of dry-eyed grief. She could barely function. Despite this Zach had to leave her alone. He couldn't stay and reassure her while there remained a very real chance he could still find his little sister.

When he'd left them, Ion had promised to report back if he discovered any news. As of today, they still hadn't heard anything at all from him. June had managed to get herself together, but Zach could tell she was a nervous wreck. She'd already phoned him three times since eight o'clock that morning asking if he'd heard anything, anything at all. Finally, he'd gently told her that she'd be the first to know if he did. He planned to call her later in the day even if he had not.

His small apartment in Texas City felt cramped, so he didn't stay there long. He drove south to Galveston, figuring he could grab a meal and take yet another walk along the seawall and Stewart Beach. This time of the year, with the exception of spring break, was his favorite next to autumn. The thousands of tourists hadn't yet descended on the island, and while the Houstonians came down on the weekends, the pleasant weather and lack of crowds made everything nice.

Abruptly he realized nothing would be nice again until Nantha came home. He headed down to the pier and Joe's Crab Shack, where he could grab a shrimp po'boy and a beer.

Even then, he showed Nantha's photo to everyone who walked by his table, just in case one of them might have seen her. No one had. He refused to let this dampen his spirits. After all, he still had time until darkness. After his meal, he'd do another circle of the seawall.

He'd simply keep searching until he met Shayla and Maddie at Broken Chains, signed the contract and handed over his retainer fee. Then and only then would he truly feel as if he wasn't simply spinning his wheels.

While he looked, he'd ask every business to put up a poster. Earlier, he'd had the foresight to print up some missing person posters. He'd left some with his mother, asking her to go around her neighborhood and get them up. For himself, he stuck close to the businesses, restaurants and shops. After traveling all around Broadway, The Strand, the seawall and the pier asking store owners to put them up, he realized he'd need to print more. He stopped back into the same print shop where he'd had the first batch done and ordered again. They ran them off while he waited, declined to charge him anything. He thanked them, the kindness of the small gesture warming his heart. He also noted they already had one posted to their window.

Making a second round to hit all the places he hadn't the first time, as the sun began to set, he ended up with a few hundred of the posters left. Exhausted, he decided to go home and shower, maybe grab a sandwich before heading to Broken Chains to meet Shayla and Maddie.

As full darkness fell, he drove back toward Harborside Drive. Across from the cruise ship terminals, there were various parking lots as well as commercial businesses and warehouses. Some of the older buildings hadn't been repaired since Hurricane Ike tore through and were still boarded up. Broken Chains was hidden down an alley between two such buildings. Most humans viewed the area as dangerous and stayed away. The bar's Vampire and Shifter employees made sure to clear the alley before opening for business each night.

As he made his way toward the alley, he glanced around before making that last right turn. There, the sign with no letters, swinging in the night breeze. If any human chanced upon it, they'd definitely believe it a remnant from the time before the hurricane.

Zach stopped, inhaling deeply, waiting before he actually tapped the code out on the door. He'd always loved the moment before entering. The atmospheric setup—the dead-end alley, towering medieval door. The precise number of knocks in a certain cadence, and the vetting before one was allowed in. He wondered what happened if a human accidentally made it this far and tapped on the door. He wasn't sure, though he knew for certain they would not be allowed inside. Broken Chains was for paranormal entities only. Among the entire world owned by humans, this place was theirs alone. A safe haven.

Once he'd made it in, he stood still and scanned the premises, a peace settling over his weary body. The muted lighting, the clinking of glasses and dishes, the sound of the band tuning their instruments and the hum of quiet conversation. For whatever reason, the bar was even more crowded on this Wednesday night than it had been the evening before. Mid-week point, perhaps? The pleasant buzz of noise made him feel welcome, at home.

Once again, as Zach made his way through the crowd, he was glad the bar didn't allow smoking. Shifters had sensitive noses, and a room full of cigarette smoke made most of them feel nauseous. The last time Zach had visited a human bar, the smoke had been so thick he hadn't even ordered a drink before turning around and walking right back out. These days, the humans had become health conscious, and more and more establishments banned smoking.

Shayla and Maddie had said they'd meet him here at eight. He'd arrived half an hour early, and judging from the lack of places to sit, he hoped they'd gotten here even earlier. If not, they'd all be standing and circling the room like hawks until someone actually got up and vacated their table.

The band continued to warm up. There were five of them. A different group from the night before. Broken Chains constantly rotated their musical act. Zach had heard everyone wanted to play there, and competition was so tight that they were booked months in advance. He liked the fact they changed up the music. Something for everyone that way. From the sound of their warm-up, this band sounded like they played eighties music. He shrugged, continuing to wade through elbow-to-elbow people in search of the two women.

He reached the back edge of the bar and turned to go down the other side. Nothing, though every single table was full. A few other Shifters whom he'd spoken with previously waved. He waved back, though he didn't stop to talk.

Once he'd made a complete circuit of the packed room, he climbed the narrow staircase to check the second floor.

There weren't as many people up here. He felt like he could breathe. There they were. They'd taken a table near the back, as far away from the balcony railing to below as possible. He approved of their choice, where it would be quieter.

Shayla and Maddie spotted him. Shayla waved. As he made his way toward them, dodging a waiter with a tray of drinks, he realized a third woman had joined them. A blonde with short, spiky hair and too-perfect alabaster skin. He stopped in his tracks. Something about her… Then he knew. The hair on his arms rose, and he pushed back the urge to growl. *Vampire.* His entire family had been blessed—or cursed—with the ability to instantly recognize a Vampire, even one who blended well with the human population. Though Shifters and Vamps had long ago forged a truce and these days the two got along, he couldn't help his initial visceral reaction. Hopefully he'd been far enough away that no one at the table would have noticed.

Resuming his progress, he inclined his head toward the newcomer before pulling out the remaining empty chair. From the cold way the Vampire regarded him, he guessed she felt the same way he did. Inherent enemies couldn't help their initial reaction. It was in their DNA.

Still standing, he kept one hand on the back of the chair. He really wanted to know what she was doing here. This was to have been a private meeting between him and the Shadow Agency.

"Evening," he said as a greeting, including all three of them in his glance, though he slid his gaze away from the Vampire as quickly as possible without appearing rude.

"Hey there, Zach." Shayla's wide smile made him catch his breath. Tonight she wore her silky black hair pulled back in her trademark complicated braid. The hairstyle showed off her high cheekbones, sensual lips and striking eyes. She was, he thought, absolutely stunning. Even his inner Wolf sat up and took notice.

She gestured gracefully toward the Vampire. "This is Carmen Vargas. I'm sorry you haven't had a chance to meet her before now. She's the third partner in the Shadow Agency."

Third partner? This was new. Privately, he wondered how wise that decision might be, but as an about-to-be client, he figured the Vampire could go places neither he nor the others could. Beggars couldn't be choosers. Right now, he could use all the help he could get locating his sister. If a Vamp could help find Nantha, he'd let her.

He finally lowered himself into the chair, directly across from the now-glowering Vampire. Shayla glanced from him to Carmen and back again. "What?" she asked, spreading her hands, showing off her bright blue nail polish. "I'm picking up a strange vibe. Do you two know each other?"

"No," Zach answered. He forced himself to relax, aware the other Shifter, Maddie, had gone into full alert. Seemed his inner Wolf wasn't the only one paying attention. "We don't."

"It's okay," Carmen interjected, finally taking her gaze off him. "Sometimes age-old instinct trumps common sense."

In the interest of getting along, he let that comment go. After a second of startled consideration, Maddie laughed. "Don't worry, Zach. The same thing happened to me the first time I met her."

Of course it had. Despite Zach's dislike, Carmen had a point. Age-old instinct could be difficult to overcome. Still, it would help if he tried to make a start. He forced himself to meet the Vampire's gaze. "You're right, I'm wrong. My apologies." He took a deep breath and continued. "I know lots of Vamps, and this hasn't happened to me in a long time. I'm not sure why I let myself get caught up in it this time."

For whatever reason, his remark made Carmen laugh.

Shayla touched his arm. "I think it might be because Carmen is the most emphatic Vampire I know. Though most can't see past her beauty, once you get to know her, you'll wonder how you didn't notice. She's very, very Vampiric."

Shaking her head, Carmen only laughed harder. "Thank you," she finally managed. "I guess."

"You're welcome." Shayla pulled a manila folder from her bag, fixing each of them with a stern look. "Now shall we get down to business?"

Zach nodded, glad to have Shayla to distract him from his lingering animosity. "Definitely."

"Um, drinks first?" Carmen protested, arching one perfectly shaped brow. "We waited for you," she told Zach. "And I'm thirsty. I need some refreshment before we discuss business."

"Sounds good to me," Maddie agreed, lifting her hand to signal a waitress. Instantly, a short woman with purple-and-pink hair appeared at their table. Shayla ordered white wine, Maddie, a wheat beer, and Carmen asked for a glass of an Argentinian weaver's blood, straight up. For himself, he went with dark beer, earning an approving look from Maddie.

Shayla slid a manila folder across the table. "Our contract," she said. "Take your time reading it."

Tuning out the noise from the bar downstairs, he read over the contract. It seemed straightforward, so he went ahead and signed. Since he'd had no idea what kind of retainer they might ask for, he'd made sure to bring a thousand dollars in cash, ten one-hundred-dollar bills neatly folded inside his wallet. If that wasn't enough, he'd negotiate, or find an ATM.

Turned out, one thousand dollars was exactly what they asked him to put down. The contract had also spelled out other fees, but to his surprise the document said if they weren't able to accomplish their goal for whatever reason, they'd refund his money. All of it.

In other words, they guaranteed success or their services were free.

Chapter 4

"I like your confidence," he said, palming the money and handing it over so that no one else could see. Shayla took similar care, closing her hand over it and lowering it into her purse. He was glad she hadn't decided to make a production out of counting it on top of the table. The bar might be full of other Shifter, Vamps and Merfolk, but that much cash might prove too big a temptation for some.

Underscoring everything, he felt the buzz of his attraction to Shayla, making him hyperaware of her.

Their drinks arrived and Shayla asked them all to do a toast. He felt a little uncomfortable clinking glasses with a female Vampire holding a glass full of blood, but he managed to keep his revulsion hidden, he thought.

Once they'd all taken sips from their assorted drinks, he leaned in. "Now tell me your plan. I want to know what steps you're going to take to find my stepsister."

Shayla nodded. She reached into her purse and pulled out

several sheets of paper and a pen. "I need you to fill out this questionnaire. Once I know more about Nantha—where she lived, went to school, worked and who her friends are, I can go back under and start asking questions."

"Why all the focus underwater when Nantha disappeared on land?" Maddie wanted to know.

"Good point," he agreed. "I'm thinking that's what her father is doing also."

"Maybe, but how many young people are going to reveal any secrets Nantha might have had to her father?" Shayla smiled gently. "You know how that is. I feel much more confident they'd be willing to talk to me. And the more we can learn about her life undersea, the more we can look for clues as to who might gave grabbed her and why."

She had a point. Sort of. "Unless her abductor is human."

"And that's where I come in," Maddie interjected smoothly. "Carmen is assisting me. We're exploring the human possibilities, among others."

He nodded and began writing down the answer to the questions. Luckily, Nantha had confided in him. Otherwise, he wouldn't have had a clue.

As he wrote, Shayla leaned over, trying to decipher his handwriting upside down. "Good," she commented. "I'm glad to see she's from Coral. That's my hometown, and I know it like the back of my hand."

Carmen watched silently, continuing to sip on her drink. Maddie checked her phone. "My brother just texted me. He's a Pack Protector. I filled him in on all this. He says there's already an investigation open."

Relieved, he nodded. "I contacted them, and they said they'd look into it. They didn't seem really concerned."

"Yeah." Maddie looked down, clearly not sure if she should finish speaking. When she raised her head and met his gaze, he saw determination in the set of her chin. "He says since you didn't get a ransom note and there's no indication whatsoever that Nantha is in danger, we have to consider the possibility that she might simply have run off on her own."

"No." Zach focused his attention back on the questions. "The human police said something similar when I reported her missing. But Nantha's not like that. She'd never do anything to worry her family. If she wanted some time away, she would have at the very least left us a note."

Maddie nodded. Shayla simply watched him, the compassion in her lovely eyes making his throat close up.

"Are you sure?" Carmen asked. "Because just about everyone has secrets they don't want their family to know."

His instinctive response—to snarl at her—he pushed back down. Instead, he mentally counted to five, taking slow and steady breaths before answering. "I'm sure. Nantha is one of my best friends."

"I'm sorry, I have to ask this." Color high, Shayla cleared her throat, though she didn't look away. "Were you and Nantha romantically involved?"

"What?" He couldn't believe her question. The supposition made him feel nauseous. "Of course not. She's my sister, for hound's sake."

"Stepsister," Carmen drawled. "Correct me if I'm wrong, but there's no blood relation there at all. And from what I can tell, this Nantha is one hot babe."

"She's pretty." Brotherly pride mixed with revulsion made him swallow hard. "And, yes, I do have to beat back human suitors when she's visiting on land. But all Merfolk are blessed with good looks." He jerked his head toward Shayla. "You all know that."

"I'm sorry." Shayla sounded genuinely regretful. And,

he thought, a tiny bit relieved. "But it's something we had to ask."

Not *we. She.* Did she really think so low of him to even consider the possibility that he and his baby sister were having an illicit love affair?

"I can see from the look on your face that the idea repulses you." Carmen again, detached and observant. "So we'll put that possibility to rest. Please, go ahead and fill out the rest of the questionnaire. We're especially interested in knowing about any boyfriends Nantha might have or have had. Past ones would be of special interest."

Boyfriends. Question sixteen. He paused, taking a moment to think. Nantha always had a crush on someone, but it seemed to change every couple of weeks. He knew she dated, but she'd never mentioned anything serious.

All three women nodded when he passed this information on. "I'll look into it when I go back to Coral," Shayla said. The low thrum of her voice reached deep inside of him, sparking arousal. To hide this, he swallowed hard and focused on the questionnaire.

Once he'd answered all the questions to the best of his ability, he slid the paper across the table. Shayla took it and began reading. She asked for clarification on one of two things—he'd listed a few odd jobs where Nantha had worked, but only a couple of places where he thought she might hang out. As for hobbies, the only one that came to mind was reading.

"Surely there must be more," Shayla pressed. "What about exercise, working out? Or fishing? Does she like any sports?"

"No. She's actually pretty quiet." He thought for a moment, then sat up straighter. "Music. She loves to sing and dance."

Nodding, Shayla scribbled that down on the form. "Most

Mermaids do," she commented. Picking up her glass, she drained her wine. He realized both Carmen and Maddie had already finished their drinks, as well.

Eyeing his still mostly full beer, he took a sip. Briefly, he considered slugging it all down, but decided against it, especially since Shayla didn't seem nearly as affected by him as he was by her.

He slid his own folder across the table. "I had some fliers printed up. I spent the day going around the island having them put up. They're laminated, so they should do well under water. Feel free to take them with you if you think they might help."

"Perfect!" Shayla beamed at him, which made his heart skip a beat. "I can definitely use them. I think they'll really help."

"I hope someone who knows where she is sees them," he said, his chest suddenly tight.

Shayla slapped some money on the table. "Drinks are on me," she said. "I don't know about ya'll, but I need to go. It's been a long day for me."

The other women stood, as well. Relieved he didn't feel obligated to sit and make small talk with the others, he pushed back his chair and did the same.

Below, the band played a steady stream of eighties hits. He knew once they got downstairs, it would be damn near impossible to hear anything.

Apparently, Shayla realized this, too.

"We'll get to work immediately," she said, holding out her hand. He reached out, and again, the instant their fingers connected he felt a jolt straight to his core. From the way her eyes widened, he had to think she felt it, too.

"You've got my cell number."

"Yes." After she released him, he shook hands with the other two women, keeping his face expressionless when he touched the Vampire. He knew his feelings were irrational, and while he didn't completely understand them—after all, he even had a couple of Vampire friends—he didn't have time to indulge in self-analysis. Getting his sister back was all that mattered.

Leaving his unfinished beer on the table, he followed the women downstairs and out of the bar. Once they reached the end of the alley, the three women went in the opposite direction. At a slight loss, he stood and watched until they disappeared from sight.

Now what? He could get in his car and head home to his place in Texas City, but he knew his mother would still be awake and frantic. Keeping her company would be the best thing to do. Plus, he needed to fill her in on what he'd accomplished today with the fliers, as well as tell her about hiring the Shadow Agency. He also needed to know if his mom had heard anything from Ion.

When Zach arrived back at his mother's house, she met him at the door. "Don't you ever check your messages?" she asked, her voice shaking. "I sent texts, too."

This was so unusual it worried him. Eyeing her, he realized she looked unusually pale. Her blue eyes were red and puffy, as if she'd been crying. And more than her voice shook. Tiny tremors rocked her slender frame.

"I'm sorry," he said, pulling her close for a quick hug. "I didn't hear my phone. It's been a crazy kind of day." He pulled his cell from his pocket and checked. Four missed calls, an equal number of messages and texts from his mother saying simply, "Call me immediately."

Dammit. When he raised his gaze to meet his mother's, he saw tears now streamed down her cheeks.

Dread momentarily paralyzed him. "Nantha?" he asked, hardly able to force the words out past the lump in his throat. "Do you have news? Is she…" He swallowed hard, unable to finish the sentence.

"Oh, no. Not that." His mom gave him a quick, fierce hug. "It's okay, honey. She's still alive," June said. "Sorry, I should have realized you'd think the worst. Come with me." And she turned and went toward the kitchen, knowing he'd follow.

Which he did, right on her heels. Oddly enough, his horrified assumption of the worst appeared to have calmed her. Hand steady, she reached for a folded piece of white paper on the counter, and handed it to him. "Take a look. This is crazy."

"What is this?" he asked, accepting it. "Who's it from?"

"Read it," she managed, before turning away. Despite that, he could see that she covered her mouth with one hand in order to muffle her sobs.

Dread coiling low in his gut, he opened the single sheet of paper, noting the way it had been precisely folded into three exact, equal sections. He also noted the high-quality paper; not your ordinary, run-of-the-mill copier paper. Interesting. And then he began to read.

TO THE FAMILY OF THE MERMAID KNOWN AS NANTHA, it began. Typed, not handwritten. All in caps. Swallowing hard, he forced himself to continue reading.

SHE IS ALIVE, the missive continued. AND OF NO USE TO US. IF YOU WANT HER BACK, YOU WILL DO WHAT WE SAY. WE ARE WILLING TO EXCHANGE HER FOR TWO OTHER MERMAIDS. BUT THEY MUST BE VIRGINS. MORE INSTRUCTIONS WILL FOLLOW.

And that was all. No way to contact the letter writer, no instructions, other than asking for two virgin Mermaids.

"What the hell?" He read it again to be sure he'd gotten it right. "Is this someone's idea of a joke?"

But now his mother was crying so hard she couldn't answer. He hugged her, wondering what kind of son of a bitch would even think of writing such a thing. "Have you told Ion?" he asked gently.

"I've asked him to come immediately," she managed. Communicating with those under the sea could be touch-and-go. Apparently, she'd actually managed to make contact.

A knock on the patio door made him freeze. Zach spun around, ready to do battle. When he realized who it was, relief flooded him. "It's Ion," he said, releasing his mother so he could unlock and open the door. "He must have gotten your message."

"Zach." Though he only had eyes for his weeping wife, Ion jerked his chin in a quick nod at Zach as he rushed to pull June into his arms. "What is this?" he asked, kissing her forehead. "Speak to me, darling. You said it was urgent. Tell me, what's happened?"

His questions only made her cry harder. Ion glanced over her shoulder at Zach, one brow raised in question. "Do you know?" he mouthed.

"Yes. She—we got a letter," Zach responded, unable to keep from reading it one more time. "About Nantha. It's crazy. It doesn't even make sense."

Ion gently steered June to a chair. "Sit, love," he ordered. "Let me take a look at this."

Zach handed it over, watching as the Merman silently read it. And then reread it.

"What do you make of it?" Zach asked when Ion raised his gaze from the paper to meet his. "Do you think it's genuine?"

"Unfortunately, yes. It doesn't read like a prank. The letter writer is definitely serious." He read it once more, exhaling sharply when he got to the end. "This isn't good at all. But, on the plus side, this means my daughter is still alive."

Zach nodded. "If they're telling the truth, yes."

At his words, his mother shot him a teary-eyed glare. "Think positive," she admonished him. "Nantha *is* alive. She has to be."

"Of course she is," Zach replied, keeping his voice gentle. "I have no doubt about that."

Reading the missive once more, Ion frowned. "The request for virgin Mermaids has me stymied, I must admit. It sounds like something from ancient legends."

Zach nodded, aware of what the older man meant, and didn't dare say out loud within his mother's hearing. Sacrificial virgins, meant to appease either some mythical god or monster.

Insanity, right? But clearly, the letter writer believed what he or she had written.

"Well?" June demanded, wiping at her eyes with the back of her hand. She stood, looking from her husband to her son and back again. "What are you going to do about this?"

Again, the two men exchanged silent looks. Zach knew they'd talk later, in private.

"I've hired a paranormal private investigation firm to help search," Zach said. He went on to tell them about the three women, one Mermaid, one Shifter and a Vampire.

His mother recoiled at the last, but didn't comment.

"I want to meet with them," Ion declared. "Especially the Mermaid. It would help me tremendously to have someone else helping me under the sea."

"I want to meet them, too," June put in, her voice fierce and determined. "Since one of them is a Shifter, she may be able to find a way for me to help."

"Fine." Zach didn't see the harm in setting up a gathering. In fact, it might actually help to have the others see who else was involved. "I'll see if they're available to meet tomorrow night at Broken Chains."

Both Ion and June nodded. Like everyone else in the paranormal community, they'd visited the bar more than once. While there were several others up north in Houston, Broken Chains was the oldest and most well-known.

"I've also involved the Pack Protectors," Zach continued. "They've promised to keep an eye out."

Though June nodded, Ion scowled. "I don't see how they could help. They can't search under the sea."

"We don't know that's where she is," Zach said.

"You'd better hope she's under the ocean," Ion shot back. "She's got to have seawater or she'll die."

June's eyes welled up again at his words, making Ion curse. He gathered his wife close, murmuring soothing words to her. Zach took that opportunity to leave the room.

Stepping out onto the patio, he stared into the darkness. Nantha was somewhere out there, scared and worried, held captive by some fools with insane ideas about sacrificial virgins. He wondered if she knew that one thing had apparently been what saved her—that she wasn't a virgin.

Shaking his head, he dug his phone out again and punched in Shayla's number. She answered on the second ring and listened intently while he told her about the letter. "It's true, what your stepfather said," she told him. "Centuries ago, virgin sacrifices were a thing. Or so the legends go. The humans claimed it was to appease a dragon or, even earlier, various gods and goddesses. Under the sea, the dragon usually was a giant squid. Once in a while, in really ancient times, I've read about an angry sea god, Poseidon or one of his demigods."

"But those were all ancient tales. Some of them might have even been myths," she continued. "I'm not sure why someone would be trying to resurrect those stories in to-day's world. Poseidon has a temper, but even he's moved beyond asking for virgin sacrifices."

Poseidon? He decided not to ask.

"Maybe someone is trying to start a new religion, or a cult?" he asked. "Have you heard anything about something like that?"

"No. But not only will I let the Pods know, I'll definitely ask around when I go visit again. Which will be soon. I plan to put up those missing person posters you gave me and visit the neighborhoods where she went to school and worked."

"Good." He told her about Ion's request for a meeting with the Shadow Agency.

"That's fine," she immediately said. "As long as you're okay with it. You are the client, after all, so what you say goes."

"Tomorrow night?" he asked. "Say around eight, at Broken Chains?"

"Let me get with the others, but I'm sure that'll be fine. I'm going to call and see if I can reserve a private room for a few hours. It'll be easier to talk that way."

Once he agreed, she ended the call, promising to let him know if anything changed.

He wandered back inside, noting his mother and Ion had disappeared to their bedroom. He knew he should head back home to Texas City, but it had been a long day, and his mother kept the guest bedroom bed made up for situations like this. He grabbed a bottle of water and went to bed early.

When he woke the next morning and wandered out into the kitchen to grab some coffee, his mother had started frying up some bacon. The smell made his mouth water.

"Good morning," she said, smiling, her posture relaxed. "I'm glad you decided to spend the night. I know it's a lot farther for you to go into work, so I figured a good breakfast would help."

She seemed so pleased with herself and so much happier than she'd been the previous night, that he didn't have the heart to tell her he'd taken two weeks' vacation. Plus, if he told her that, she'd want him to hang around the house most of the day. He needed to get back to the heart of the island as well as make a few phone calls. He hadn't yet informed the Pack Protectors about the note, and he knew they'd definitely want to know.

Dutifully, he took a seat at the table, happy to eat his mother's cooking. It revived his spirits to see her looking so much better.

"Where's Ion?" he asked, once he'd cleaned his plate and pushed it away.

She smiled. "He headed out at first light to talk to his contacts in his underwater city. He'll be back by afternoon. He also wanted me to tell you he's sorry, but considering what's happened, he's going to have to postpone your meeting with Teredia."

Teredia. He blanked for a second before remembering she was the Mermaid Ion had wanted Zach to marry. Though Zach hadn't met her yet, Ion had claimed the alliance would help Nantha tremendously, by virtue of family connections. In the photo he'd shown Zach, Teredia was stunning.

When Zach had asked why someone who looked like that would need an arranged marriage, Ion had laughed. "It's complicated," he'd said. "I'll let her tell you, if you'll agree to do this for your sister."

Zach had given his tentative agreement, with the caveat that he could back out if Teredia and he weren't a match.

He didn't have much of a social life—engineers weren't known for their scintillating conversational skills—so he'd told himself it wouldn't hurt to try and be open to new experiences. Then he'd promptly put it to the back of his mind. Clearly Ion hadn't.

"That's fine." He waved his hand dismissively. "I can't even think about that right now. But I'm glad Ion's going to be back tonight." He told her about the meeting at Broken Chains that night at eight. "Can you make sure and let him know?"

"Of course." She carried his plate and hers to the sink. "I'm looking forward to meeting your friends. I just wish it was under better circumstances."

He started to point out that they weren't exactly friends, but decided against it. Whatever she needed to believe to make herself feel better was okay with him.

"Thanks for breakfast, Mom." He kissed her cheek. "I've got to go. I'll see you at Broken Chains, tonight."

The sadness in her gaze echoed how he felt in his heart. He sighed and left. He knew the drive back to Texas City would feel twice as long as usual, but he wanted to go home and change before making those phone calls.

On the way there, his cell phone rang. Caller ID showed Unknown Caller. His heart skipped a beat. While it was possible someone was calling who'd seen his poster and had information about his sister, he had a gut feeling this was something else.

"Did you get the note?" a low voice growled. Masculine, he thought, though the voice-garbling software made it difficult to tell.

"I did." He kept his tone even, stifling the rage that filled him. Somehow, he managed to keep it contained. "How did you get this number?"

"Never mind that," the anonymous person said. "Have you considered my offer?"

Though there were many ways Zach could have responded to that, he knew he didn't have time to waste. "Consider it? I have no idea where I'd find virgins, never mind virgin Mermaids."

"Really?" The caller sounded unconcerned. "If you don't, then my little captive's father should know. Ask him. Otherwise, tell him his daughter is going to die. You have one week. No longer." And then, with a click, the person ended the call.

Stunned, Zach stared at his phone. He punched Redial, but only got a recording stating that the call could not be completed as dialed.

Clearly, this meant the letter writer had been serious. While he could infer from this that Nantha was still alive and they might be able to save her, he knew beyond a shadow of a doubt he couldn't be part of some sort of sacrifice. Two innocent lives for his sister's? No.

But would Ion feel the same way? For the first time ever, Zach wasn't certain his stepfather would do the right thing.

While this was something else he'd discuss with the Shadow Agency, he decided he wouldn't tell June just yet. Due to the letter's implications, he could only imagine her reaction. No, when and if he decided to fill Ion in, he'd need to catch the Merman alone before he went back to the ocean.

For the first time, he wondered why the captors had chosen to reach out to him rather than Nantha's father, especially since they wanted virgin Mermaids.

Chapter 5

Shayla got to Broken Chains early, before the place had even begun to fill up. The band hadn't even arrived yet. Johnny, the bartender, looked up when she entered, his expression surprised. "You're really early," he commented.

"I rented a private room," she told him, smiling. "Can I get a ginger ale?" The soft drink had become a favorite. And it was far too early in the day to drink.

"Of course," he said, pouring the beverage into a glass without ice, just the way she liked it. He checked a clipboard. "You've got room three. I'll start a tab."

"Thank you." Carrying her drink with her, she headed toward the back of the bar, where bright red double doors separated the main area from the private rooms. Rumor had it that all kinds of deals were conducted in those four windowless spaces. Shayla didn't know for certain, as she'd never rented one before.

Lately, every time she set foot in Broken Chains she

marveled at how this place—a bar, for shark's sake—felt so much like home. But here was truly the first place she'd ever been where no one was judged for any reason. Talk about diversity—Shifters and Vampires and Merfolk, and who knew what else, all coexisted in harmony. The knowledge, as well as the experience of finally feeling as if she belonged somewhere, made Broken Chains her home away from home.

Once she stepped through the double doors, she stood in a short hallway that ended with a full-length mirror decorating the wall and reflecting her image back at her. There were two doors on each side, numbered. Number three was the last door on the right.

She went to it, grasping the knob. Giddy with anticipation, she opened the door and stepped inside.

The perfectly square room looked like a conference room. Beige walls, boring artwork framed in walnut, dark hardwood floors and a large round mahogany conference table with six upholstered chairs.

At first disappointed, she shook her head and laughed. What had she expected really? Red upholstered couches and gilt coated lamps? This wasn't a whorehouse, after all.

For whatever reason, she thought of Zach. It had been a long time since she'd battled such a fierce attraction to a man. Of course, since he was her client, this was not only inappropriate, but dangerous. She needed to keep her full attention on the investigation.

Setting her tote bag down on the table, she pulled out her laptop and powered it up. Might as well check the internet connection before the meeting. Maddie had also promised to be there early so they could get everything set up. Carmen, too, though, like Maddie she'd had to work so would have to come straight from her job. As long as they were here before Zach and his family.

Shayla opened a thick manila folder. She'd printed out all of the research she'd done on virgin sacrifices, both in human history and Merfolk. She'd been tempted to ask her father to speak to Poseidon, but she knew all kinds of trouble came from getting the Sea God involved.

She slipped off her high heels, rubbing her aching feet together before taking a seat. While she loved the way the red-soled, spike-heeled shoes looked, she still hadn't gotten used to walking in them. That hadn't stopped her from buying several pairs. She figured she might as well build up her collection.

Now to deal with the business at hand. Time to make notes and see if she—along with Maddie and Carmen—could come up with any sort of plausible theory as to who might be holding Nantha. All before meeting with the young Mermaid's parents and Zach at eight.

Maddie arrived thirty minutes later, when Shayla had just gotten into the research. Distracted, Shayla looked up when the door opened, slightly disoriented.

"Hey," Maddie said, by way of greeting. "You seem really lost in thought."

Shayla indicated the papers scattered all around her on the table. "Research." She glanced at her watch, surprised to see thirty minutes had already passed. She'd also just about drained her ginger ale.

"Great." Maddie pulled out a chair. "Fill me in."

Shayla told her what she knew about the note and the follow-up phone call that Zach had received.

"Virgins?" Maddie asked, her tone incredulous. "So are we to infer from this that young Nantha is not?"

"Apparently." Shayla shrugged. "She's seventeen, after all." And her people were known to have a very casual attitude toward pleasures of the flesh.

Maddie grinned. "I know what you mean." She indicated the stack of articles. "What have you found out?"

"I don't have anything but folklore."

"Ah. The old virgin sacrifice trope?"

Shayla nodded. "Yes. For all I know, that could be nonsense inserted just to cause a smoke screen and throw off searchers. I just hope whoever has this young Mermaid understands how badly she has to be in water every so often."

Maddie nodded, her gaze troubled. "We've got to find her," she said. "It's not only our first case, but I can't help but think of my own little sister. I can't imagine how I'd feel if something like this happened to her."

"Agreed." Shayla thought of Zach, of the way his hard features softened when he spoke of his stepsister. Seeing a man like him, so strong and rugged, at such a loss, made her feel as if she'd do anything to wipe that look of pain from his face.

"Since we don't know if the demand for virgins thing is real or a smoke screen, we've got to find out if there are any other missing Mermaids," Shayla continued. "I've already left word with the Pod—our Mer-council. Surely they'll have records if anything like that has happened."

"Right. And both you and Zach have contacted the Pack Protectors. So there's that."

Shayla nodded, struggling not to show her frustration. "You know in human disappearance cases, the first twenty-four hours are the most important. They say the chances of the victim being found alive diminishes exponentially for every hour after that. We're at day four now."

"That can't be good." Maddie sighed. "This is the part where I wish we had more experience as private investigators."

"I agree, but I'm not sure how even experience would help in this instance," Shayla said. "We have no witnesses, no evidence, nothing except this weird sort-of-ransom note. According to Zach there's not even a way to contact them."

"Yet," Maddie said darkly. "I'm sure that's next."

The door opened, and Carmen glided into the room. Quickly, since Zach and his family would be there soon, Shayla and Maddie filled her in.

"Missing Mermaids," Carmen mused. "If there are, we've got to find the reason. That's what will lead us to the perps. Revenge? Lust? Love? Or is it something else?"

No one spoke, because no one had an answer. Shayla divided up the research, and they all began reading.

As before, time seemed to fly. A waiter appeared, bringing a pitcher of ice water and a tray of glasses. Carmen ordered a bottle of blood. Both Shayla and Maddie decided to stick with water.

Finally, Zach and his parents arrived. The instant Shayla caught sight of him, all the air seemed to leave the room. He ushered them inside, fussing over his mother, a tiny female Shifter with delicate features and neatly braided hair. Shayla's gaze drifted past her to the stepfather, a tall, angular Merman whose mouth fell open in shock when he met her gaze. Crud. She should have thought of this. For whatever reason, she hadn't considered the possibility that he'd recognize her.

"You're..." Clearly stunned, he couldn't finish.

"I'm Shayla," she said firmly, holding out her hand. "One of the owners of the Shadow Agency."

"Sorry," Zach said, turning. "Shayla, this is Ion, and my mother, June. And this is Maddie and Carmen. They're the other two partners." He took a deep breath. "They're all helping search for Nantha."

June nodded, her gaze slipping past Carmen to return to light on her son. Meanwhile, Ion continued to stand, apparently frozen in shock. He didn't take Shayla's hand, though he did perform an awkward sort of bow in her general direction.

Of course, Zach noticed. "Ion, what's wrong?"

Slowly, the tall Merman swiveled his silver head to meet Zach's gaze. "Is this some kind of joke?"

"What?" Clearly puzzled, Zach frowned. "I'm not sure what you mean."

"Princess Shayla." Ion turned to face her, bowing again. "I am honored by your presence, though I admit to being confused. What ruse is this?"

Great. Now her secret was out in the open. Shayla sighed. She'd really hoped Zach's stepfather would have the sense to keep her underwater status to himself. She hadn't told anyone, not even her closest friends. Glancing at them, she swallowed hard. Even Maddie and Carmen stared, their expressions both stunned and confused. Of course, she couldn't blame them. They'd had no idea she was anything other than an ordinary Mermaid.

Meanwhile, Zach looked from her to his stepfather and back again. "Princess?" he asked, his tone incredulous. "What the hell are you talking about?"

Stomach churning, Shayla readied herself to explain. She dreaded the moment when the easy acceptance vanished from her friends' sweet faces, replaced with either misplaced envy or awe or something even worse. She hated the way people treated her when they realized she was royalty. This had been one of the reasons she'd chosen to live on land.

The steady thump of a bass guitar managed to penetrate even this small room. The music had started. She actually wished they were out in the main bar, so there'd be a distraction.

"Your friend is a royal princess," Ion informed Zach, his tone icy.

Zach eyed her, a question plain on his face. Slowly, she nodded. "True."

He didn't respond. Would his opinion of her change? Would he consider her an entitled, spoiled royal dabbling in playing at becoming a private investigator?

Would they all look differently at her now?

"I live on land now," she said, directing her comment to Ion. Aware of the avid curiosity in her friends' faces, she knew she'd have to give more information than she wanted to. "I might be royalty under the sea, but here I'm just an ordinary Mermaid."

Carmen, bless her heart, laughed. "That's priceless," she said.

Neither Maddie nor Zach cracked a smile.

"Look, ya'll," Shayla said, spreading her hands in a gesture of supplication. "Please, don't be weird. I'm just me. Nothing has changed."

Slowly, Maddie nodded. "Okay," she said. "I guess."

Though Zach nodded, too, the tightness in his jaw didn't relax. Shayla wished she had the right to touch him, to press her lips against the pulse beating at the base of his throat and reassure him that nothing had changed.

"Your Highness," Ion began.

"Please," she interrupted. "Call me Shayla."

"You were engaged." Ion crossed his arms and leaned back in the chair. "I remember the hoopla, because you were supposed to marry Prince Richard from Gill. When he died, instead of choosing another, you decided to come live on land."

Inwardly wincing at the accusation in his tone, she glanced from him to his wife. "Just like you chose a Shifter," she gently pointed out. "You can't truly hold that against me, now can you?" But many did. In the great underwater cities, the royal line of succession was considered inviolate. The fact that she'd chosen to abandon her heritage once and for all was something some people considered inexcusable.

But in spite of that, her parents had been her strongest supporters. After all, her brother had succeeded to the throne. When he married and had children, the line of succession would bypass her completely.

She considered restating this fact to the other Merman, but not only did he probably already know, she owed him no explanations.

Fury and disappointment blazed from his silver eyes. She'd been looked at like that a lot after her heart had broken when Richard had died. Some people thought she'd lost her mind. None of this mattered to her, especially since she'd removed herself from all of the underwater world.

She sighed. If Ion didn't want her handling his daughter's case, that was his problem. Zach had hired her and until he fired her, she'd continue investigating.

Zach stood. "Look, I'm not sure what's going on, but whatever it is has nothing to do with the search for Nantha."

"That's right," June said, putting her hand on her husband's arm. "Please don't let politics interfere with the search."

At first, Ion didn't respond. Shayla's heart sank. Luckily, right then the door opened, and a waiter came in to see if anyone wanted a drink.

While everyone placed their drink orders, Shayla rolled her shoulders, trying to ease some of the stiffness. She looked up to find Zach watching her, which made her heart skip a beat. As their gazes locked, he smiled. "It's okay," he mouthed.

Though his smile made warmth blossom inside her, just like that, the pressure in her chest eased. Hoping her desire for him didn't show, she ordered her usual white wine, aware that once the waiter left, she'd need to regain control of the meeting, as well as herself.

As soon as the door closed behind him, she cleared her throat. "Ion, I'm sorry that you apparently have objections to working with me, but your son has employed our agency to find your daughter. In light of that, I won't be offended if you want to leave. Otherwise, I'm going to have to ask you to keep your feelings to yourself."

As the elder Merman peered down his nose at her, she braced herself for a possible explosive reaction.

Instead, to her relief, he nodded. "You're right," he said. "My apologies."

"None needed." Exhaling, she pulled out her questionnaire and slid one across the table to him. "I've already had Zach fill this out, but I'd like to get your input, too. I know you'd be more familiar with your daughter's activities at home in Coral."

Accepting the form and a pen, he lowered his head and began to write.

"Ahem." Carmen, tilting her head. "While he's doing that, I think you owe us an explanation."

Her heart squeezed. "Do I?" Maybe if she kept things light, nothing would change.

"Yes," Maddie interjected. "You do. *Princess.*"

Ion glanced up at that, his mouth tightening. He didn't comment, returning his attention to filling out the questionnaire.

Though he didn't speak, even Zach watched her with a look of expectation.

"Fine." Shayla shrugged. "I'm a Mermaid princess. One of many. My brother took over the kingship once my father retired. Once he's married and has children, I won't be anywhere near close to being in line for the throne." Chin up, she took a deep breath. "My fiancé died a few years ago. And I've chosen to live on land rather than under the sea. That sums it up nicely."

To her surprise, both Maddie and Carmen simply nodded. Zach reached across the table and squeezed the back of Shayla's hand. "I'm so sorry. How long ago did this happen?"

Surprised, she could only gape at him. Finally, she found her voice. "Two years now."

"How…"

"The initial report said he was eaten by a shark," Ion interjected, without looking up. "A freak accident. Mermen simply don't die this way. We can outswim everything." He shrugged. "It was believed he was drunk, but the coroner's report revealed he'd been poisoned. No one knows by whom. The general consensus was that it was some chemical in the alcohol he drank."

Again, the grief. And the guilt. As if she somehow could have stopped it, as though if she'd been there, she could have saved him. She bowed her head, taking the time to get herself together before speaking.

Maddie and Carmen had her back. "That's terrible," Maddie said, the hard edge to her tone a warning. "And I don't understand why you feel the need to rehash it all right now."

"Exactly," Carmen interjected. "Unless you, Ion, had some part in his death."

June gasped. Ion whipped his head up, fury flashing in his silver eyes.

The situation had just deteriorated rapidly.

"Enough." Shayla pushed to her feet, so hard her chair crashed to the floor. "This meeting is not about me. Or you, Ion. It's about finding Nantha. And unless you can stay on topic, I'm afraid I'm going to have to ask you to leave."

Instead of apologizing or changing the subject, Ion glared at her. She realized that this Merman apparently believed the crazy rumors that had floated around about her.

His next words confirmed that. "The sea claimed him. A Merman who had no reason to die, but did. So tell me, Princess Shayla. You fled the sea after his death. Are you happier now that you're free of him?"

Shayla gasped.

"Ion!" Both Zach and June spoke at the same time. "That's enough."

"Sorry," he said, sounding anything but. "Her marriage to Prince Richard of Gill would have forged a huge bond between two cities. The economic repercussions were enormous. He suffered greatly before he died. And people say she's always wanted to live on land. Now that she's single, she can."

Shayla lifted her chin, shaking. "You don't know me, and I can bet you never knew Richard. You have no idea how I felt when I lost him, no clue how his death broke me. How dare you? Excuse me," she said to her friends, Zach and his mother before stalking from the room. Either Ion didn't realize or else he didn't care, but she could have him hauled into court for speaking to her like that.

Though she wouldn't. Because that would start all the gossip and finger-pointing up again, and she sure wasn't up for dealing with it.

Once out in the pulsing noise of the bar, her anger slowly bled out of her. She took a deep breath. Royalty had enemies, though she usually managed to steer clear of them. Crazy reactions like Ion's were one of the downsides to being a princess.

A hand on her shoulder had her whirling around, fists upraised.

"Hey." Zach. He leaned in close to her ear, so she could

hear him. The warmth of his breath on her skin made her shiver. "I'm sorry about my stepdad."

"It's not your fault. I should be used to that crazy kind of drama, but I'm not. I don't know if I ever will be." She had to put her mouth almost on his ear, tempted to use her tongue, though she didn't. "It's one of the reasons I left home. The gossip and craziness made my grief even worse."

He nodded, taking her arm and steering her toward the back of the bar, where the band wasn't as loud. She fought the urge to lean into him. "It must be hard, losing someone you love like that."

"Yeah." She tried a laugh, but it fell short. "That he drowned seemed like kind of a bitter irony. Your stepdad wasn't the only one who felt like the sea settled the score. I mean Merfolk and sharks usually coexist. If they don't, we outrun them or kill them. There had to be something else. And there was. He was poisoned. To this day, they haven't found out who did it."

"Yikes." He winced. "Again, I'm sorry. That must have been really hard on you."

The kindness in his eyes made her swallow. She eyed him, wondering how she could be talking to Zach about her ex-fiancé whom she'd truly grieved while simultaneously aching to touch him. The masculine confidence he exuded made her feel a way she'd never felt nor expected to feel. Protected. Safe. Cared for.

Dangerous territory. Blinking, she forced herself to concentrate on the topic at hand.

"It was," she allowed. "I confess there were a lot of nights when I wondered. I tried to live inland, in the rolling hills of central Texas, near a big lake. It seemed reasonable. I'd be as far as possible from the sea, but near water."

"I take it that didn't work?"

"No. I got sick and nearly died, so I had to come back here. Mermaids need the ocean, salt water, to survive."

He still leaned in, close enough for her to see the way the hair on his arms stood up. Why? Could it be he felt as attracted to her as she did him? Her entire body went warm at the thought.

"At least you learned to cope with it." He tilted his head, studying her. "You seem well-adjusted and confident."

She liked the way he tried to encourage her, to find the positive. "Now, yes. But not then. Once I returned to live close to the ocean, I wanted vengeance. I was sick with it. I swam the seas, sang to every ship I saw. There were nearly several shipwrecks before my father and brothers tracked me down and dragged me back to home. I took my pain and anger out on the wrong people." She shook her head. "Luckily, no one was hurt or died."

"Luckily." He shifted his weight from one foot to the next. His broad shoulders, rugged features and overall general hotness earned him constant coveting glances from other females, though he didn't appear to notice.

When he took her arm, Shayla had to grin. "I'm over it now," she said. "The revenge part, that is. As for the grief, it comes and goes in waves. Mostly, I guess I'd say I'm at peace."

"I'm glad." His deep voice rumbled in her ear. "And now you're smiling again. I was worried for a moment there that you and Ion were going to do battle."

Refusing to let bitterness spoil her mood, she shook her head. "I've found it's better to try and rise above people who make comments like that."

"I agree." And then he placed a quick, soft kiss at her temple.

She froze. Just that simple press of his lips on her skin had her craving more. Every fiber of her being ached to lean into him and put her arms around him and pull him close. For a better kiss. A *real* kiss. The kind that would make her toes curl in her shoes.

Dang. What had gotten into her? She wanted him. She might as well admit the truth, if only to herself. Hell, whenever they were within ten feet of each other, all she could think of was how it might feel to slide her hand over his muscular arm, splay her fingers across his chest, tug his face down to hers for a kiss. Because she hadn't felt this way since she'd lost Richard, the strength of her desire stunned her. More than that—a small shiver of foreboding skittered up her spine. It had her worried.

The Shadow Agency had just gotten started. If she wanted the business to be a success, she couldn't afford to lose her focus, even for a distraction as tempting as the sexy Shifter. And as for him, she knew he'd never forgive either her or himself if they didn't recover his sister.

Neither could let physical attraction get in the way of that.

The problem was, she could tell he felt the same. The way he looked at her when he thought she wasn't watching—as if he'd like to do all the same things to her she ached to do to him. Plus more. Her body tingled down low at the thought.

It had been a long time since she'd welcomed a man into her body. For Merfolk, this could only happen when in their human shape, of course.

Shaking her head to clear her thoughts, Shayla brought her attention back to Zach. He watched her, his gaze dark and knowing, as if he knew the spiral her thoughts had taken.

"Are you ready to go back?" he asked. "Or would you prefer I ask Ion to leave?"

She considered. "I can be professional, as long as he

can. I have to tell you, though. One more outburst like that, and I won't be held responsible for my actions."

He eyed her. "Maybe I should get him to go first then. He's beside himself over Nantha's disappearance. I have no idea what he might say or do."

"I was kidding." Though only partly, which she kept to herself. "Let's go back and see what happens."

"Are you sure?"

"Of course." She lifted her chin and turned to make her way back to the private room. "Hopefully Ion will have finished filling out the questionnaire. Once I have both of your answers, I'll have a better starting place of where to go and search."

"Wait." He tugged her back, up close to him, sending a shiver up her spine. "There's more. Neither of my parents know about the follow-up phone call or the fact that whoever has Nantha has now given me one week to come up with the payment they requested."

Shocked, she stared. "You haven't told them?"

"No." Expression grim, he grimaced. "My mother's going to freak out when she learns we have one week or my sister will be dead."

"We've got to tell them," she informed him immediately. "Maybe it will help once they learn Maddie's brother is a Pack Protector. It's possible he can trace the call next time they phone you."

"I hope so. And I know you're right. But fair warning. I think my mother's going to get hysterical."

"Come on." Now she grabbed his arm, pulling him back the way they'd come. "She'll have to settle down. Everyone needs to focus one hundred percent on getting Nantha back. One week is actually more time than I expected."

Chapter 6

When they opened the door to the private room, everyone instantly went silent. Zach figured they were all discussing Shayla's newly discovered royal status. He really didn't care about that. All he wanted was to find his sister. Then and only then would he let himself think about anything else, like the strength of his attraction to her and vice versa.

Ion stood and, avoiding looking at Shayla, jerked his head toward the door. "Zach, I need a word in private," he said. Which turned out to be perfect. That way, Zach could tell him about the phone call without his mother listening in.

"Sure. Let's go out into the hall."

But once they stepped out of the room and closed the door behind them, Ion grimaced. "This isn't far enough." He pointed to the closed door. "I can't take a chance of being overheard. Do you mind if we step outside for a few minutes?"

Curious, Zach agreed. They made their way through the packed bar to the exit. Once in the alleyway, they went a few feet away from the entrance. The cooler night air felt good on his overheated skin.

"Listen," he began. "There's something I—"

"Wait," Ion interrupted, looking from left to right as if he thought they might have been followed. "I need to tell you about that Mer-Princess you hired. Shayla. Her fiancé drowned, and she hasn't been right since."

Zach nodded. "I know about that. It's got to be difficult for her to lose someone she loved to the sea."

"Exactly." Ion seemed to pounce on the word. "In fact, it was rumored at one time she blamed other Mermaids. Claimed someone poisoned him. And when she thought humans did it, she went off and started singing to their ships. Luckily, the king intervened and put a stop to that."

Again Zach nodded, not sure what his stepfather was getting at.

"You need to be careful around her," Ion proclaimed. "Many in my circles consider her mentally unhinged."

Despite the fact that Ion hadn't detailed exactly what circles these were, Zach kept quiet. He didn't see the point in fanning the flames.

"And now," Ion continued. "You've hired someone to look for Nantha who might actually be behind your sister's disappearance."

"What?" Zach blinked. "You can't be serious."

"I am. If she's not directly behind this, there's a strong possibility that she knows who is."

Zach wasn't sure how to respond. On the one hand, he didn't want to flat out accuse Ion of talking crazy. On the other, Nantha had nothing to do with Shayla's fiancé's death. This was crazy talk and he suspected Ion knew it. The older man's grief had completely clouded his judgment.

Ion sighed, correctly interpreting Zach's silence. "At least consider it," Ion demanded. "I know to you it might sound far-fetched, but so does a demand for two virgin Mermaids."

"I will. As a matter of fact, I'm going to bring it up with Shayla in private." Which he would, if only to let her know the craziness apparently had never gone away. "When I see how she reacts, I'll have a better handle on the possibility of it being true."

"Don't. Don't mention it to her. Just keep an eye on her and see if she does anything that might lead us to Nantha."

"Ion, she's going to be searching for Nantha under the sea. I really hope she's successful. And if you really believe it's possible she's somehow involved, it makes sense for me to discuss it with her."

At that, Ion looked down. "You can't. She's a member of the royal family. I live there. The consequences of accusing her of a crime like this—especially if it turns out to be false—would mean my imprisonment. Maybe even my death."

As Zach watched his stepfather, he realized the older man was serious. "I'll be careful."

"No." Ion sounded panicked now. "I shouldn't have said anything. Forget I mentioned it."

As if he could. "Finding Nantha before something bad happens to her supersedes everything else. Even that."

After a moment, Ion sighed. "You're right. But if you can, please don't mention my name."

"Of course."

"Now what were you wanting to say?" Ion asked.

Zach told him about the phone call.

"One week?" Terror edged the older man's voice. "Did you ask to speak to her?"

Proof of life. Damn. He wished he'd thought of that. "I

did not," Zach answered regretfully. "I was so stunned by the call that I couldn't think."

"Well, if you hear from them again, demand to speak with her. And let them know that you're working on fulfilling their demands."

"What?"

"To buy time," Ion clarified. "We need all the help we can get."

Whew. For half a second, Zach had thought Ion was seriously considering coming up with a few virgin Mermaids.

"Let's go back in. We've got to fill in Mom."

Ion winced. "How about you wait until your mother and I leave. She's been hysterical due to how long it's been since Nantha disappeared. If she finds out her supposed captors are only giving us a week, she'll lose her mind."

Zach nodded. "How are you holding up?" he asked quietly. "I know this has been weighing heavy on all of us, but you..."

For an instant, Ion's patrician features crumbled. He swallowed hard, and visibly got himself under control. Until he opened his mouth to speak and all that would come out were a few disjointed syllables that sounded as if he was gasping for air.

He cleared his throat and tried again. "I'm doing the best I can," he managed. "I want my baby girl back."

"We all do." Zach squeezed the older man's shoulder. "Now let's return to the meeting. Will you please be civil?"

Ion slowly nodded.

As they turned and walked toward the door, Ion's words replayed over and over in Zach's mind. *Proof of life.* Not once had he ever allowed himself to consider the possibility that Nantha might be dead. Not once.

And now, he had to. Hell hounds, he hoped that caller

phoned again. Because he knew he wouldn't sleep well until he spoke to Nantha and knew she still lived.

As soon as they reentered the room, Ion refused to look at anyone but his wife as he informed the others that he and June had to go. He waited by the door for June to collect her things, his gaze averted so he wouldn't accidentally meet anyone's gaze. The air felt heavy in the small room, and no one seemed to know what to do with themselves. Shayla, Maddie and Carmen occasionally glanced at each other, but they mostly watched as June fumbled with her tote bag while Ion made no effort to help her. Finally, Zach went over and quietly helped her rearrange everything. "It'll turn out all right, Mom," he murmured, kissing her cheek. "I promise to stay in touch. If I hear anything, anything at all, I'll let you know."

She nodded, her mouth working soundlessly as she gazed at him with tears in her eyes. Finally, she walked to the door, taking her husband's arm as she murmured a quick goodbye.

The tension that had vibrated in the room went with them. Shayla exhaled. "Whew," commented Maddie. Even Carmen, still silently sipping her blood drink, appeared relieved.

Exchanging a quick look with Zach, Shayla asked Maddie if her brother could trace the call.

"Let me see your phone," Maddie demanded. Once he'd handed it over, she used her own cell to make a call. They all listened silently as she repeated what Zach had just told them to whoever was on the other end. "Sure, I've got the number," she said, looking up. "Zach, what's your cell phone number?"

Once he'd given it to her, she passed it on. "Okay," she said. "Let me know what you find out."

After ending the call, she slid his phone across the table

to him. "That was my brother Tanner, the Pack Protector. He's going to see if he can trace the call."

"That'd be fantastic," Shayla said, her green eyes glowing with excitement. Even Carmen's usually stone-faced expression changed.

Dragging his gaze away from Shayla, he forced himself to consider what his stepfather had said about her. He had to ask her about it, but he wouldn't do it right now, in front of her friends.

A few minutes later, Maddie's phone rang. Immediately all chatter ceased. Everyone went silent, watching as she answered.

"Yes," she said. "I see. Well, thank you for trying."

Attempting to contain his disappointment, Zach eyed her, pretty confident he knew exactly what she would say.

"He couldn't trace the number to a person," she said, exactly as he'd feared. "But, he was able to tell the call came from land rather than under the sea."

"On land?" Shayla spoke, the surprise in her voice echoing his own. "That's interesting."

"Is it?" Carmen interjected. "All this means is if Nantha's captors are Merfolk, they came up on land to make the call. Much more difficult to trace that way, so that makes sense."

"Even more specific," Maddie continued. "He says the call originated in Houston. Not any of the towns in between there and Galveston, but Houston. That's a huge city."

"That could mean anything." Zach dragged his hand through his hair in frustration. "Merman on land, human working with a Merman, hell, it could even be a Shifter."

"Or a Vampire," Carmen said grimly. "Though kidnapping people isn't really our thing." She pushed to her feet.

"I need to go hunt. I think I'll go explore the area down by the pier and see what I can find out."

Maddie stood as well. "I've got to leave, as well. My brother has promised to see if he can narrow the call's origination down even farther—North Houston or South. He wanted me to bring him a later dinner, so I'm going to do that."

Zach and Shayla said their goodbyes. Once the others had gone, Shayla sighed. "Can I see the note?" she asked. "I'd like to take a look at the writing style and syntax."

"Sure." Pulling his wallet out, he removed the slip of paper and unfolded it before passing it across to her. He waited in silence while she read it, trying to figure out the best way to approach bringing up what Ion had told him. It was awful, pretty terrible, and he couldn't come up with a way to ask her without sounding accusatory.

"Do you mind if a take a picture of it?" she asked, pulling out her cell.

"Of course not."

She snapped several photos. "Thank you," she finally said, handing it back to him. He took it, folding it neatly and putting it back in his wallet. Still he couldn't seem to figure out the right opening statement.

Apparently, Shayla noticed. She touched his arm, the light contact making him ache for more.

"Zach, are you all right? I know all of this has been tough on you. You seem a little off tonight."

He started to nod, and then didn't. "I'm struggling to figure out the best way to ask you something," he admitted.

Raising her head, she met his gaze. "Just go ahead and ask." Her candid look told him she felt she had nothing to hide.

There were several different ways he could phrase the

question. He mentally reviewed each one and simultaneously discarded it.

"Just ask," she urged. "It's about my reaction after my fiancé drowned, isn't it? I'm guessing Ion said something."

Relieved, he nodded. "You knew."

"I saw your stepfather's reaction when he looked at me. Once he got past the initial shock of who I am, all he could think about was how I was after Richard drowned. I'm not proud of it, but it's pretty common knowledge where I come from."

Richard. A good, steady-sounding name. It sounded more human than Merfolk, actually.

"I went crazy for a little bit," she admitted. "I said some things I shouldn't have. My grief got tangled up with rage and regret and…" She swallowed hard, momentarily looking away. "I hated the thing that I was. I no longer wanted to be a Mermaid. The irony of knowing that I could swim in the same sea that took Richard's life… It felt like too much to bear."

He watched as she took a deep breath, and then squared her shoulders and lifted her chin. "I'm better now. But I admit, sometimes I still wonder how such an awful thing was possible. Poison? Who would do such a thing?"

"I take it they never caught his killer?"

"No." The simple word conveyed all her frustration, sorrow and anger. Yet she managed to still stand tall, her bearing regal.

Hell hounds, the urge to touch her had him clenching his hands into fists to keep from reaching out to her, despite everything.

"Every royal has enemies," she continued, her expression grim. "Mine used my breakdown against me. I take it your stepfather is one of them."

"I don't think he considers you an enemy," he said,

aware he had to be careful for Ion's sake. "But he says he's heard rumors. You know he's worried sick about his daughter. We all are."

"I know." To his shock, she leaned in and impulsively bumped her shoulder to his. Even this, the slightest of friendly movements, had his body tightening with desire.

"We'll find her, Zach. I promise you. No matter what it takes." She began gathering up the papers both he and Zach had filled out, placing them back in her manila folder. "Now at least I have a place to start. If I can talk to her friends, I might be able to find out who took her."

Though his mouth had gone dry, he managed to speak. "Hopefully. But what if this isn't personal?"

"Ninety-five percent of child abductions are by someone the child knew," she pointed out. "And while technically, I know none of you think of Nantha as a child, she's still pretty young. A teenager."

He nodded. "By human standards, she's still a child at seventeen."

"Here's what I'm going to do. I'm going back home to talk to her friends and coworkers, see where she hung out and find out if she had any male beaus. I'll also put up the rest of the posters you gave me."

Her brisk, no-nonsense tone made him feel slightly better. More settled. "When?" he asked.

"Tomorrow morning, right after dawn. If there's anything down there that might help us locate her, I'll find it." She flashed him a smile, confident and sexy. Again, he felt that twinge of connection. "Maddie's brother said he'll continue trying to trace that phone number. And Carmen is excellent at skulking around the waterfront at night, talking to the drunks and other denizens of the underworld, to see if she can learn anything."

He had to grin at her choice of words. "Skulking?"

She smiled back, which of course had him wanting to kiss her. "That's what she calls it. She takes pride in being the most Vampire-like Vamp she can be."

Even he disliked those Vampires who tried to come off as hipster humans who happened to be immortal and believed they were cool because they liked to prowl the night searching for blood. He had to appreciate Carmen's approach, even if she made him a bit uncomfortable.

"I'm thinking I need to head home," he said, as exhaustion washed over him. "But please, call me as soon as you get back from under the ocean tomorrow."

"I will." She scribbled something on a piece of paper and held it out to him. "As for you, here's all three of our numbers. If those people call you again, let Maddie know so she can have her brother try and trace it."

He took the paper, glancing at it before folding it to put in his wallet near the ransom note. "And I'll make sure to ask to speak to Nantha."

"Proof of life," she agreed. "Always a good thing."

Though he'd never hated a phrase more, he nodded. Nantha had to be alive. He didn't know what he'd do if she wasn't.

Early the next morning, as Shayla prepared to go back to her home under the sea, those three words haunted her. Proof of life. As she dove under the waters and began the long swim, with each stroke of her arms and flip of her tail, the phrase repeated over and over in her mind like a mantra.

None of what had happened made the slightest bit of sense. She'd done some research into abductions, and most of them were done by someone the victim knew—a family member in most cases. If there was a ransom demand, it was usually for money. Not some weird request for virgins.

That's why she suspected this wasn't about a ransom. If it was, if the abductor was truly serious about wanting an exchange with virgin Mermaids, she'd have to guess he or she was a human who'd somehow stumbled onto learning about the existence of Merfolk. Only a human would have such a crazy idea as demanding virgin Mermaids, as if such beings would have some sort of magical powers.

But then what? What did the captor plan to do with virgins once he had them? Surely they wouldn't be used as a sacrifice.

For the first time, Shayla allowed herself to wonder if Nantha had truly been abducted at all. Though Zach refused to even consider the possibility, maybe the teenager had run away. Which would make the odd ransom request a smoke screen. While she didn't know Zach's stepsister, she could picture a seventeen-year-old giggling over the request.

Maybe that was one possibility she could consider. At least, add it to her list. It would fit too, except for the fact that they'd been given a deadline. One week. And then what? Did they mean to kill Nantha?

Hopefully, today she could find something out. Some hint, some clue, that might give her insight into what exactly had happened.

The farther out she swam, the deeper the ocean and the cooler the actual temperature of the water. She stayed down about one hundred feet, keeping her eyes open for sharks, giant squid or other natural enemies to her kind. So far, so good. Nothing but the occasional school of fish, most of them preoccupied with finding food.

She continued to swim, determination fueling her, overriding her exhaustion. Though she really craved a nap when she got home. Nothing too long, just an hour or so, enough to rejuvenate her. But, no, there was too much to do and not enough time. The nap would have to wait. She'd stick to her plan, and see if she could learn anything new.

When she reached her parents' house, she swam inside. The kitchen—her mom's usual hangout—was empty.

But this time her dad sat in his recliner in the den, arms crossed, as if he'd been impatiently waiting for her.

"Dad?" Surprised to see her father, Shayla rushed over for a hug. "What are you doing home?"

Though he got up from his chair and hugged her back, he didn't crack a smile. "I came to wait for you," he said, confirming her suspicion. "Your mother told me you were coming today."

The gravity in his voice had her worried.

She tried teasing him. "Well, you sure don't look happy to see me."

"I…" He shook his head, a reluctant smile curving the corner of his mouth. "I came to speak to you, before your brother summons you before the court."

"Summons? I don't understand. Why would he do that?"

"There have been rumors swirling around court, though no formal complaint has been made against you. Apparently the family of one missing Mermaid named Nantha believes you might have had something to do with her disappearance."

"What?" Stunned, she didn't bother to hide her shock and dismay. Ion. "That's crazy." She showed him the flyers she'd laminated. "I've been hired by her stepbrother to find her. And her father, Ion, knows this. I met with him last night. He wasn't very nice—in fact, he spouted off similar accusations, but I never would have believed he'd go this far."

Her words didn't appear to reassure her father. If anything, her statement deepened her dad's frown. "Then why would he make such an accusation? He's saying you were involved with the abduction of one of your own people, Shayla. This is very serious."

He had a point. Why would Ion do such a thing? What did he hope to gain by this?

"I don't know." She hesitated. "Though I have my suspicions. Ion didn't say anything to me, but he spoke to his stepson, Zach. Apparently, he's one of those who still believe I'm out to avenge Richard's death."

Instantly, her father's expression cleared. "I see. Now this at least makes a modicum of sense. I've never heard of this Ion, though your mother did tell me you were searching for a missing Mermaid. Let me call your brother and let him know." Picking up the red phone that went directly into the palace, he paused. "Are you free for lunch later? That is, if Merc agrees you don't have to come in just yet?"

Since Merc liked to play practical jokes on her and had since they'd been guppies, she wouldn't put it past him to insist she spend several hours answering questions at the palace.

"Dad, lunch sounds great, but do you mind if I head out before you talk to Merc? You know how he is. And I have a lot of places to cover before I have to return to land."

He nodded. "You have a point. As long as you don't get too busy and forget about me."

"I won't." Studying her notes, she reaffirmed her planned schedule out loud. "I should be over near Seaweeds at lunchtime," she said. "Do you want to meet me there?"

"Sure. But, Shayla, tell me again why you're searching for this missing girl here. As I understand it, she disappeared while on land."

"We don't know that for certain." She sighed. "She and her father, Ion, were visiting his wife on land. They were about to return to the sea when she vanished. Apparently, she had a mischievous streak, and at first they thought she might be playing a joke on them." She told him about the ransom note, and then the phone call Zach had received.

"Virgins?" The former king appeared dumbfounded. "To be honest, that part right there sounds like a joke. From someone who is either not very bright or hasn't kept up with their mythology." He shook his head. "Virgins. Honestly. What they're asking is inconceivable. As if we'd go out and round up a couple of innocents and demand they be willing to let themselves be handed over like chattel."

"I know." His outrage ignited her own. She'd been so intent on the weirdness and reason for the request that she hadn't stopped to think of the other aspect of it. "Right now, I'm focusing on who might have had some sort of grudge against her. I plan to speak to her friends, visit places where she worked and find out if she had a boyfriend. Meanwhile, if they contact Zach again, he's going to ask for proof of life."

Her father winced. "That's realistic. I have to say, none of this makes sense. I fail to see what the abductor would hope to gain. Surely he or she must be aware no one would try to trade other Mermaids—virgin ones, no less—for her. Sadly, the only conclusion I can come to is that the person making the request is mentally unhinged."

"I agree that's a possibility. That's why it's imperative we find her as quickly as we can. I've talked to the Pod—as has Ion—and her stepbrother has brought in the Shifter Pack Protectors. There are a lot of people looking for her, but right now we don't have a single clue where she is."

And Ion gunning for her to be questioned and possibly arrested had her wondering how badly he actually wanted his daughter to be found.

"What do you think of all this?" her father asked. "Do

you have any theories? I'm interested to know. And of course, I'll help you in any way I can."

She sighed and then told him everything, every single possibility that had occurred to her, including her new questions about Ion and his motives. The former king listened in silence, and when she'd finished, he quietly pondered her words.

"Have you looked into the mythological significance of virgins, specifically virgin Mermaids?"

"I tried." She shrugged. "I did see some studies indicating that originally we were believed to be half bird, half woman, then later half snake." Her smile felt more like a grimace. "I'm not sure how I feel about that. But I also read that later, the image of a half woman, half fish came into play. And I know all of the stuff about virgins, specifically sacrificial, but I can't tie the two together. A virgin Mermaid? Why?"

"Why indeed." He took a deep breath. "Maybe we should ask Poseidon. He knows everything."

"Poseidon?" Shayla froze. The ancient god of the sea terrified her, even though she'd only met him once. "You can't be serious."

"I am. Why not? You know he and I are good friends."

"The great Poseidon has better things to do than worry about one lost Mermaid." The second the words left her mouth, she winced. "Though of course, I'd welcome his help if he were so inclined to give it." Unfortunately, as everyone knew, Poseidon's help always came with a cost. She reminded her dad of this.

"That's only if he finds the request boring or stupid. He'd find this interesting, believe me." Her father spoke with assurance. "He loves a good mystery. And if anyone would know about the whole virgin mythology, he would."

She took a deep breath. "But I'm not sure we could afford the price. Despite what you say, you know he'd demand some sort of payment."

"That's possible," he agreed. "Though sometimes he's willing to wager on the outcome. Let me talk to him and see what he thinks."

"Just don't promise something you can't deliver." Mermaid lore was full of stories of Merfolk who'd thought they could outsmart the God of the Sea. It never ended well.

"Gotcha." He leaned in and kissed her cheek. "Though since it's a long journey to Poseidon's court, I'm going to have to take a pass on lunch. We'll do it next time. When will you be back?"

Staring at him, she battled mixed emotions. "Are you sure you want to involve him? Couldn't you wait a few days and then see if we still need help?"

"You said the caller gave you one week. I don't see how the situation could be any more urgent."

Again, he had a point.

"Fine," she conceded. "But I'm really disappointed you're standing me up for lunch."

He chucked her under the chin. "Something tells me you'll survive until the next time you visit."

"You're probably right. I do plan to check in pretty regularly. It shouldn't be more than a few days, if that."

"Good." With a jaunty wave, he left. On his way to seek out a cantankerous old god. The thought made her shudder.

Because she had a lot to do, Shayla tried not to worry about him. Aware she needed to get busy as well, she took off to begin her planned journey.

Chapter 7

Swimming back toward Galveston, instead of scouring the ocean floor for artifacts like she usually did, Shayla used the time to think. This entire scenario with Nantha missing, the request for virgins, and with Ion going to her brother and insinuating Shayla might have had something to do with it had her wondering what exactly everyone might be trying so hard to hide. Because her gut instinct told her all of this weird, extraneous stuff, was a smoke shield hiding the actual truth.

But why? Why go through so much trouble? If Nantha had run off, why wouldn't she just contact her family and let them know, so they wouldn't worry? If someone had actually abducted her—for whatever reason—why ask for something as improbable and impossible as virgin Mermaids in exchange? Surely, the abductor would know no one would trade one innocent life for another.

As she pushed her body through the sensual heaviness of

the deep ocean, she considered alternatives. Out of respect for Zach—and belief in his opinion of his stepsister—she'd disregard for now the option that Nantha had vanished of her own free will.

Which would mean she'd truly been abducted. But for what purpose? None of Nantha's friends claimed to know anything about a boyfriend or stalker. Shayla had also talked to people she'd worked with and her teachers in school. Again, no red flags had surfaced.

Her thoughts kept returning to Ion. He'd deliberately tried to implicate her in his daughter's disappearance. What she didn't understand was why.

Maybe her father's idea had more merit than she'd first thought. If anyone could cut through the murky water, Poseidon could.

The instant she stepped onto dry land and retrieved her things, she looked at her cell phone. Two missed calls, one message and a text. Her mother had texted, her father had called, and the second call had come from an unknown number. She punched the button to listen to the message, astonished when she realized someone from the Pod had contacted her. Of course, she'd filed a report with them as soon as she'd taken on Nantha's case.

Of course she called them back first. Her parents could wait.

But she got voice mail. Disappointed, she left a message with her name and number. Her mother had texted a simple please call me when you get this, so that's what Shayla did next.

"Is Dad okay?" she asked the instant her mother answered.

"Yes. He's on his way back. He didn't have to visit Poseidon after all."

"Good." Then, realizing this meant something had happened, she asked, "What's going on?"

"Have you spoken to your brother?" Blythe asked, excitement making her voice high-pitched. Without waiting for an answer, she continued. "The Pod has contacted him. Apparently, they've learned of a trio of young Mermaids who were attempting to lure fishermen."

Which was against the law. The Pod and king, who at the time had been Shayla's father, had made such acts illegal and criminal. In these days where everyone had a cell phone that could take videos, the danger to the underwater kingdoms was too great.

Still, from time to time, a few wild and unruly teenagers became so full of themselves and their Mer-beauty that they couldn't resist trying out their songs on unwary fishermen. One time back in the 1970s, a couple of idiotic sixteen-year-olds had even caused a foreign tanker ship to sink. The Pod had worked hard to cover that up.

The last thing any Merfolk wanted was for humans to learn of their existence. Just like all the other paranormal beings, they'd enacted laws to keep that from happening.

"Interesting," Shayla commented. "I wonder if that's why someone from the Pod left me a message."

"Probably." Blythe's voice rose even higher. "Because there's more. They told your brother that one of the young Mermaids was Nantha Deangelo."

"What?" Though Shayla had been walking back up to her house, she stopped in her tracks. "Are you sure?"

"Yes. The two who were arrested confirmed it."

"Two?" A chill snaked up Shayla's spine, only partly because she remembered her own imprisonment for the same crime. "Mom, what happened to Nantha?"

"That's just it." Her mother took a deep breath. "The girls were hysterical. They say she was captured. The very men they were trying to lure to their deaths grabbed Nantha and fled."

* * *

When Shayla phoned and asked him to come over to her house as fast as he could, Zach broke speed records. He was lucky he didn't get a ticket.

He rushed up the sidewalk. She opened the door before he even reached it.

"What is it?" he asked. "What's happened?"

"I've received some news about your sister. Come inside. Have a seat. You'd best be sitting down when I tell you."

Sitting down? Zach's gut twisted as he followed her into the kitchen. "So help me, if she's dead, just spit it out."

"She's not dead. At least, not that I know of. Sit." She pointed to the kitchen table as she went to the fridge and retrieved two bottles of beer. And then she proceeded to tell him what her mother had said.

"She what?" Staring at the beautiful Mermaid sitting opposite from him, Zach struggled to process the news. "I can't…"

She slid a beer across the table. "Here. I have a feeling you're going to need this."

Grateful, he took a deep drink. Once he'd carefully set the bottle down, he met her gaze again, ignoring the usual jolt of attraction. "You're saying my baby sister disappeared on purpose, at first."

"Right."

"And then she was getting her kicks trying to drown human fishermen when she was actually captured."

Shayla nodded. Without taking her eyes off him, she sipped her glass of wine. "And the humans who grabbed her know she's a Mermaid. This could spell disaster for not only our kind, but every paranormal species. The Pod is meeting with your Pack Protector and your council. They've invited the Vampire Council and all the others."

He swore. While what had happened carried a huge potential for disaster, he couldn't yet get past the shock of the betrayal. Nantha—sweet, always laughing, the baby girl Zach had carried around on his shoulder. His stepsister, Nantha, had let her entire adoring family think her dead or in danger. She hadn't given a single thought to how much pain her disappearance might have caused them.

And then she'd ended up getting captured after all. "I don't know whether to be furious or worried," he mused out loud.

"Hopefully if the other two Mermaids got a good look at the fishermen and their boat, we might have a chance of locating them. They're being interrogated by the Pod right now."

Dragging his hand through his hair, he nodded. "That would be helpful."

"Yes." She smiled at him over her wineglass. "It would."

He felt the pull of that smile, like a lure drawing him to her. For one crazy instant, he wondered how she'd react if he climbed up over the table and kissed her.

Instead, he forced himself to focus on her bewildering news. "Despite the gut-wrenching knowledge that my baby sister lied to us, the end result is the same. She's being held captive."

Her smile faded. "True."

"So if her captors are a couple of fishermen, what's with this demand for virgin Mermaids in exchange?" he asked, somehow keeping his voice level. Despite that, the warmth in Shayla's long-lashed emerald eyes told him she understood the emotions raging through him. "What's that all about?"

"The Pod is working to determine if that's real or if someone else who knows that happened is trying to cash in on your sister's capture," she said. "Consensus right now is that whoever has Nantha is most likely who sent the note. And called you. No one understands the virgin Mermaid request, though. That part is still unexplained." She swallowed. "And of course, we still need proof she's alive."

He winced. "About that. I didn't get a chance to tell you with all this going on, but they called again." Despite his attempt to sound unaffected, his voice broke. Dammit. "I asked to speak with her, for proof of life. As soon as I did, the caller hung up."

She went silent, no doubt reaching the same awful, stomach-turning conclusion he had. "Maybe," she ventured, summoning up a smile that had to be just for his benefit, "he didn't have access to her right then. He'll probably call back."

God, he hoped so. Right now, that was the only possibility he was prepared to face. "They'd better. I appreciate your effort to be positive." Restless, he got up, wishing he could get his hands on something to punch.

His inner Wolf, awakened by the turmoil inside him, grew restless. Zach realized right then what just might help release some tension. He needed to change and hunt. Let his Wolf out to run.

He decided that he would, after he finished this meeting with Shayla. His favorite place was north of Galveston Island, near his home in Texas City. Since he knew he'd need to deliver this news personally to his mother, he'd invite her to shape-shift and hunt with him that night after he told her.

"Does Ion know?" he asked. "I can only imagine how hard he'll take this news."

"I'm not sure." Shayla's mouth tightened. "But I'm thinking he would have been notified." She looked down before raising her head and meeting his gaze. "There's something I need to tell you. Ion went to my brother, the king, and filed a formal complaint against me. He claimed I had something to do with Nantha's disappearance."

Zach struggled to make sense of her words. "Why would he do that? I don't understand."

"Neither do I. If he's so worried about his daughter, why would he let his feelings against me take precedence over that? He must realize how much I intend to help search for her."

"I'm concerned about Ion." Zach took a swig of beer. "He's been acting odd ever since Nantha went missing. At first, I put it down to his concern over her disappearance. But he's been treating my mother weird, shutting both of us out. And now this."

Realizing he'd picked up his beer again, he took another gulp and then set it back on the table. "I'd better go," he said, his throat aching and his eyes stinging. "My mother's going to be devastated when she hears this."

The kindness in her expression nearly undid him. "I understand. I'll call you if I receive any new information."

Later, when he pulled up to his mother's house, he killed the car engine and sat in the car instead of immediately going in. While he'd rehearsed numerous different ways to give her the news, in the end he understood the delivery didn't really matter. The end result remained the same. Nantha had done the inconceivable. And her blithe disregard for everyone else had resulted in her placing her own life in danger.

Finally, he got out of the car and headed up the sidewalk. There was a slight possibility that Ion, who'd surely been informed by now, had immediately traveled here to commiserate with his spouse. But judging by the way Ion had taken to remaining under the sea except for the occasional weekend, Zach doubted it.

Sure enough, when he walked into the house, he found his mom sitting in her recliner, reading.

"Zach!" She smiled and jumped up, giving him a quick hug. "Such a pleasant surprise."

"I wish it was." Gently he steered her back to her chair. "I think you should sit down."

His words wiped the smile from her face. She dropped back into her chair, hand to her chest. "It's Nantha, isn't it?" she asked. "Please don't tell me she's been killed."

"It's not that," he reassured her. "But I do have bad news of another kind."

She listened intently as he told her the information Shayla's Pod had passed on. June's expression changed as she realized the truth. "You're saying Nantha did this on her own? Let us believe she'd gone missing and worry ourselves sick?"

Slowly he nodded. "And because of that, she's gotten herself in real trouble."

June grimaced. "Does Ion know?" Then, before Zach could answer, she answered her own question. "Of course he does. The Pod would have notified her father first."

If she wondered why her husband hadn't come to her with the news, she didn't say it out loud.

"This is incredibly frustrating," she said, pushing herself up out of her chair, her jerky movements revealing her inner struggle. "I feel like I should do something, but I don't know what. These fishermen who grabbed her—do they mean her any harm?"

"That I don't know." He reminded her of the ransom note and call. When he told her of the most recent conversation and how he'd asked for proof of life only to have the call abruptly end, she blanched.

Inside, his Wolf had grown more and more agitated, likely in response to Zach's riotous emotions. "I thought

I'd go hunt tonight," he said. "It's been a while, and my inner Wolf is restless. Do you want to join me?"

Immediately she nodded. "That might be the only way I can release some of this tension." She checked her watch. "Let's go now. It's certainly dark enough."

"Sounds great." He jingled his car keys.

"Oh, wait." The eagerness vanished from her expression. "Maybe I should stay here in case Ion shows up."

He managed to bite back the first thing that popped into his head. Casting aspersions against his stepfather would only make his mother feel worse. Instead, he managed to shrug. "That's up to you. But don't you think it's more likely Ion will arrive in the morning?"

Though she still hesitated, she finally nodded. "You're probably right. He hasn't come after dark since the early days of our marriage." The regret in her voice made him sad.

"Well then, come on." He needed to get her into the car before she changed her mind. "It's time for a little mother/son hunt."

"Yes, it is." Though her attempt at a smile was wobbly, it was a start.

He felt a little bit of the grimness inside lighten. "It's been way too long."

Once they reached the park, he noted there were two other cars in the lot. "I wonder if those people are still out on the trails," he mused. "Most times, humans won't go hiking after dark."

"That's true." She shrugged. "I'm not concerned. For all we know those cars could belong to other Shifters who came out here to hunt just like we did."

She had a point. "Are you ready?" he asked, his inner Wolf already half-giddy with anticipation of knowing he would soon be set free. "Meet you back here when we're finished?"

Instead of answering, she jumped out of the car and ran toward the woods. Feeling better than he had since Nantha vanished, he laughed and ran after her.

Once she entered the forest, she veered from the hiking trail, pushing through underbrush. He followed, knowing she wouldn't stop until they were sufficiently remote from all things human.

The smells here were different. Damp and musky, the earth seemed raw and primitive. The thicker undergrowth gave way to smaller paths, natural ones made by animals. Here, a Wolf could feel at home. Here, the hunting would be abundant.

"Does this look good?" June asked, dropping to all fours without waiting for his confirmation. She already knew, because they'd come here to shape-shift before.

With a nod, he moved on past her, wanting to give her a little privacy while shifted.

For a second, he knew a sharp instant's regret that he could never share a hunt with Shayla. If she had been Shifter, he knew she'd make a beautiful Wolf. But she wasn't and would never be, so it was foolish to even think about. He tried to picture her in her natural shape, with a vibrant, shimmering tail, but couldn't. All he could think about was how she'd look naked, in his arms.

Pushing the thoughts away, he focused on his Wolf, eager to break free. Finally, he judged he'd gone far enough and began removing his own clothing, folding it neatly and placing it inside the backpack he used for exactly this purpose. And then he cleared his mind of everything but the moment at hand and dropped to the ground and began the change.

The sparkling lights, like fireflies, surrounded him.

They seemed brighter this time, somehow. His Wolf, eager to burst free, tried to rush things, which always, without exception, meant pain. Zach forced his beast to wait, giving his human body time to make the adjustments to take him from man to beast.

His bones lengthened and changed shape. With excruciating clarity, he felt his pelt begin to grow, his skull become more angular. A flash of pain, here and there, quickly gone. Finally, filled with savage joy, he stood as Wolf, breathing in the moist scent of the damp earth and forest. In this form, his body felt compact, more muscular and much more in tune with nature. Wild and free, the burdens of his human existence fell.

When Wolf, he used his sense of smell first and his vision second. Scenting the breeze with his nose, he determined his mother had already taken off and was heading north. Low to the ground and moving fast, he went after her.

He picked up the scent of others hunting in the woods this night, and by tacit agreement he avoided them and they him. Every once in a while, someone would organize a group hunt and several of the local Shifters would hunt as a pack, but with the popularity of drones these days, and the danger of exposure, those had become few and far between.

This, though, was different. A much-needed run through the forest, crashing through the underbrush at breakneck speed, uncaring if the smaller creatures heard him coming and fled. He'd hunt later. For now, he'd enjoy being a Wolf.

His mother must have felt the same way. At one point, she zipped past him, a lupine grin on her face, tail high in a jaunty wave. They ran circles around each other, and when they reached the meadow, he tackled her the way he'd used to when he'd been a younger pup. She rolled, and he went with her, joyous camaraderie filling his heart. This moment, his worries and cares as a human were nonexistent, as he lived completely in the moment.

They passed several hours in this fashion. Because of their dual nature, part human, part Wolf, shape-shifting regularly kept them healthy and vital. When they changed back to human, their focus would feel sharper, their senses keener. All due to the experience of becoming their other self. This was how life as a Shape-shifter had always been, each side taking something from the other and giving back a different set of rewards.

Most times after the play ended came the hunt. And tonight would be no exception. He caught a careless rabbit and feasted, aware his mother most likely was doing the same somewhere else in the forest.

When he'd finished, he knew the time as Wolf had come to an end. Since time passed differently while in his Wolf form, he had no idea of the exact hour, but the sky had begun to lighten. That meant it would soon be dawn. Time to change back to human and go home.

When he arrived at the car, he saw his mother had gotten there before him. She waited in the passenger seat and waved at him.

"I feel much, much better," she said, once he'd gotten in and started the engine.

"Me, too." Though worry about Nantha had already started creeping back in, he pushed it away. His mother must have been doing the same thing, because neither of them spoke as he drove back to her house.

Once there, she invited him inside. "It's so late—or early, as the case may be."

He checked the clock, not surprised to see it was past four.

"You might as well see if you can grab a few hours of

sleep before you head back to the city." She underscored her point with a yawn.

"You're right," he replied, not bothering to keep his weariness from showing in his voice.

Once inside, he saw how eagerly she glanced around the house, unable to keep from hoping Ion had shown up. Zach went to her and put his arm around her slender shoulders. "He'll be here tomorrow, I'm sure."

"I know." But her smile seemed sad anyway. "I'm going to go lie down. If you're still here when I get up, I can fix you eggs and bacon."

Though he hadn't planned to hang around that long, how could he abandon her when her husband apparently already had? He'd need to stay until Ion showed up, which better be first thing in the morning. Like in a few hours. This morning.

"Sounds great," he said, releasing her. "I've got to head back before noon, but I'll try to catch a few hours shut-eye first." And he wondered when Nantha's captors were going to call him again.

As it turned out, Zach didn't have to wait long for a second phone call. Again, Caller ID showed Unknown Number. And again, the caller used some sort of voice distortion software, making it impossible to tell if the voice belonged to a male or a female.

"Well?" the person demanded. "The clock is ticking. Have you got me what I want?"

"I'm not getting you anything until I know my sister is alive," Zach said, his voice flat and hard. "I need to speak to her."

Silence. His demand must have shocked the abductor. So he repeated it. "I want to talk to my sister. Now."

The caller swore and ended the call.

Furious, Zach punched Redial. As before, he got the

same recording. The call could not be completed as dialed. What did the refusal to let him speak with Nantha mean? His gut twisted. His baby sister had to be alive. The alternative wasn't acceptable.

The next night, Shayla called a meeting at Broken Chains. Maddie showed up before Carmen, so Shayla filled her friend in on the news.

"Wow." Maddie indicated the beer bottle. "I'm guessing Zach didn't take it well."

"No. But then, who would?" Shayla sighed and took a sip of her wine, waiting while Maddie caught the waiter's attention and ordered a drink.

"Are you okay?" Maddie asked, once she'd asked for her usual beer. "You look exhausted and stressed."

"Thanks." Grimacing, Shayla shook her head. "This case is weighing on me more than I thought it would. I can't stop thinking about Zach."

Tilting her head, Maddie studied her. "Are you…interested in him?"

Shayla sighed. "I'm not sure. Probably. Yes." She briefly covered her face with her hands. "I have feelings. I haven't allowed myself to explore, and I'm not at all sure he feels the same way."

"I thought so!" Maddie exclaimed, leaning forward. "I'm glad. It's about time."

The waiter delivered her beer just then, also bringing Shayla a second glass of wine, even though she hadn't finished her first.

"I have no expectations," Shayla confessed, after the waiter moved away. "He and I have never discussed it. The awareness is just there, simmering under the surface. At least on my part. Right now, it's a business relationship, you know that."

"Pffff." Maddie almost spit out her beer. "Why can't it be both?"

Shayla considered. "It's our first case. You know as well as I do that it can make or break the Shadow Agency. I want this venture to be a success. I can't jeopardize that simply because I'm attracted to him."

"I do, too. But he's a Shifter, and I strongly suspect he's Pack, like me. We're very physical beings. And I can see the electricity sparking between the two of you."

Intrigued, Shayla eyed her friend. "Can you really? Because it all felt one-sided to me. Maybe once his sister is found, we can pursue it and see where it goes."

Again Maddie made a rude sound. "Why wait? Throw the guy a bone. I'll bet he could use a little 'comfort' right about now." She winked.

Despite herself, Shayla felt her face heat. "I can't be the one to make the first move."

"Come on, now. You're a freakin' Mermaid! Isn't that what you people do, entice men?" Maddie leaned forward, taking Shayla's hand. "I know you were devastated over losing Richard, but it's been two years. In all the time I've known you, this is the first time I've seen you show interest in a man."

Chapter 8

Shayla didn't respond. She didn't have to. Her friend was right. And Maddie knew it, judging from the look on her face as she took a long drink of her beer.

"Promise me you'll at least try," Maddie pressed. "Even if it's just a little release-the-tension sex. I don't know a single male Shifter, or male anything for that matter, who wouldn't be up for that."

"Up being an appropriate term," Carmen drawled. She'd glided up to the table without anyone noticing. Though her sudden appearance startled Shayla, and Maddie too, since she'd jumped, they'd come to realize that was just her way. "Sorry," she told Shayla, sounding anything but. "I couldn't help but overhear most of that. Maddie's right. You've got to grab your chance for fun, for happiness, when you can. You know as well as anyone how quickly things can change."

Like what had happened with Richard. The familiar

pang of grief came, though the sharpness of it had lessened over time. "You know what?" Shayla said, smiling at both of her friends. "You may be right. I'll never know until I try."

"That's the spirit," Maddie crowed. Carmen nodded, pulling out her chair and signaling the waiter, who immediately brought her a glass of her favorite blood.

"Such service," Carmen purred, looking the young waiter up and down with her long-lashed eyes. "Thank you very much."

He colored and dipped his head in acknowledgment. When he noticed the way Carmen's gaze fixed on the pulse beating at the base of his throat, he shook his head in bemusement and hurried off.

"Tasty treat, that one." Carmen smiled as she took a sip of her drink. "Mmmm. So where are we on the case?"

Shayla filled her in quickly, not leaving anything out. When she finished, Carmen sat in silence for a moment, digesting the words.

"Karma's a bitch, ain't it," she finally drawled. "You know, Shayla, if that girl made those fishermen fall in love with her, that's likely why they grabbed her. If that's the case, she's probably safe." She frowned. "The only thing that doesn't make sense is the request for virgins in exchange. That makes me think more of sacrificial rather than adored captive."

"Exactly." Shayla finished her first glass of wine. "My father even mentioned talking to Poseidon."

Both women stared. "The God of the Sea?" Carmen asked. "Seriously?"

Maddie closed her mouth. "Poseidon's a real...person?"

"Being," Shayla corrected. "He's kind of like the ultimate King of the Ocean. Immortal, powerful, et cetera, et cetera."

"All-knowing, all-seeing?" Carmen didn't bother to hide her skepticism. "If that's true, he could solve this case for us. I hope your father asks him. And soon."

"The only problem is Poseidon always demands a high price. More than money or things. Sometimes, the end doesn't justify the means. Now that we know more of the story, I don't think my dad will bother Poseidon."

"Unless you ask him to."

"Which I won't," Shayla said, her voice firm. She and Carmen had a stare-down for a few seconds. The Vampire had a bossy streak and knew it. The only way to deal with that was to be just as forthright.

Finally Carmen dipped her chin and conceded. "Fine. But think about how the client would feel if he knew there was such a simple solution."

"Contacting Poseidon isn't ever simple. And there's no guarantee he'd even help. He's been known to be quite capricious." Which was putting it mildly.

At least Carmen didn't try to argue with her this time. She simply took another sip of her drink, eyeing Shayla. "Then what else do you have planned to help solve this case?"

"I'm not sure. The captor has given us a short timeline. But until Zach is allowed to speak with his sister, we don't even know for sure she's alive."

"I've got my brother trying to trace the calls," Maddie said. "And both the Pack Protectors and the Pod are involved."

"Now that we know she did this deliberately and got snared in her own trap, our focus has shifted," Shayla pointed out. "The Pod are interviewing the other two Mermaids to pin down location and time. Once we have that, we can find out which fishing boats were in the area."

"Assuming whoever nabbed her is a commercial fisherman," Carmen pointed out. "If it was just a couple of guys out in a private boat, you might have a bit more trouble."

"True." Shayla smiled. "But we can talk to the marinas in the area and ask to see their surveillance cameras. Those will show anyone who went out fishing that day."

Carmen nodded. "You sound like you're pretty confident."

"I am. This additional information will help us find the kidnapper much more quickly."

"Before the week deadline is up," Maddie added, her voice hopeful.

"Do you have any idea if the fisherman was near Galveston?" Carmen asked. "Or farther down the coast, by Corpus or South Padre?"

"No. Mermaids sometimes swim great distances. Nantha and her friends could have been anywhere in the gulf. Louisiana, Mississippi, Alabama, even Florida. Though I'm hoping they were close to Texas. It'll make this guy much easier for us to locate."

"I'll chat up the local fishermen," Maddie said. "Though I don't think any of them will readily admit to seeing a Mermaid, once they have a few drinks they might mention someone they'd heard of who has."

"I'll go with you." Carmen shifted her weight in her chair. "And if there's anything else either of you can think of that I can do to help, let me know."

Shayla nodded. The band was about to start, which meant they'd soon have to shout in order to be heard. In actuality, she wanted to take a break from talking about this case. And about Zach. Right now, more than anything, she needed to relax and recharge. Listen to music and hang out with her friends. Maybe even dance.

"What's this about Zach?" Carmen asked. "That's who you two were discussing when I walked up, right?"

Maddie grinned and answered. "That's right. I'm trying to convince Shayla to loosen up and have a fling."

"Please." Shayla fixed both her friends with a mock stern look. "I really don't want to talk about him anymore. Can't we just have a few drinks, enjoy the music and each other's company?"

Both Maddie and Carmen laughed.

"That's a cop-out," Carmen said. "I never figured you for being one who'd back down from a challenge."

"I'm not backing down. I just want to give it a rest for one night. Can't we do that? Please?" She took a long, deliberately slow drink of her wine to keep herself from saying anything even remotely combative. They definitely didn't need to start arguing among themselves. They'd been friends first, long before they'd formed the Shadow Agency and before a sexy Shifter named Zach had strolled into the bar.

Carmen, however, loved nothing more than a good fight. "I think you're afraid," she began, leaning forward. The lazily amused smile she flashed made Shayla clench her teeth. That, too, was unusual. Most times she found Carmen's machinations entertaining.

Looking from one to the other, Maddie laughed. It sounded forced, as if she, too, sensed the underlying tension. "Come on, you two. The workday is over. Can we just hang out and relax? The case will still be there tomorrow. So will Zach."

"Agreed," Shayla said instantly, greatly relieved. Though Carmen was a bit slower to respond, finally she nodded.

The music started, cutting off further conversation. Tonight's band played upbeat dance music. Several couples got out on the small dance floor. This started a steady stream of single men approaching the table, asking one or the other of the three women to dance. Which was fun and perfect for Shayla's state of mind. While out there shaking and moving, she didn't have to think.

She danced until her feet hurt and she couldn't catch her breath. Back at the table alone, she begged off accepting another dance invitation, claiming she needed to take a break. She didn't invite the man—who appeared to be a Shifter—to sit down, even though he waited, clearly hoping she would. Finally, he got the hint and walked away.

Shayla motioned for a drink refill, and the waiter brought it, telling her someone at the bar had bought it for her. She shot a bland smile in that general direction, careful not to make eye contact. Though on any other night she might have welcomed masculine company, all she could think about was Zach. She wished he hadn't left, wished even more that she could have experienced being held in his arms while moving around the dance floor to a slow ballad.

Because if she'd had that opportunity, she'd find out if he wanted her. One of the things Merfolk excelled at while in human form was the art of seductive dance. She usually took great care to rein it in, like tonight. But with Zach, all gloves were off. She wanted him with the same intensity that she craved water. She wanted him as if she needed him to exist.

Stunned, she took a large slug of her wine. How had something this intense managed to slip by her? She'd known she found him attractive—hell, what woman wouldn't? But this longing, this desire, it went deeper than that.

She couldn't stop thinking about him. And not just because of the case.

When her phone rang and Caller ID revealed Zach's

number, Shayla's heart skipped a beat. Though she wondered if she'd be able to hear over the music, she answered, cupping her hand around the phone at her ear to help.

"Are you still at Broken Chains?" he asked, sounding surprised. "I can hear the band."

"Yes." Again the longing. "We're hanging out, doing a little drinking, some dancing. I'm thinking we might close the place down." Especially since both Maddie and Carmen were still on the dance floor. They'd only been back for a minute or two here and there before someone else appeared to drag them back out. Since Shayla had perfected the art of cold disinterest, she'd reached the point now where men were leaving her alone. If she wanted to dance she simply picked one, got up and asked him. As of yet, no one had turned her down.

"Wow." Zach went silent, which was a good thing as she wouldn't have been able to hear him over the guitar solo.

As soon as that song ended, the band announced their last song and launched into a slow one. The bartender yelled out "Last call," and the waiter appeared to ask if she needed one more drink. Though Shayla shook her head, Maddie and Carmen rushed up, both asking for another. Maddie looked flushed and out of breath, but happy. Even Carmen appeared tons more relaxed. Their dance partners had followed them back to the table, but both women waved them away.

"What time does the bar close?" Zach finally asked.

Shayla half turned away so she could continue the conversation. "In an hour. It's nearly five a.m.," she said. Out of respect to their Vampire clientele, Broken Chains closed at 6:00 a.m. "What's wrong? I have to think the only reason you would call me this late is because something happened."

He sighed. "I couldn't sleep and I just wanted to hear your voice."

Her heart stuttered, and she nearly choked. Catching both Maddie and Carmen eyeing her, she got herself back under control. There were several ways she could respond to that, none of them anything she wanted her friends to hear. She wasn't even sure she'd have the courage to say them out loud. Especially not in front of an audience. The music helped, but both Shifters and Vamps had really good hearing.

"Are you okay?" she asked, her voice softening as the last notes of the song played. The band thanked the room, people drifted back to their tables and many of the other customers began to leave. The band began packing their instruments. At least she could hear much clearer. But then everyone else could also hear her.

"I'm trying to be." His candor shocked her. "But there are times when it's not working. My mom and I hunted tonight. We got back about an hour ago. She didn't take the news well and both of us needed to blow off some steam. I hope that enabled her to get some rest."

Clearly, it hadn't helped him. Yet the knowledge he'd been thinking of her while lying awake in his bed made her feel tingly inside. She fell silent while she tried to think up something to say.

"I'm sorry." His tone changed, becoming clipped. "I can tell you're busy. Tell Maddie and Carmen hello for me. I'll talk to you tomorrow." Abruptly, he hung up.

Shayla stared at her phone, wondering if she should call him back and ask him what had just happened.

"Earth to Shayla." Maddie nudged her. "What's going on? Who was that? You're acting strange."

"Even weirder than normal," Carmen interjected. "What gives?"

"It was Zach," Shayla admitted. "He's having trouble sleeping. That's all."

Her two friends exchanged a look. "Really?" Carmen drawled. "That's interesting. Does he want you to come over?"

"No. It wasn't a booty call or anything like that. He's worried about his sister."

"Uh-huh." Maddie shook her head. "So he called you at five a.m.? Nope. I think it was definitely a booty call."

This time, the good-natured teasing just made Shayla smile. Because inside she wished it had been a booty call. Who knew, maybe she could have helped steer the conversation that way. Maybe the fact that she'd been in a bar instead of at home in bed had given Zach second thoughts. "Are you guys ready to go?" she asked.

"Sure." After downing the last of their drinks, Maddie and Carmen gathered their things. They made it a rule to stay together for safety's sake, especially this late at night, or early in the morning. This rule was generally to protect Shayla, since both Carmen and Maddie could easily protect themselves.

Along with several other patrons, they filed from the bar and into the long, narrow alley. Once they reached the street, they turned right, still moving along with a few others. The group thinned as they left the warehouse area, many melting away to return to their own homes or haunts.

Shayla couldn't wait to get home and climb into her bed. She knew once she closed her eyes, she'd dream of Zach.

Dammit. Staring at his cell phone after hastily ending the call, Zach cursed whatever urge had compelled him to give in to the need to hear Shayla's voice. What if she'd been sleeping instead of hanging out at the bar? How would she have reacted to having a client wake her?

He needed to remember that's exactly what he was to her. A client. No more, no less. These aching longings to see her, touch her, hear her, were aberrations he should put aside. At least until Nantha was found. After that, maybe Shayla would be amendable to exploring a different kind of relationship. Hopefully, one that involved nakedness and limbs tangling in the bedsheets.

He burned at the carnal images as he imagined Shayla, her perfect skin gleaming, under him in his bed. The stab of desire made him groan. Already aroused, he almost rushed to take a cold shower to cool himself off.

But he didn't. Instead, he handled his arousal with the same methodical precision he applied to daily problems at work. Not by giving himself release, oh, no. He wanted that to be with Shayla. He'd let the need continue to build, the better to savor the rush and the eventual explosion when they came together.

So instead, he forced himself to think of other things. Like where the hell was Ion when his wife needed him?

Somehow, he must have dozed off. When he next opened his eyes, the sun had fully risen, and he could smell bacon frying. Which meant June was already up and making breakfast. Perfect. He'd grab a bite to eat while waiting for Ion. And then once his stepfather had showed, Zach would head back to his own home before planning the rest of his day.

Hopefully, Ion would have some more information about Nantha. He'd think his stepfather would have talked to the Pod or something. Because right now, Zach felt as if they'd reached an impasse. Aside from somehow rustling up a couple of virgin Mermaids who were willing to become sacrifices, Zach had no idea what to do. Other than talk to Shayla and the rest of the Shadow Agency and see if they could come up with any other ideas. The caller had given them one week. With each passing day, they were running out of time.

"Good morning!" Smiling at him, June appeared chipper and in an excellent mood. Only the dark circles under her red-rimmed eyes and the downward slant to her mouth told a different story. Like always, when she was upset, she liked to keep busy. She cooked and cleaned, often baked. Like now. It appeared she'd actually been up a while. Three cakes, several dozen cookies and a batch of muffins were testament to how badly Nantha's disappearance—and her husband's conspicuous absence—had affected her.

"Mornin'," he said, managing to smile back.

"I hope you're hungry."

"I am." His stomach rumbled, as if to prove a point.

"Good. Because I made enough to feed both you, me, Ion and a small army."

Her rueful smile tugged at his heart. He could feel the twinges of a headache coming on. "Mom, I'm sure Ion will be here soon."

"He'd better be." Filling a plate with scrambled eggs, bacon, toast and several strawberries, she carried it over to him. "In the meantime, eat as much as you want."

"It looks delicious." And smelled like heaven, too. "Have you already eaten?" he asked as she poured him a mug of coffee, setting it in front of him before she retreated to stand over by the stove, where she had a clear view out the window of the ocean.

"I'm not hungry." Grimly, she drank from her coffee cup, still staring.

"Come on, Mom," he coaxed. "Please come and sit and have breakfast with me. I won't feel right eating unless you do."

The loudness of her sigh told him she knew exactly

what he was doing. Still, it worked. She put a little food on a plate and sat down across from him.

Now he could dig in. His mother even took a few bites, though mostly she just watched him eat.

"Ion's not answering his phone," she finally said, her inner pain coming through clear in her voice. "I'm not sure why."

"Maybe he went too deep," Zach reassured her. The Merfolk had developed phones that worked underwater, but only to a certain depth. If they traveled beyond that, the phone stopped working, until they came back up.

"Maybe," she allowed. But she didn't sound convinced. Still, she took a couple more bites of scrambled egg, nibbled on a piece of bacon, and some of the tension seemed to dissipate from her posture. "This has really affected him, Zach. And now knowing she did it deliberately? I just don't understand why Nantha would do something like this. I mean, she likes a good joke and can be mischievous, but nothing like this. It's not like her at all."

A few days ago, he would have said the exact same thing. Now, he had to wonder if he'd truly ever known his baby sister at all. Because the Nantha he'd believed he knew would never have hurt her family like this. Not for anything or anyone. There had to be more to the story. Or, being a teenager, she hadn't really thought things through.

And Ion's rapid personality change made Zach wonder if there was something the Merman knew, some secret he kept hidden from his wife and stepson.

After Zach had eaten his fill, he helped his mother bag up the leftovers and stow them in the fridge. He tried to shoo her out so he could do the dishes, but she refused. "You know I have to stay busy," she told him. "If I don't have something to occupy myself, I think too much."

He understood. Instead, he poured himself another cup

of coffee and carried it out to his mother's huge back porch. From there, one could see not only the ocean, but all up and down the beach. He even had a clear view of the rocky outcropping that the Merman used when he came ashore.

Aside from a few humans sunbathing, the beach appeared deserted. As for the sea, while Zach could make out the silhouette of a tanker way out in the bay, he saw no signs of any larger sea creature breaking the surface of the water.

Noon came and went and still no sign of Ion. Though he knew his mother no doubt kept trying to reach her husband, Zach stepped outside and dialed his stepfather's number. The call went straight to voice mail.

Damn. He glanced at his watch. He really needed to get back home.

Impulsively, he placed a call to Shayla. She answered on the first ring, sounding surprisingly chipper for someone who'd closed down a bar a few hours earlier.

"Any news?" he asked. "My stepfather hasn't come to fill my mother in and he's not answering his phone. She's getting pretty worried about him."

"Nothing," she replied, the warmth in her voice instantly making him want her. "But I'll be sure to let you know if anything changes."

"Same here." He ended the call, turning to go back inside when his phone rang. Thinking Shayla must have thought of something else she wanted to say, he answered. "What'd you forget?"

"Zach?" Not Shayla. The unknown caller. "I understand you wanted to speak to your sister."

Instantly every nerve went on alert. "That's correct."

"Here she is." Silence, then someone moaned.

"Talk to your brother." This time, the caller forgot to digitally alter his voice. Clearly a man.

"Zach?" Nantha. Sounding weak, but still Nantha. Alive. "It's me. I'm… I'm sorry." She sounded as if she was about to cry.

Nantha's tears were one thing Zach had always been powerless against. Now, though, his relief was so great he couldn't allow them to bother him. "Are you all right?" he asked.

"I'm alive. They don't hurt me. And now that they know I have to be in the seawater, I feel much better. I almost died, I think—"

"Enough." The abductor came back on the line. This time, he'd gone back to disguising his voice. Though tempted to tell him not to bother since he'd already heard him, Zach kept his mouth shut.

"Now, you have your proof of life. What about my demands? Are you ready to make the exchange?"

"Virgin Mermaids are kind of hard to come by," Zach said. "Surely there must be something else you want. Money, maybe?" He held his breath, hoping the caller didn't demand some outrageous amount like ten million dollars. Coming up with that would be as impossible as finding two virgin Mermaids willing to be sacrificed.

"Five days," the caller snarled. "And then she dies." He ended the call.

Zach swore. And swore again. He went back inside the house to find his mother cooking something else. This time, she appeared to be mixing batter with a grim sort of determined concentration.

"I talked to Nantha," he said.

Her expression lit up, just like that. "She's alive?"

"Yes. I didn't get to talk to her long, but it was definitely her."

June cried out. She gave him a fierce hug. "Thank goodness." Grabbing her phone off the kitchen counter, she smiled through her happy tears. "I need to tell Ion."

But as she listened, her smile slipped a notch. "No answer," she finally said, ending the call. "I don't understand what's going on with him. I know he's heartbroken and I understand he's searching under the sea, but he doesn't answer the phone at all anymore, never mind return my calls when I leave a message."

She lifted her chin, trying for bravery, though hurt shone from her eyes. "It's like once Nantha disappeared, he did, too."

"I'm sorry, Mom." He didn't know what else to say. "Hopefully once everything gets back to normal, he will, too."

"I hope so." Sniffing, she returned her attention back to her baking. "I'm making an angel food cake. Your favorite."

"I've got to go," he told her, dropping a careful kiss on her cheek. "Are you going to be okay here alone?"

"Yep." Her instant response came too quickly. "And I'll keep the cake refrigerated so you can have some the next time you're here."

"Sounds good." As he turned to go, she caught at his arm.

"Zach, please find your sister. I know she's done wrong, and she might be in a heap of trouble down there under the sea, but she's still my girl. I love her." Her voice wobbled, and her eyes filled with tears.

"Of course we're going to find her." He took her hand. "Don't you ever doubt that."

"I don't." Her immediate answer made him smile. "Promise you'll call me if you learn anything?"

"I promise." As he let himself out the door, he cursed Ion. While he understood his stepfather's pain, his mother needed her husband, too. They should have been able to lean on each other for support during this trying time. Instead, Ion had pulled away, retreating into his own world.

Chapter 9

As he got into his car, Zach found himself thinking of Shayla. Wondering where she was, what she might be doing. He even got his phone out with the intention of calling her. Instead, he stopped himself.

Shayla had become a distraction of epic proportions. And right now, he couldn't allow himself to be distracted. Once Nantha was found and returned home safely, then and only then could he afford to explore the connection between them.

Mind made up, he dropped his phone into the cup holder and started the car to head home. He'd just gotten to the seawall where he planned once again to look for any sign of Nantha, when his phone rang.

Shayla's name popped up on the screen. His heart skipped a beat. "What's up?" he asked.

."I have a plan," she said, sounding upbeat and well rested.

"Great. What is it?"

"I've got some work to do before I can talk about it, since it's so urgent. Once I know more, I'd prefer to discuss it with you in person, along with Maddie and Carmen. Can you meet us at Broken Chains tonight? I'm thinking early, before the band shows up. How's six sound?"

"I'll be there." Deliberately he kept his tone business-like. If she noticed, she didn't comment. He had to admit he was interested to hear her plan.

Shayla felt energized. The idea for saving Nantha had come to her while showering. She couldn't believe she hadn't thought of it before.

It would work. It had to. The time had come to be pro-active rather than reactive.

She practically inhaled an early dinner before heading to Broken Chains. When she arrived, shortly after five thirty, to her surprise, there were still quite a few other customers there.

"Happy Hour," the waitress told her when she asked. "We have a special one for Saturdays. People come after shopping. They usually leave before the second crowd ar-rives." She smiled. "The late-night customers, the ones who come to hear the band and drink and dance."

"So there's not really any time the bar is less crowded?" Shayla asked.

"Between six a.m. and noon, but we're closed then."

They both laughed. Shayla went ahead and ordered her wine. She hoped everyone arrived right about the same time. She didn't want to reveal any details of her plan until they were all present. And she knew her friends would im-mediately start bugging her to spill.

To her surprise, Zach walked into the bar less than five minutes after her drink arrived. Since there wasn't live music yet, she'd taken a table downstairs, the same one in the back corner that she'd come to think of as hers.

As soon as she saw him, her entire body tingled. She was about to wave, but he saw her, so she didn't have to.

Approaching the table, he locked his gaze on hers. She resisted the urge to lick her lips.

"Where are your friends?" he asked, pulling out the chair next to her.

She shrugged. "Not here yet. You're early."

"So are you." He grinned as the waitress, unasked, brought him a beer. "How'd you know?" he asked, after thanking her.

Her smile was deliberately coy. "I've seen you around in here. Don't look so surprised. A guy who looks like you must be used to that."

Zach's thunderstruck expression made both women laugh. The waitress walked off, still chuckling.

"Was she serious?" Zach asked, as he took a sip of his beer.

"Of course she was." Tilting her head, she studied him. "Seriously, are you kidding me?"

He frowned. "About what?"

Maddie and Carmen arrived then, saving her from answering. Still frowning, Zach greeted them.

"What's with the sour face?" Carmen asked, blunt as always.

Unfortunately, this question made Shayla laugh again. "Zach's not used to receiving compliments," she said, and told them what the waitress had said.

Maddie and Carmen looked from Shayla to Zach and back again. "Okay," Maddie commented.

Carmen shook her head. "Come on, Shayla. You're just as bad. Men are falling all over you if you even so much as smile at them."

"No, they're not."

Shayla's instant protest had the other two women giggling.

"See?" Carmen finally said.

Shayla glanced at Zach, who shrugged. The waitress, who evidently had been paying attention to every one of them, brought Maddie's usual beer and Carmen's tall glass of blood.

"Bavarian opera singer," the waitress said, in response to Carmen's arched brow.

"Perfect." Carmen flashed her dazzling white teeth. "Thank you."

Once the waitress left, Zach leaned forward. "Okay. We're all here. Tell me your plan."

"Yes," Maddie echoed.

Shayla took a deep breath. "You know how the captor wants two virgin Mermaids? We'll tell him we got one."

"What?" Carmen spoke first. "Are you serious?"

"Perfectly serious."

As of yet, Zach hadn't reacted. Instead, he crossed his arms and leaned back in his chair. "Where are you planning to come up with a virgin Mermaid?"

"It won't be a real virgin," she assured him. "But they won't know that. Not up front."

"I don't follow," he said slowly.

"I'll do it," she told him. "I'll pretend to be a virgin Mermaid. I can be the bait to get Nantha back."

Immediately Maddie and Carmen protested. "No way. That'd be too dangerous," Maddie said.

Carmen was more direct. "Don't be stupid here, Shayla. We kind of like having you around."

Zach just stared, his expression shut down. She couldn't read his thoughts at all.

"I'm serious," she reiterated, her eyes locked on his.

"Clearly we've got to make some kind of an exchange. And we can't endanger any innocents. I'm a Mermaid, and it looks like I'm going to have to do."

"What makes you think they'll believe you're a virgin?" he drawled, his gaze intense.

Though she could feel her face heat, she stood her ground. "How are they going to know I'm not?" she countered. "There's only one way to tell for sure, and I'm not letting them go anywhere near there." With a rush of horrified shock, she realized what she'd just said also applied to his sister. And since the abductor already claimed to know Nantha wasn't a virgin...

"Of course, maybe they'll take my word for it," she hastened to add.

Carmen laughed. Maddie just shook her head and took a deep drink of her beer, her expression troubled.

But the person whose opinion most mattered said nothing. Shayla eyed him and waited.

Finally, he shifted in his chair, locking his gaze on her. "You know what?" he said, his tone firm. "I don't like you putting yourself in danger like that."

She grimaced. "It's not like we're going in blind. We have backup—each other. Besides that, what other options do we have?"

Expression furious, he considered. She saw in his gaze the moment he decided to go along with her plan.

"You're right. It's an excellent idea, and it just might work."

Maddie groaned. With eyes only for each other, Shayla and Zach ignored her.

"I'm glad you think so." Her original excitement had come back, thrumming in her veins. "What should we do next? Do you have a way to contact them?"

"No. But I should be talking to them soon. All I need

to do is wait for them to call me again, which they hopefully will. When they do, I'll just say I could only come up with one Mermaid, and they'll have to take it or leave it."

"Perfect." Delighted, Shayla sipped her wine. "I feel better now that we have a plan. But, Zach, please don't say anything to Ion or your mother. I can't let the Pod find out about this or they'd put a stop to it. Somehow they seem to frown on royal princesses putting themselves in danger."

"You won't be at risk." Zach's immediate response made her feel all warm and fuzzy. "I won't let anything happen to you."

"Zach, you don't know Shayla that well," Maddie put in. Shayla shook her head at her friend.

"She can be impetuous," Carmen added. "She doesn't always think things through. And I for one am worried this is one of those times."

"Maybe you could pretend to be the Mermaid," Maddie said, meaning Carmen.

"Wouldn't work," Shayla answered. "Especially if you have to swim. With my natural tail, I can swim faster than a Great White. I can definitely outswim any human."

"What if they shackle you?" Carmen interjected. "I really think you should rethink this idea. There's got to be a better way to rescue Nantha."

"If there is, we haven't come up with it," Shayla said, glancing at Zach, glad he agreed with her.

But now, his expression appeared troubled. As he met her gaze, he shook his head. "Maybe they're right," Zach said slowly. "Shayla, I can't let you put your life in danger. We've got to come up with a better idea."

"I can take care of myself," she protested, thinking furiously. "Plus Carmen can go with me. We can both be the virgins they want. She's immortal and freakishly strong."

Carmen grinned at the compliment. "Agreed."

This addition to her plan appeased both Maddie and Zach. "I like it," Maddie said, smiling.

"Me, too," Zach agreed, finally leaning back in his chair.

Shayla couldn't help it—she laughed. "I give up. I love the way none of ya'll think I'm strong enough."

"It's not that," Zach hastened to explain. "It's just we feel better knowing we have backup."

Slowly, she nodded. The warmth in his eyes made her blood heat.

"By the way," he said, low-voiced. "I love the way you laugh."

Instantly, she blushed. Carmen and Maddie laughed. And once again, things were back to normal.

Though he'd agreed to try it, the more he thought about it, the less Zach liked Shayla's plan. Having Carmen as backup was reassuring, but Shayla was a royal Mer-Princess. But, as she'd pointed out, at least they were doing something as opposed to before.

The women chatted away, drinking and laughing, as if two of them hadn't just decided to put themselves in grave danger. And now that Shayla had brought it up, the virgin aspect bothered him. He hadn't thought of his sister that way at all. Thinking about what Nantha's captors must have done to her to make that determination had him clenching his teeth and plotting their death. How dare they?

He also realized the idea of anyone putting their hands on Shayla was enough to make him go ballistic. Damn Nantha. What the hell had she been thinking to pull a stunt like this? Not only had she endangered her own life, but the lives of others.

Of course, the fact that she wasn't a virgin had probably been what saved Nantha's life, at least if the sacrificial theory was correct. He truly didn't understand the whole virgin thing. Virginity was overrated as far as he was concerned.

Looking up, he realized all three of the women had gone silent. They stared at him, Carmen with her perfectly arched brows raised, Maddie with a look of amusement quirking her lips and Shayla with what had to be exasperation. "Overrated, huh?" she asked, making him realize he must have spoken his thoughts out loud.

"Just so you know," she continued before he could speak, lifting her chin to meet his gaze. "I'm hoping we can stall them long enough to get your sister free. I'm not planning on being around them long enough for them to be able to check out whether I'm a virgin or not."

Relieved, he nodded. There was no way someone as passionate as Shayla could be untouched. As soon as he had the thought, he squashed it. While her love life was none of his business, at least she wasn't at risk of being sacrificed—or whatever it was they wanted to do to the poor virgins. However, the abductor might be so infuriated to learn he'd been lied to, he might just kill her and be done with it. Even with Carmen there to back her up, there was no way her safety would be guaranteed.

He didn't know what he'd do if he lost her. A shudder snaked up his spine at the thought. "I still have reservations," he began.

"We'll be fine," Carmen said immediately.

Shayla echoed her response.

"You know I feel really left out," Maddie interjected, sitting up really straight. "I want in. Let me be part of this, too."

Shayla included him in her smile. "I only need one other 'virgin' Mermaid. Maddie, I think it would be better if you stayed here to hold down the fort. You know we just started advertising. It might not be long before someone else might need our services."

Though disappointment clouded her pretty features, Maddie nodded. Meanwhile, Carmen looked like a cat who'd just finished eating a canary. "No worries, Zach. I can pretend to be a Mermaid," she drawled. Swiveling her head around to eye Zach, she smiled. "And I can protect her."

"Thanks," he told Carmen, before turning back to Shayla. "I'll agree to go forward with this plan. But I'm going with you."

"What?" Shayla shook her head so vigorously, that her long, inky hair whipped around her head. He ached to wrap his fingers in that hair, and pull her to him. "No, you're not. Having you there would negate the entire thing. They'd know it was some sort of setup."

"I disagree. Since I'm supposedly the one making the exchange, it's only right that I'd be there to make sure everything went off without a hitch." He folded his arms, aware he wasn't going to budge on this.

Again they locked gazes. His entire body tightened and his mouth went dry. Even now, the attraction sparking between them felt palpable. Talk about the worst possible timing. He refused to look away until she agreed. Finally, she nodded. "Fine. You're right. When the abductor phones you again, set up the exchange."

Relieved, he smiled. Now he could only hope his sister was all right. And that he and Shayla and the Vampire could pull this off without anyone getting hurt. Except, he amended grimly, the abductors. They could rot in hell for all he cared.

"I'm going to say I told you that I know he is the son of a famous movie producer and that he wanted to make both of you famous. That's how I got you to agree to go with me to meet him."

"Perfect," Shayla exclaimed, the admiration in her beautiful eyes making them glow. "Good thinking."

His body stirred in response. Whatever it was about this woman, the connection between them begged to be explored. Which he would, once all this craziness was over.

After finishing his beer, he excused himself and left. On his way toward the exit, he couldn't keep himself from glancing back over his shoulder. As he'd hoped and suspected, Shayla was watching him, too. Once again, their gazes locked, and that zing of attraction sparked.

Damn. Resolutely, he turned back around and headed for the door.

The next day, he kept busy. After slugging down his first cup of coffee, he went back to Galveston Island to begin another round of checking posters and asking people if they'd seen Nantha. Though he knew she was being held captive somewhere, he still cherished a hope that someone might have spotted her right before she was grabbed. At least then, he'd have a basic idea what general area she might be in.

Also, staying busy kept him from wondering if her captor would call him again. Since the clock was rapidly ticking, he figured the calls might escalate to every day.

When his phone rang, he actually jumped. Again, Caller ID said Unknown Caller.

"Well?" the abductor asked, again using the voice distortion software. "Your sweet little sister is just about out of time."

"I have what you want." Zach didn't bother to hide his rage. "Two virgin Mermaids. They think they're going on a fun adventure, so they're coming willingly. I told them you're related to a well-known movie producer and want to make them famous." He took a deep breath. "They bought it. When and where do you want to meet?"

His response apparently surprised the other guy, judging from the silence on the line. When he spoke again, he sounded uncertain. "You seriously have them? Are you sure they're virgins?"

"Very sure." Zach put a slight sneer into his voice. "I took the time to have them examined by a doctor. I told them it was to make sure they were healthy."

"Wonderful." The man appeared to believe him. "We will meet tonight down by the Pleasure Pier."

"That's too crowded," Zach protested. "There's too much of a chance of being seen."

"And that's exactly why I chose it. Your sister will be in human form. Make sure the other two are, as well. We'll meet there, and you can take Nantha, while I'll leave with the others. Ten tonight. It'll be good and dark by then."

Though every internal alarm clanged a warning, Zach agreed to the meeting. As soon as he hung up, he phoned Shayla and told her the plan.

"Perfect," she said. "The only thing we've got to be careful of is the darkness." Her brusque tone told him she was already thinking ahead. "Let me get ahold of Carmen. We'll meet you at the pier at nine. That'll give us time to scope the place out."

If he hadn't known better, her confidence would have him believing she'd done this before.

"Fine." Hating himself, he ended the call and began to pace. He had just a few hours to come up with a foolproof plan to ensure he didn't mess this up. He decided to arrive an hour early.

Fifteen minutes before nine, he parked his car and killed the engine. Despite his best efforts, the uncertainty of the situation had rendered him unable to mark out a clear and certain path. He'd actually jotted down several different variables, each a potential action by Nantha's captor. For those, he'd come up with possible reactions, which made him feel slightly more prepared.

The two women sat on one of the numerous benches on the long pier. They looked like typical tourists. Shayla had chosen to wear a bright floral sundress while Carmen wore neat Bermuda shorts and a tank top.

Shayla looked at him as if he'd sprouted two heads when he told her what he'd done. "You outlined every possible scenario?" she asked in disbelief. "That's unreal."

"I'm an engineer," he said with a shrug. "That's just how we think."

Carmen snickered. "He's right, you know. One of my best friends is an engineer, and that's exactly how she is."

Surprised to find her an unexpected ally, he grinned. "Truth. And it comes in handy ninety percent of the time."

Shayla snorted and rolled her eyes. With that, the tension that had crackled in the air around them dissipated like smoke in a stiff breeze.

Still, time seemed to crawl. Finally, at 9:45, they all looked at each other.

"Let's do this," Shayla said. "I'm ready."

"I am, too," Carmen chimed in.

"Okay, Mermaids. Remember, the cover story is that this guy is the son of a famous movie producer. He's offered you both a chance at fame and fortune."

The two women exchanged amused glances. "Got it," they drawled.

Even at this late hour, there were still plenty of people on the pier. While this made Zach a bit nervous, he also found it oddly reassuring.

They were early, so they had plenty of time to wander

around and check out the pier. Shayla and Carmen were acting like vapid schoolgirls, hanging on to each other and giggling. Since he figured Shayla would know better than anyone else how a virgin Mermaid would act, he pretended to humor them. All the while he kept a sharp eye out for anyone resembling his younger sister. To his immense disappointment, he didn't see her.

Yet. Or so he told himself.

Right before ten, Zach picked a spot closer to the carnival rides and stationed himself there. He had Shayla and Carmen take seats on a metal bench. Their backs were to the ocean, and a snow-cone shack provided a buffer to their right and a corn-dog stand to their left. This way, they could only be approached straight on. Much more easily defensible. Carmen caught his eye and dipped her chin, indicating her approval.

A few minutes after ten, Zach felt as wound up as a starving wolf closing in on a plump rabbit. He scanned the face of every single person who came in their direction. None of them had his stepsister's unique blue eyes.

"Excuse me." A man wearing a Houston Astros baseball cap bumped into him, hard enough to make Zach stagger. "I'm looking for the men's room," he mumbled, sounding drunk.

Instinctively, Zach recoiled. But the stranger leaned in close. "If you want your sister, follow me." And then took off, weaving through the crowd.

"That was him," Zach said. "We need to go after him."

They rushed after the man, keeping his baseball cap in their sights as he dodged people. He appeared to be alone, which meant if he truly planned to turn over Nantha, he'd stashed her somewhere else.

They couldn't risk losing him.

Finally, he left the pier, heading for the parking lot of

a crowded seafood restaurant. Though Zach found that choice both odd and questionable, he had no option but to go after him. Patrons were coming and going, and cars circled the lot searching for a place to park.

"I don't get it," Zach murmured to Shayla, who stuck close by his side. She shrugged, her attention focused on their quarry. Carmen's was too, her expression intense.

Instead of going inside the restaurant, the man went around to the back. More parking, most likely for the staff, and an industrial-size trash Dumpster enclosed on three sides by a six-foot fence.

The man stopped in front of the Dumpster and waited for them to catch up. He looked the two women up and down, leering. "Are these the two you promised?" he asked, his voice husky.

Zach had to bite back his disgust. He bet Shayla and Carmen did too, though he didn't dare look at them to see.

"Where's my sister?" Zach asked.

"She's here."

"Prove it." Somehow, Zach suspected she wasn't. He wouldn't be surprised if this guy didn't make a grab for Shayla and Carmen without turning over Nantha. At least he knew the two of them would be prepared in case this happened.

"Just a second." Boldly, the man circled around the women, inspecting them. "I need proof they're Mer."

Damn. The one thing they hadn't prepared for.

Maybe he hadn't, but Shayla must have. Still pretending eager anticipation, she pulled a photo from her pocket and handed it over. "Here. It's me, with my fish tail. It'll have to do, since obviously I can't change into my Mermaid shape right here."

He studied the photo before passing it back. "What about you?" he asked, turning to Carmen.

With a bored expression that didn't quite hide her rage, she, too, handed over a photograph. This had to be something she'd doctored, so Zach hoped it looked convincing. Evidently it did, as baseball cap guy nodded and returned it to her.

"Now, about my sister?" Zach asked, his hard voice matching his expression.

"Right." Moving toward the Dumpster, the other man slid it open. Inside, a clearly terrified Nantha stared out at them. A second glance showed she was not only gagged, but her hands were tied behind her back.

Chapter 10

Zach saw red. The effort to contain a rage unlike any he'd ever felt had him struggling to keep his inner Wolf contained. His beast snarled and fought like a crazed beast to escape. It took every ounce of strength Zach had to keep him contained. He knew better than to shift to Wolf unless absolutely necessary.

Shayla must have noticed. She bumped him with her hip. "What's all this?" she asked in a petulant voice. "Where's the movie guy? What's the deal with the girl in the Dumpster?"

"Yeah," Carmen chimed in. "Is this some kind of a hoax? Because I'm thinking it's not very funny."

Their playacting bought Zach the time he needed to get himself under control. "All in good time," he told Shayla. "Be patient."

Though they huffed and puffed, they nodded. Then he turned to the stranger. "Release my sister," Zach demanded.

"Get her yourself."

As Zach helped Nantha climb out of the garbage-filled Dumpster, he first removed her gag. Instead of speaking, she gasped, sucking in great lungfuls of air. Tears welled up in her huge eyes, and she began shaking.

"It's okay," Zach told her, his fingers fumbling as he struggled to remove her bonds. "You're safe. You're coming home with me."

He barely had her free when she caught sight of Shayla. Her eyes widened as she stared, clearly shocked. "Your Highness?" she asked. "What are you doing here?"

Before Shayla could answer, two men appeared from around the back side of the Dumpster. They were both armed, with their pistols pointed directly at Zach and Shayla. Another gun suddenly showed up in the hand of the guy in the baseball cap. "Nobody move," he ordered.

Zach shoved Nantha toward Carmen. If anyone could get his sister to safety, she could since Vampires had supernatural speed. "Carmen. Take her and run," he shouted.

To her credit, the Vamp didn't hesitate. She snatched Nantha up as if she were weightless and took off, holding the young Mermaid in her arms as she sprinted away.

Though Zach braced himself for the three men to shoot, they did not. Instead, they kept their attention—and weapons—on Zach and Shayla. Zach considered jumping them, since regular bullets couldn't kill him, only silver ones could. But he figured bullets most likely would be fatal to Shayla, and he simply couldn't risk her getting shot.

At any moment he figured someone would comment on Carmen's freakish speed, but no one did. Had to be because they were human and had no idea only Vamps could run that fast.

"Now we're short a Mermaid," ball cap guy commented. "Though, maybe, from what the other one said, we might have a very important Mermaid." He swung his gaze around to lock on Shayla. "What did she mean when she called you 'Your Highness'?"

"I have no idea," Shayla said, still using the petulant, spoiled tone. "And this is getting boring. Where's the movie guy? I'm here because I was promised he'd make me a star." She looked him up and down, her upper lip curling. "And what's the deal with the guns? Put them away, right this instant."

One of the men laughed out loud. Ball cap guy simply frowned. "Drop the act," he ordered. "You can't possibly be that stupid."

Shayla opened her mouth and then, after exchanging a quick glance with Zach, closed it. Because they both knew he was right.

"We have her," he told his cohorts. "But now what do we do with her escort?"

"He's with me," Shayla put in hurriedly. "I'm not going anywhere without him. If you want to take me, you've got to take him, too."

Instead, ball cap guy shook his head. With his gun still leveled on Zach, he squeezed the trigger and shot him point-blank.

Pain seared like fire through his gut. Zach doubled over, his forehead beaded with sweat. While a gut shot like this would be fatal to a human, to a Shifter it was merely excruciatingly painful. And inconvenient, since Zach would need to have a few hours to heal.

"You can't leave him here to die, boss," one of the other guys said. "That'll bring on too many questions."

"True. Bring him and the girl with us. Let's get out of here before someone sees."

Thankful for small blessings, Zach grimaced and grunted in pain as they loaded him up in the back of a minivan. Shayla climbed in after him, the expression in her eyes telling him she was struggling with fear and concern. "Are you all right?" she whispered in his ear.

He managed an almost imperceptible nod. "Not a silver bullet," he whispered back. Then louder, "Please, do something to stop the bleeding."

Shayla nodded, removing her jacket and pressing it up against his wound. He groaned, because it hurt like hell. "This should do it," she told him. Then, clearly remembering she was playing a part, she huffed. "Why did you shoot my agent?" she demanded, a tremble in the false bravado of her voice exactly right. "And where are you taking me? What is all this about?"

But no one would answer. The driver started the engine, and the truck took off. Every bump, every turn, every jolt, brought Zach a fresh stab of pain. His body had already started the healing process, which brought another kind of pain. But once he'd healed, he'd have a definite advantage. No one worried about defending themselves from a guy with a gut shot wound.

Zach had been shot! First instinct, Shayla panicked. While she wasn't normally a violent person, the knowledge that these men had harmed him made her wish she was a Wolf Shifter so she could change and rip out both their throats.

She wanted to protect him, heal him and avenge him. But then she remembered Shifters couldn't be killed unless by fire or a silver bullet, and it was unlikely these men's bullets were anything but ordinary.

But still…

As soon as some of the color started returning to Zach's face, Shayla knew he'd be all right. Shifters were well known for their almost magical self-healing abilities and while she'd known he wouldn't die, watching him suffer had been another form of torture. With her gut still twisted in knots, she took deep breaths, trying to calm herself down.

Meanwhile, their captors continued to drive. They didn't speak much, not even among themselves. She wasn't sure what exactly they might have planned for her, but she'd gotten a good look at Zach's stepsister and she suspected it wouldn't be good. The other Mermaid had been supernaturally pale, her complexion more like that of a recently risen Vampire than a denizen of the sea. While Shayla had no idea what these men had done to Nantha while holding her captive, whatever it had been hadn't been healthy. No doubt they had something similar planned for Shayla.

She wondered exactly how long it would take Zach to return to normal. Hopefully, sometime between now and when they arrived at their destination, wherever that might be. She'd need his help to keep them from hurting her.

Right about now, she could have used Carmen's Vampiric strength. But at least Nantha was safe. Mission accomplished. Now she just needed to figure out a way to get her and Zach to safety.

"Where are we?" Zach's groggy voice startled her out of her thoughts. "I can usually see pretty damn good in the dark, but I can't see a thing."

"Still in the van," she replied, stretching. "I must have dozed off. They tied me up before they left. I'm guessing they went to get a good night's rest before starting in on me tomorrow."

A rustling sound told her Zach had shifted his position. "They didn't even try to restrain me." The grim satisfaction in his voice made her smile.

"Because you were gut shot. Most people don't recover

from a wound like that. Luckily for both of us, they don't have any idea what you are."

"True." His stomach growled. "Right now what I am is hungry."

Only a man could think about eating at a time like this. "Sorry. I don't have any food. But would you mind untying me?"

"Okay. But I want you to make it so it looks like you're still tied up when they come back."

Unbelievably, she found his fumbling around in the dark arousing. Her breath caught in her throat as he slid his fingers down her arm, searching for the rope. When he found it, he slipped his fingers under it, giving her a brief relief from the pressure. And then, it tightened again as he worked to undo the tie. She held her breath, not wanting to cry out or do anything that revealed how painful her wrists had become.

Finally. Freedom. She bit back a small moan, as he rubbed the spot where the rope had been. It tingled as blood began to flow back. "Oh, thank you," she breathed. "That feels so much better. I can feel my hands again."

Next he freed her feet. She held herself absolutely still while he trailed his hands down her sides, along the curve of her hip. Was it her imagination, or did he linger there slightly? But, no, he felt down the outside of her thighs, all the way to her ankles. There, the rope had been tied tighter, and she could no longer feel her feet at all. When he finally released her, she couldn't suppress a cry of relief.

"Let me rub it." His voice sounded husky. Dizzily, she wondered if touching her affected him the same way it did her.

Bad timing, she chided herself, even as she arched her body toward him. They had no way of knowing when their captors might return.

Still, knowing that did nothing to prevent the yearning, swift and sure, coursing through her. She'd long known she wanted him, though she'd been less certain of his feelings. Even now, while she secretly panted over him in the dark like an unhinged fool, he caressed her ankles, his confident, sure touch bringing the blood flow back.

A second later, a sound outside the van had them scrambling to redo the ropes.

A light came on, showing her that the van had been parked inside a garage or warehouse, which explained the utter enveloping blackness. A door opened and several men came in. Two from earlier and a couple that she hadn't seen before. Baseball cap guy was one of them.

"Are they in the van?" A man in a white lab coat asked. There were three dressed this way. Shayla figured this either meant they were doctors or lab technicians.

"Yeah. But we couldn't get two virgins. One ran away with the Mermaid we were using for trade."

The three men conferred among themselves.

"Have you verified her untouched status?"

"Of course not!" Clearly shocked, baseball cap guy stepped back. "I'm not letting myself get tempted that way. Look what nearly happened to John."

"You simply cannot allow the examination to become sexual," the first white-coated man admonished.

"Pretty hard to do when she starts singing to you."

"Then gag them."

"We've tried that. But they hum, which also affects us." All three of the lab coat men produced ear plugs. "That's why we wear these. No sound, no temptation."

Shayla had to admit, albeit begrudgingly, that they certainly had figured out a solid plan. Except there were things about Mermaids they apparently didn't know. Singing wasn't the only way to cast a beguiling on a human.

With enough skill, a strong Mermaid could use a sentence or even a slow smile. And she, as a Princess of the Sea, definitely had been trained well.

Not that she ever practiced what she'd been taught. She'd always considered such methods invasive and wrong to inflict on innocent human males. This, however, was not one of those circumstances. This was out-and-out war.

Before she acted, she needed to warn Zach. While she wasn't sure if Shifters were more resistant to beguiling than humans, she didn't want to take a chance of catching him in her snare. If the attraction between them would ever have a chance of developing into something real, it had to be genuine.

"Zach," she whispered, making her voice urgent so he'd understand the seriousness of what she had to say. "When I start speaking to them, block your ears."

"They have earplugs," he shot back.

"I know. I need to take care of the other men first. Then I'll deal with the ones in lab coats. I have other methods besides my voice."

Though his eyes widened, he simply nodded.

"Don't listen and don't look at me," she reiterated. "I don't want to accidentally beguile you."

"I get it," he said, frowning. "But if every Mermaid has these skills, why didn't my sister use them?"

"Not everyone has the experience or training," she began, breaking off as the group of men moved closer. Baseball cap guy opened the sliding side door and stepped aside. "Oh," he said. "I forgot to mention we shot the guy who was with the Mermaid. It's a gut wound, not looking good. We brought him with us because we didn't want to take the chance of leaving him there to die and being able to alert the police."

The white-coated men stared. "What do you intend to do with the body one he's...expired?"

His cold clinical tone as well as his choice of words had Shayla gritting her teeth. She'd had just enough warning to rearrange herself so it appeared she was still tied up, though she'd clenched her hands into fists.

"I dunno." Baseball cap guy didn't sound concerned. "Probably just bury the body. Unless you people need body parts for any of your experiments."

Experiments? What the...?

"I think we're good." Smiling smugly, the tallest white-coated man signaled his friends, and they all put in their earplugs.

Nonetheless, Shayla lifted her head and began to sing. "Go to sleep, go to sleep," she crooned. A lullaby. Immediately, all of the men without ear protection closed their eyes. Every single one dropped to the ground as if they'd become boneless.

The three in the white coats glanced back at the others, unfazed. One of them produced a wickedly long needle, the metal tip glinting in the light. "I'm just going to give you a little shot," he said. "This will help you get some rest, calm down and make you much more compliant with our wishes."

"I love compliant," she said, even though they couldn't hear her. Then she smiled, invoking the megawatt, utterly false movement of her lips that could charm even a charging grizzly.

All three of her adversaries froze. Shaking the rope off her hands, she gestured at them to remove their earplugs. With the slow and deliberate motions of sleepwalkers, they complied.

And then she sang. She sang a song of longing, of aches

and needs and fears. Of truth and shadows, coming together in peace and harmony. Of love.

Rapt, they listened to every word, every note. And when she'd finished, she quietly asked them to drop the needle and hand over any weapons.

Apparently, none of the lab-coated men was armed. After the needle dropped to the cement floor with a clatter, they continued to stand motionless, as if awaiting further instructions. Their glazed expressions and slack jaws spoke of how deeply she'd enchanted them.

Aware she and Zach would need to move quickly if they were to escape, she ordered the men to lie on the floor near their comrades and sleep. Once they'd done so, she and Zach could grab any guns the others might have. Just in case anyone else showed up.

She could only hope Zach had healed enough to go fast. She didn't think they could use the van, but with any luck there'd be other vehicles outside.

"Okay, Zach," she said, turning to look at him. "You can take your fingers out of your ears now."

But though he twitched his hands, he lay supine with his eyes closed, as if he'd followed her instructions to the letter. As if…he'd somehow heard, even with his ears plugged.

How was this possible?

Horrified, she tried to figure out what to do. Why hadn't Zach done as she'd asked? Fingers in the ears, gaze averted?

Since she didn't have time to dwell on the why or how, she knew she'd need a solution. Stealing the van appeared to be the only way she'd get him out of there, because she was afraid if she gave him an order to snap out of it, all the others would do the same. And if that happened, every single one of them would be filled with an intense desire to love her, to have her and hold her and never, ever let her go. Which is what had gotten Nantha into trouble in the first place, singing the siren's song to unwary fishermen.

Something Merfolk were expressly forbidden to do.

Right now, she needed to focus on getting them out of there. Then she could worry about how to undo what she'd done and return Zach to normal.

She spied a large, metal garage door right behind the van. Since all the entranced men had lain down alongside it, the path to back out was clear. All she needed to do was to locate the button to open the door.

There, on the wall, just like in every other suburban garage. Relieved, she hopped out, her feet tingling from being immobile for so long. She punched the button, and as soon as the door began lifting, she jumped back into the van, this time in the driver's seat. Except she had no keys.

Eyeing ball cap guy still slumbering, she got out again and made her way over to him, stepping over the others, careful not to disturb them. Gingerly, she reached into his jeans pocket, praying she'd chosen the one that had the car keys.

There! As her fingers closed around them, she exhaled. Pulling Zach's fingers from his ears, she leaned close and whispered. "Zach. Get up and come walk with me." To her relief, he instantly complied. Whew.

Heart pounding, she glanced outside at the night sky before climbing back into the van. The last thing she needed was for more of these men's crew to show up at the last minute.

But no one did.

Counting her blessings, she started the engine and put the van in Reverse. Only once they'd reached a main road did she realize how badly she was shaking. She pulled over, sucking in one deep breath after another, trying to calm herself.

Meanwhile, Zach appeared to have fallen back asleep. Glancing at him, she let her gaze roam over his perfectly chiseled features, the stray lock of hair falling over his forehead. Though she could wake him now, she decided to let him slumber. He'd be much easier to deal with later, once they were out of danger and safe.

While she knew she could get him back to normal, the thought of an amorous, besotted Zach made her heart race. Except that while she wanted him badly, she wanted him to come to her with honest desire and need, not because of a beguiling song-spell sung by a Mermaid.

She decided for right now to focus on simply getting them to safety. Since she had no idea of their location, she put her home address into her phone and asked for directions. Once the robotic voice began to give them to her, she put the van back in Drive and pulled out onto the road.

Two hours and forty-seven minutes later, she pulled up in front of her house. After she parked, she flexed her hands. They'd begun cramping from her iron grip on the steering wheel.

The dashboard clock said it was 3:10 in the morning. Despite that, she pulled out her cell phone and called Maddie. When her friend answered, she explained a tiny bit of what had happened and asked Maddie to come over. Once she'd agreed, Shayla dialed Carmen.

Of course that call went to voice mail. As a Vamp, Carmen was a creature of the night. Though normally she'd be either out partying with her other blood-drinking friends or hunting, she'd carried Nantha to safety. No doubt she'd either escorted the young Mermaid to Zach's mother's house or had taken her to the sea, depending on what Nantha had asked her to do. Most likely the sea, as only salty ocean water would have the healing properties she needed. She'd be arrested immediately, but it couldn't be helped.

Shayla left Carmen a message, simply stating that she was needed, and asked her to come over as soon as possible. She knew once Carmen got the message, she'd head this way, probably beating Maddie.

Turning to face Zach, Shayla gave soft orders that he was to follow her from the van and into the house. Robotically, he complied. Though she didn't know him all that well, she understood enough of his nature to know he'd hate this. Heck, anyone would.

She'd need the other women's help once she got him out of the beguiling. Sometimes men became combative when they woke. And that was with human men. She had no idea how a Shifter would react.

Deciding they'd need to attend to the practical matters, such as getting rid of the van, first, she had Zach sit on the couch. Once he had, she told him it would be okay to take a nap.

Instead of complying, he merely gazed at her as he slowly removed his bloodstained shirt. The wound on his stomach had already begun to heal, the skin knitting back together and looking pink. Amazing, the rejuvenating powers of Shifters.

She let her gaze travel slowly from his stomach, up across his broad and muscular chest, to his ruggedly handsome face. His pupils were dilated, and his skin flushed. When he stood, she saw the force of his arousal pushing against the front of his jeans.

Her knees went weak and she struggled to catch her breath. Even though she was well aware he was not in his right mind, she couldn't help but be affected.

There was no way she would be taking advantage of him while he was in this state. Sexual desire was one of the major effects of a beguiling. It wasn't anything personal. She could be any woman, as far as he was concerned right now.

"Settle down, big boy." Waving her hand in front of his face to break his intense concentration, she gestured at the couch. "Let yourself rest. Close your eyes and lean your head back. This will all be over soon."

Instead of complying, he held his ground. Towering over her, he closed the distance between them with a few steps. "Mine," he said, as he reached for her.

"No." But her protest came out weak. She knew if she insisted, that he'd back off. Beguiled or not, Zach wasn't the kind of man to force himself on a woman.

Even if part of her wanted him right now.

There was nothing forceful in the way he touched her. In fact, the way he slid his fingers down her face felt gentle and seductive. "You're so beautiful," he mused, as he tucked a wayward strand of her hair behind her ear. Though his pupils were still huge, she swore she saw awareness in his gaze. Had he somehow come out of the beguiling on his own? She began to wonder. Especially when he tugged her closer and breathed a trail of kisses down the side of her neck. "I want you," he whispered.

Dizzy with desire, she shivered. Tempted—oh, she was tempted. But if and when she and Zach ever got together, she wanted it to be clear of any kind of complications, like him getting accidentally caught up in her beguiling.

"No," she said again, more loudly and forcibly this time. She also stepped back. "Zach, you're not yourself. You need to stop."

"I am myself," he insisted. "Never been better." He touched his wound, drawing her gaze to his six-pack. "It's healing nicely, don't you think?"

While he definitely sounded normal, she needed to make sure.

A second later, someone knocked on her front door. Relieved, she hurried to answer. Carmen stood on the doorstep, and as soon as Shayla opened the door, Carmen hugged her. Though fast and hard, this was so out of character that it left Shayla without words.

"I'm so glad you two got out of there," Carmen said, brushing past Shayla and stepping inside. She sniffed the air, frowning slightly. Then her eyes widened when she caught sight of Zach, shirtless. She spun around to face Shayla. "Am I interrupting something?"

Though Shayla could feel her face heating, she shook her head. "No. He was shot, and his shirt was bloody. The wound is healing nicely, though."

"I thought I smelled blood." With a satisfied smirk, Carmen strolled over to Zach and got close to examine the wound. "It looks almost as good as new."

He looked at Carmen, his eyes cold. While he didn't recoil exactly, he clearly didn't welcome her getting near him.

"I need to make sure he's no longer under the beguiling spell," Shayla murmured for Carmen's ears alone. "Sometimes they can get a little violent when they're brought out. If that happens, will you help me restrain him?"

"Of course." Judging by the Vamp's satisfied grin, she'd actually relish this.

Chapter 11

Shayla took a deep breath. Then she spoke the ancient Greek words that would remove any trace of Mer-magic from him. Bracing herself, she waited to see how he'd react.

He blinked, clenching his jaw. He glared at Carmen, his expression hostile. "Where's my sister?" he demanded. "What have you done with Nantha?"

"She insisted on waiting in the car until I could judge how pissed off you were."

"Bring her inside." When Carmen didn't move, he added, "Please. For all we know, she might have already jumped into the sea so she doesn't have to face me."

"Are you okay?" Shayla asked cautiously. "You were a little out of it earlier."

"I'm fine. I just need to see Nantha."

"I'll go get her." As Carmen turned to do exactly that, another tap on the door told them Maddie had arrived.

Once she'd joined them, Shayla and Carmen filled her in on everything that had happened. Then Carmen slipped outside to retrieve the errant Mermaid. Shayla could only hope Zach wasn't right and that his sister was still where she was supposed to be.

A moment later, Carmen returned with the meek, blonde Mermaid teen. Nantha looked everywhere but at her big stepbrother, so she didn't see how his expression had softened.

She swallowed hard. "Hi," she said, her voice trembling.

No one spoke. Shayla figured Zach probably had something he wanted to say.

And she was right. "Nantha?" The tone of Zach's voice when he spoke his stepsister's name was also a command for her to look at him.

Slowly, the teenager raised her chin. Visibly trembling, she finally met her brother's gaze.

"Why?" he asked, a wealth of emotion in the single word. "What you did almost destroyed us. Me, your father and June."

At that, she hung her head. "I'm sorry." They all had to strain to hear her. "I just wanted to have fun. I really didn't mean for anyone to get hurt."

Inwardly, Shayla winced, though she kept her face expressionless. This was between Zach and his little sister. And later, she knew Nantha and Ion would have it out, as well. She almost felt sorry for the young Mermaid. Almost.

"There are a million different ways to have fun," Zach pointed out. "None of them involves worrying your family or luring innocent fishermen. Not only that, but you endangered Shayla and Carmen here."

"Not to mention your brother," Carmen put in, her hard voice matching her expression.

"I'm sorry." Her blue eyes huge and glistening with unshed tears, Nantha sniffed. "Really, really sorry."

"Come here." Zach held out his arms. Nantha ran to him, and he enveloped her in a bear hug. "Do you have any idea how worried we were?" he asked, smoothing her hair back from her face.

Watching them, Maddie smiled slightly. Shayla felt a catch in her heart, wondering if Nantha would ever understand the depths of a family's love. Even Carmen appeared to soften slightly, though she still held herself rigid and stiff. She moved over to stand next to Shayla, clearly uninterested in watching the touching and tender reunion between Zach and his sister.

"What'd they want the Mermaids for?" she asked Shayla, pitching her voice low.

"I don't know."

"What? Why didn't you find out what they were planning on doing with the Mermaids once they had them?"

Put that way, it was a damn fine question. Luckily, she had a damn fine answer.

"Because I was too busy trying to figure out how to get both Zach and myself out of there. He'd been shot, and while the wound had started healing, he still wasn't a hundred percent."

"Fair enough." Carmen shrugged. "But you know if they're up to something, they're not going to stop. For all you know, they could already be holding other Mermaids captive."

Hearing this, Nantha raised her head and stepped away from her brother and toward them. "They do have other Mermaids. I was going to tell you this, Your Highness."

Ignoring the title, Shayla nodded. "How many?"

"Two, maybe three." Gaze troubled, she looked from Shayla to her brother, and then back again. "They want our blood. They took some of mine, and they ran some kind of test on it. That's when they came back and said I wasn't…pure."

"Blood?" Carmen's nostrils flared, as if she could smell it. "Why? Are they Vampires? Or do they have a Vampire they're feeding?"

Nantha's shoulders sagged. "I don't know. But as far as I can tell, they seemed to be human. I heard them talking. I think they're making something with the blood. One of the others even told me they took so much blood from another Mermaid that it killed her."

Horrified, Shayla gasped. "I'm going to have to let my father and brother know about this. I'll also need to text the representative from the Pod and fill him in."

"I'll need to inform the Pack Protectors as well," Maddie said.

Nantha nodded. "I'm pretty sure my father will go to the king, too." She swallowed. "I'm waiting to be arrested."

"You will be." Shayla almost reached out to comfort the younger Mermaid, but held back. The time had come for Nantha to pay the consequences of her reckless actions.

"What about the men?" Nantha asked. "They'll continue what they're doing if no one stops them."

Shayla, Maddie and Carmen exchanged a look.

"Are you thinking what I'm thinking?" Maddie asked.

"Yes," Shayla replied. "We have to work to stop these men before any more Mermaids are hurt or killed."

Zach took Nantha home, phoning ahead to alert his mother. As she had on the phone, June broke down in tears at the sight of her stepdaughter, wrapping her up in her arms and refusing to let her go.

When June finally released her, Nantha glanced around, partly in dread and part eagerly. "Where's Dad?"

June's happy expression crumpled. "I've been trying to reach him. He's under the sea, but he won't answer his phone."

"I tried, too," Zach said. "No answer. I ended up leaving a message asking Ion to call back as soon as he could. I don't know what's up with him, but he's sure busy all of a sudden." He glanced at his sister. "What the heck does he do these days that keeps him so busy all the time?"

She fidgeted, looking down. Finally she sighed. "All I can say is I'm not the only one with secrets. My dad's aren't mine to tell. Maybe you should ask him. I'm sure he'll tell you if he wants you to know."

What the hell kind of an answer was that? Zach shook his head. Did he really know his family? First Nantha, and now Ion? He swore if he found out his mother had some huge secret, he was going to lose it.

Even Shayla had turned out to be a royal Mer-Princess. At least she tried to downplay her lofty family connections. Though he'd much prefer her to be just an ordinary Mermaid, especially since he still harbored hopes of them getting together. When and if they did, he knew it'd be so hot they'd go up in flames.

"What's the deal with you and the princess?" Nantha asked, as if she'd read his mind. When she shot him a sideways glance, he believed he understood. She was trying to change the subject. He guessed he didn't blame her. "You know you're already promised to someone else."

"I've ended that," Zach replied, his tone curt. "As for the rest, I have no idea what you mean."

Nantha snorted. "Don't play innocent. I was only around you for a little while, and even I could see the smoldering looks you two exchange. Sparks are practically flying."

"None of your business." His short answer hopefully let her know to be careful. He wasn't going to let her try and use his personal life as a way to deflect attention from her own problems. Privately he wasn't surprised that his baby sister had picked up on the attraction Shayla had for him. He didn't know what it was about Shayla, but she drew him to her like no other woman ever had. Her combination of strength and confidence, her direct way of talking and of course her sexy, sensual body outshone any other female he'd ever met.

Nantha rolled her eyes. "Look, I'm actually happy for you. You deserve it. I'd give anything to have someone look at me the way you do her."

June looked from one to the other. "Shayla seems like a nice girl," she said. "I just don't want you to get hurt."

Mothers. He wondered why she immediately assumed he would come out the loser in a relationship with Shayla. Maybe because she was royalty. "I won't be hurt," he said. Then, deciding there was no point to beating around the bush, he added, "I like Shayla a lot, and I think she feels the same way about me. And—" he directed a hard look first at his mother, and then at his sister "—I liked her before I even learned she was a princess. We've just been so busy searching for you, Nantha, we haven't had time to date or anything."

Nantha briefly hung her head. "Sorry," she mumbled. "At least that's all over."

"It's not all over, not really. No doubt you'll be taken into custody soon. As for Shayla, she's still trying to find out who those men are and what they're doing. Plus, she wants to rescue any other Mermaids they might be holding captive."

"That sounds dangerous," June protested. "Since she's a princess, maybe she should assign someone else to work on that case."

Zach couldn't help it—he laughed. "She wouldn't do

that. The Shadow Agency is her business. I think she's actually enjoying herself."

"She's pretty famous back home," Nantha interjected. "At one point, she was engaged to another prince from a neighboring city. He was handsome and strong and rich." She sighed. "All the single ladies were crushing on him."

Amazingly, he felt a quick stab of jealousy, even though Ion and Shayla had already told him about this. He'd be interested to get his little sister's take on it. "What happened?" He kept his tone casual, as if the answer didn't matter to him.

Judging from her smile, Nantha wasn't fooled. "He died. Drowned, somehow. Which is impossible for a Merman. It turned out he was poisoned. Shayla took it hard. She fell apart. Some people say she went crazy. The whole thing almost caused an international incident."

"Ion said some pretty awful things to her. His words hurt her badly. I don't know why, but your father seemed to take an instant dislike to her."

Nantha gasped. "Did he really do that? I'm surprised. Back home, you can't just go around insulting royalty."

He thought back to the aching look of pain and anger Shayla had worn. "Unfortunately, he did. I'd venture to say that Ion isn't among her favorite people right now."

His baby sister swore under her breath. He considered chastising her for her language, but figured she was going to get enough grief from Ion when the Merman finally appeared. Well deserved, but still. Part of him couldn't help but feel a tiny bit sorry for her.

But then he considered all she'd put him—and their parents—through. "I was shot, you know," he said.

June gasped. "Where? Are you all right?"

"I'm fine. Now. I was lucky it wasn't a silver bullet."

His mother hugged him. "Thank goodness. I don't know

what I'd do if something happened to you." Releasing him, she turned to face Nantha. "See what kind of trouble you caused?"

Nantha hung her head. "I'm sorry." When she raised her face to look at him, tears glistened in her eyes. "I didn't think things through. A couple of us wanted to have some fun, and it seemed daring, at first. After that, things seemed to happen really fast, and I didn't know what to do. So I went along with it. But I'm really, really sorry."

Her apology softened June's anger. "Come here, sweetheart," the older woman said, wrapping the teenager up in a fierce hug. "I'm so glad you're all right. You have no idea how worried I was. Or how upset your father was. He's going to be furious with you, so you'd better brace yourself. And realize this. Whatever punishment he doles out is well deserved. You've got to understand you can't simply do something this awful with no repercussions."

"I do understand," Nantha whispered, the stricken look on her young face making him think she really did. "May I be excused?" she asked June. "I'm exhausted. I'd like to go to my room and lie down."

"Of course," June agreed instantly. "You'll need all the strength you can get to face your father."

"Thank you." Nantha hurried out of the room.

Zach shook his head. "I'm not done talking to her. I'll be right back." And he followed his sister down the hall.

She'd already made it inside her bedroom and closed the door. He knocked gently, three times.

"Come in, Zach," Nantha said softly.

When he stepped into her room, she eyed him for a moment silently. "I'm happy for you. Shayla is very beautiful, as well as kind. She'll make a good girlfriend."

Again, while he knew she was merely trying to divert

him from what she'd done, he couldn't help but feel pleasure at her words.

"Look," he began.

"You know Shayla left her family, her friends and the sea and went to live permanently on land. Where I'm guessing she still lives."

She was good. He had to give her that.

"Yep. She's got a waterfront house, though, so I guess she can slip into the ocean whenever she wants."

"That's smart." Nantha sounded wiser than her years. "We get really sick if we're too far away from the water for very long. That's one of the things I had to convince my captors of." As soon as the words left her mouth, her expression went stricken as she realized she'd redirected the conversation exactly where he'd tried to start it.

His stomach twisted. Taking a deep breath, he tried to make himself relax. "Nantha, what you did is awful. You caused so much hurt, fear and worry. This caused a strain on everyone, not least of all your father. You're not a child any longer, and it's time you think of others besides yourself."

Though she nodded as if in agreement, she also frowned. "I hear what you're saying. But it all turned out all right in the end, so what's the harm?"

It took a few moments before he could push words out past the anger and disappointment clogging up his throat. "Do you really believe that?" He held up his hand. "Wait. Don't answer yet. I want you to think about this. What if your father disappeared without a trace? Or me, or June? And then while you were freaking out, trying to find us, you get a phone call wanting a ransom paid. Would you truly believe no harm, no foul if we managed to get free? What about all the worry, the suffering, the searching?"

Nantha didn't immediately answer. Good. At least she was considering his words.

"Please tell me you aren't that short-sighted and inconsiderate," he continued, hoping to pound the point home.

"I didn't think of it like that," she said, her voice small. A sound from outside made her jump. They both looked out the window and saw Ion striding toward the house, his face dark with anger. June trailed behind him, her expression both worried and relieved.

"I hope you're ready to face the music," Zach warned, right before Ion slammed into the house, calling for Nantha at the top of his lungs.

With an audible hitch in her breath, she turned to Zach, as if to ask for help. The absolute panic in her expression told him that now maybe she finally understood how much trouble she was in. "Please..."

He shook his head. "You deserve to hear whatever your father has to say to you. He's been through hell since you disappeared."

Because she knew he was right, she hung her head and left her room, walking toward the living room. A moment later, Zach did the same. He thought he'd trail after her and listen in, since he sure as hell had been involved in all of this. He also wanted to prevent Ion from doing anything too drastic. His stepfather had seemed unstable lately, but that might have only been due to his daughter's disappearance. Since Nantha deserved a punishment for her actions, Zach definitely didn't intend to interfere too much.

To Zach's surprise, Ion yanked his daughter into his arms and wept. The scene was so raw, so personal, that Zach turned away.

He headed into the kitchen, where he fixed himself a giant glass of ice water. Then he waited until he heard the murmur of voices before returning to the living room.

Ion had taken a seat next to Nantha on the sofa, with June on his other side. They were talking quietly, their voices too low for Zach to hear. He walked into the room, dropped into the chair across from them and cleared his throat, feeling the need to remind them he was there.

Only June looked up. She flashed a reassuring smile before returning her attention back to her husband and stepdaughter. Despite her proximity, she somehow seemed apart, as if the two Merfolk were deliberately excluding her.

Zach's suspicions were confirmed a few seconds later when Ion stood, tugging Nantha up with him. "We're leaving," he announced, his hard voice matching the look he gave his wife.

June protested anyway. "But you just got here, both of you. Can't you wait until tomorrow at least? Give us some time together?"

Expression unyielding, Ion shook his head. "We cannot. The king has requested Nantha be brought to him immediately. I plan to accompany her, so I can plead for him to be lenient with her."

As the two moved toward the door, Ion stopped, glancing back over his shoulder at Zach. "Please pass on to Princess Shayla that I will not forget her help in this. If there ever comes a time, I will repay her."

After issuing that pronouncement, Ion and Nantha slipped out the back door.

The stricken sound June made nearly broke Zach's heart. He took her arm, and together they went outside, just in time to watch the Merfolk slip into the ocean.

"I can't believe they're gone." With her hand over her mouth, June turned to him, her expression tormented. "I'm beginning to feel as if Ion no longer considers us part of his family."

Though Zach had begun to think the same thing, he didn't admit it to his mother. "I'm sure he had no choice," he said instead. "When a king summons you, you have to go."

Her expression cleared. "You're right, of course. Once everything settles down, we'll be able to go back to the way we were before."

For her sake, he hoped so, Zach privately doubted it. Something else was going on with Ion. He couldn't quite put his finger on it yet, but he was sure it would come out eventually.

June looked troubled again when Zach told her he had leave, making him feel awful.

"But it's almost dark," she protested. "Why don't you stay over for the night and head back home in the morning?"

When he hesitated, she sighed. "Please, Zach. I don't want to be alone tonight."

Of course then he had no choice. He agreed. She got them both a beer, and they sat on the back porch overlooking the ocean and drank it while the sun set. As the sky darkened, the solar lights came on, casting a soft glow in keeping with the peaceful evening. The only thing missing was the rest of the family, he thought. Whatever Ion was up to, he'd better not seriously hurt Zach's mother.

"Tell me about you and Shayla," she asked softly.

"There's nothing to tell." He hadn't meant to sound defensive, but his reply came out that way. "I hired her to find Nantha. She did. I need to pay her the balance of her fee."

"Isn't she going to continue to investigate this case?"

"Yes. But that's something she's doing on her own, for her people. I didn't hire her for that one."

"Are you helping her?"

He sighed. He knew what his mother was doing, looking for a distraction to pass the time. Unfortunately, her questions felt intrusive, maybe because he himself wasn't sure what direction he and Shayla's budding relationship might go.

"Possibly. Look, Mom." He spread his hand. "Right now there's nothing between me and Shayla. She's cute, and I'm attracted to her. That quite possibly might be the end of it. Maybe, maybe not."

"I see," she said. Her puzzled voice contradicted her statement. Plainly, she did not.

"You'll be the first to know if that changes," he told her, kissing her cheek. "Now if you don't mind, I'm going to go in and take a shower. It's been a really long day."

"Of course. I can only imagine." She got up when he did, following him into the house. "I'm probably going to sit out a little longer and watch the waves." The sadness coloring her voice was at odds with her attempt to smile. "Thank you for staying with me. I really appreciate it."

"I love you, Mom," he said. "No matter what happens, you're going to be all right."

"Yes." Some of the color had returned to her cheeks. She squared her shoulders and lifted her chin. "I am."

"Why do they want the blood, do you think?" Carmen swirled her own drink around, watching the blood move in her glass before she took a sip. "Is it possible they're Vampires?"

"Anything is possible." Though Shayla didn't mean to sound glum, the knowledge that somewhere these crazy people were holding young Mermaids hostage and doing unspeakable things to them made her feel ill. "But I will say this. The ones I met weren't Vamps. They were humans."

At that, Carmen made a quiet growl low in her throat.

Maddie stared. "You sound like a Shifter when you do that."

"Do I?" Supremely unconcerned, Carmen continued to glower. "Humans taking blood like that is an abomination."

"Anyone capturing Mermaids, holding them prisoner, and doing who knows what to them is committing grave crimes and will be held accountable," Shayla said. "They may very well find themselves being held accountable to Poseidon himself." Her phone pinged, indicating an incoming text. She read it, disappointment clogging her throat.

Maddie leaned forward, a wolfish look in her eyes. "We've got to stop them. You two know where they were. Why don't we round up a posse and go get them?" She waved her hand around the room. "I'm sure we could get enough supernatural volunteers from this room to help us."

Shayla shook her head and held up her phone. "I just got a text from my guy with the Pod. They sent armed Mermen there to investigate. The place had been cleaned out. They're gone."

"Damn," Maddie cursed. Carmen merely flashed her fangs and finished off her drink.

"Now we're right back where we started." Shayla rubbed her temples. "I feel like I'm missing something obvious, but I can't think of what it might be."

Carmen squeezed her shoulder. "Don't worry. Once you de-stress, it might come to you. It's still there in your unconscious mind."

Though Shayla hoped so, she also knew she needed to rest. Exhaustion had her yawning. Finally, she stood. "I'm calling it an early night. I've got to go home and get some sleep."

Immediately, the other two stood. "We'll walk you out," Maddie said.

"I think I'll be okay," Shayla protested. "I don't think it's even dark yet."

"Maybe not, but there's no need to take chances. Especially after what you've been through."

After they accompanied her to where she could catch a cab, Carmen and Maddie waited until one pulled up. Then they turned around and went back the way they'd come. Shayla figured they were headed back to Broken Chains. She didn't blame them. The night was still young.

Once the cab delivered her to her house, she paid and gave the driver a generous tip. Trudging up the staircase, she let herself in the front door. She'd barely locked the dead bolt behind her when her cell phone rang.

"No," she protested out loud, even though she was alone. "Whoever it is can wait until morning."

Moving slowly, she headed to her bedroom, shedding clothes as she went. Once she reached her bed, she pulled back the covers and crawled between the sheets. She barely had enough energy to click off her light before falling asleep.

When she opened her eyes, it wasn't yet dawn. Her nightstand clock said 4:45 a.m. That's what she got for going to bed too early.

Yawning, she briefly debated snuggling back under the covers and trying for another hour of sleep. But then she remembered her phone had rung when she got home and reached for it on her nightstand.

She didn't recognize the number, and there was no message. Caller ID showed Unknown Caller.

Probably a solicitor, she muttered, deciding she'd try to sleep after all.

But try as she might, she couldn't get back to that drowsy state of mind. Her mind wouldn't shut off, and she couldn't stop thinking of Nantha and Zach and Ion.

She decided to call her father and fill him in. Of course, she'd have to wait to a decent hour. He definitely wouldn't be awake now.

Though she knew Poseidon would be. She wondered how much of this the Ocean God knew.

Chapter 12

The next morning Zach passed on his mother's offer to cook him breakfast, snagging a bagel and coffee to go instead. Now that his sister had been found, he could either return to his job or actually try and enjoy part of his remaining vacation days. He decided to do the latter, at least until he saw Shayla and found out if there was any way she might want to spend some time with him, in a non-work capacity.

The thought made him feel ridiculously happy. When he arrived home, he thoroughly cleaned his little house, did laundry and made a grocery run, all things that were long overdue. He'd abandoned regular life when Nantha disappeared. Once he had his house in order, he thought he'd feel as if the rest of his life had gotten back to normal.

Finally, with his life restored to the neat, meticulous state he preferred, he showered and changed his clothes. Then he drove south to Galveston. He spent the rest of the day going from business to business, taking down the posters and letting the workers know his sister had been found. Peoples' reactions touched him. He was hugged, prayed over, congratulated, high-fived and given a free coffee at one place.

He grabbed a sub sandwich for dinner and walked out onto the seawall to eat while looking out over the ocean. As usual, two or three freighter ships waited in the distance. He marveled at the fact that under the waves existed entire civilizations known only to Merfolk. While he knew exactly what it felt like to exchange his human body for that of a wolf, he wondered how switching legs for a huge fish tail and slicing through the water would feel.

He liked living near the gulf and enjoyed the beach as much as anyone. But the sea had never been an integral part of him, not the way it was for Ion and Nantha and Shayla. His realm as Wolf was the forest and meadows, the tall fields of grass, the texture and scent of damp earth. The polar opposite of Shayla's.

His parents' long marriage proved a Shifter and a Merfolk could survive their differences, but the last few days he'd been witness to an unraveling of sorts. He hoped this was only temporary. Surely Ion and June would find their way back to each other.

Finally, full darkness had fallen. He stood, dusting his hands on his jeans, and got back in his car. Less than five minutes later, he parked near Broken Chains, anticipation making him jittery.

Not only did he need to settle up with the Shadow Agency, since they'd solved his case, but he had to see Shayla. Even while all the drama with Nantha had been going on, he hadn't been able to stop thinking about the beautiful Mer-Princess.

When he walked in, he began scanning the crowd, hoping against hope he'd find her there. When he spotted her, sitting at a table with Maddie and Carmen, his entire insides came alive.

They looked up when he approached. Maddie and Carmen appeared pleased, while Shayla glanced up indifferently until she realized it was him. Her lovely eyes widened, and a pink flush spread across her creamy skin. Her lips parted, making him ache to taste them.

"Hi," she said faintly. "I'm surprised to see you so soon. I thought you might be home with your family, recuperating from your gunshot wound."

"Nope. It healed up almost immediately after." Grinning, he pulled out the one remaining chair and took a seat. "I came here to settle the rest of my bill now that the case is closed."

"Oh, it's not closed," Shayla said. "Your part is through. But the rest of us have decided we've got to find these guys and stop them before any more Mermaids get hurt."

Since she'd said as much before, he wasn't surprised. "I'd like to help. Count me in."

Now all three women exchanged glances. It occurred to him they might not welcome his help. Why they wouldn't, he had no idea. "What?" he asked, looking from one to the other.

In unison, all three women shook their heads.

"I want to help. In any way I can."

"You can't exactly travel under the ocean," Shayla pointed out.

"The bad guys are on land," he countered. "And I'm pretty damn good on land, if I do say so myself."

Carmen and Maddie laughed. Shayla just stared. Finally, when he thought she might out and out refuse, the tiniest smile curved one corner of her mouth.

"Fine," she said. "As long as you understand we're in charge of this investigation, not you."

He nodded. "No problem."

For whatever reason, all three women seemed to find this comment hilarious. He watched them laugh, signaling the waiter for a beer plus another round for everyone else.

The carefree sound made him happy. He leaned back in his chair, soaking in the atmosphere. The steady hum of voices talking, the band tuning up their instruments, the clink of glasses and bottles. The smell of whiskey and beer and various supernatural beings of every kind. In one sweep of the room, he picked up wolf and panther and bear. If he'd been in his Wolf form with his supersensitive nose, he could have pinpointed every single person in seconds.

The waiter brought his beer and drinks for everyone else. Zach noticed their choices hadn't changed—still wine for Shayla, beer for Maddie and the blood cocktail for Carmen.

"You're pretty relieved to have your little sister back, aren't you?" Maddie asked, after thanking him for the drink.

"It's a huge weight off my shoulders," he replied. "That's partly why I'm here. I wanted to do a little bit of celebrating."

"I would have thought you'd do that with your family." Shayla watched him, her gaze intense.

He grimaced. "There's not too much celebrating going on there right now. Ion took Nantha and went back under the sea. My mom is hurt. And Nantha…" He stopped, unsure of the right word.

"Is defiant?"

"Maybe. Unrepentant definitely. No one can seem to make her understand how wrong she was to do what she did."

"Ouch." Shayla winced. "I'm sure once she and Ion

arrive back at their home, she'll have to answer to my brother."

"That's what Ion mentioned." This intrigued and worried him. "I know what my sister did was wrong. Do you have any idea what will happen to her?"

"She'll be imprisoned," Shayla said matter-of-factly. "Like I was. My brother will let her make a statement, but he always follows the law."

"I admit I find it a bit odd that your king gets involved in matters like this."

"Maybe so, but we Merfolk are old school." After sipping on her wine, she nodded. "Merc is a very hands-on kind of ruler. But she'll still have a fair trial. Merc's just a couple years older than me, and he's quite the lady's man. It's strange to think of him sitting in my father's throne and dispensing wisdom." She shook her head, her expression amused. "That said, I rarely visit the palace, especially since Richard died."

"Are you going there soon?" he asked. "I'm really interested to learn what happens with my sister." Privately he had his doubts Ion would be sharing news any time in the near future.

"Probably," Shayla said, taking a sip of her wine and smiling at him. He felt the power of that smile low in his gut. "I'm going to have to pay him a visit. He needs to know what's going on with these humans. Taking Mermaid blood and using it for nefarious purposes is enough to start an all-out war."

"What?" Carmen asked, leaning forward. "Are you saying the Merfolk would declare war on humanity?" Maddie had also gone still. Zach wondered if she'd truly meant that or if it had been a poor choice of words.

Shayla swallowed hard. "Oh, it won't be us, exactly.

But if my father notifies Poseidon like he said he would, there will be hell to pay."

"Point taken," Zach replied. "You've mentioned him before, so I knew there was that possibility." He tilted his head, studying her. "I'll admit to being curious, though. If Poseidon exists, then what about all the other ancient Greek gods?"

"I wouldn't know about that one," Shayla admitted. "Though I'm reasonably sure they probably do. Where there's myth, there's often truth. You all know that better than anybody."

While the others began a lively debate over which of the ancient Greek gods or goddesses they'd most like to meet, Zach fell silent. He still felt like he'd missed something important, but he couldn't quite put his finger on exactly what that might be.

Shayla felt Zach's gaze on her, almost as if he'd reached out and caressed her skin. Tonight, she'd collect the final payment from him, and their business relationship would be over. Which meant…what? How did she broach the question of whether or not he might be interested in taking things a step farther?

She reached into her purse and pulled out an envelope. Inside, she'd placed a typed invoice. Sliding this across the table toward him, she felt relieved when he accepted it without comment.

He reached into his back pocket and removed his wallet. From this, he extracted a neatly folded check, which he placed in the envelope and passed it back to her. All without even checking the statement.

"Don't you want to look at it first?" she asked.

"Nope. I'd already written the check. We'd discussed

the total, and you'd collected my down payment. I'm sure it will be fine."

Opening the envelope, she looked at his check. "It's for too much." Way too much. "I gave you credit for helping so much with the investigation."

He waved her comment away. "Not needed. You did what you said you'd do. My sister is safe. You earned every penny."

Pleased, she dipped her chin in agreement and closed the envelope up, placing it inside her purse. Zach watched her, his gaze intense. The way he looked at her made her entire body feel warm. She glanced at the others to see if they'd noticed.

Clearly oblivious, Carmen and Maddie continued to discuss the merits of various members of the Greek pantheon. This may have been intentional to give her privacy; she didn't know. Either way, she appreciated it.

She took a deep breath and gathered her courage to ask Zach if he wanted to have dinner sometime. Maddie's phone rang, interrupting her. While Shayla watched, Maddie checked the Caller ID before answering. All the color instantly drained from her face. "Excuse me," she told them. "I have to take this." Answering, she pushed up from the table and headed toward the door to go outside where it was much quieter.

Carmen frowned. "That didn't look good. Do you think I should go after her?"

"No." Shayla shook her head. "I think she wants privacy. I'm sure if it's something she needs us to know, she'll tell us."

Carmen nodded, her gaze drifting past Shayla toward the door. "Oh, wow!" she said, her eyes flashing. "Catch a look at what just came in. And he's heading this way." Her voice changed to a purr. "I like what I see."

Trying not to laugh, Shayla swiveled in her seat to see who had caught her picky friend's attention so strongly. The instant she caught sight of the broad-shouldered giant striding their way, the crowd parting for him like water, she groaned. "Oh, hell."

Still fixated on the newcomer, Carmen ignored her.

Zach however, went instantly alert. "What is it?" he asked, glancing up at the man purposely coming toward them.

"My brother," she said. "And for Merc to leave his kingdom, I'm guessing there's something very wrong indeed."

Now she had Carmen's attention. "*That's* your brother? Every woman in the place is drooling."

"They always do," Shayla replied. With his mane of wavy golden hair, startling green eyes and impressive physique, he attracted women the way a large school of feeding fish attracted hungry sharks.

"You know I love a challenge," Carmen purred.

Though she nodded, Shayla didn't have time for an answer because Merc had reached them. He swept up to their table as if riding a monster wave on a surfboard. "Sis, we need to talk."

"Pull up a chair," Shayla said, pretending not to get that he wanted her to leave with him. "These are my friends, Carmen and Zach."

With a startled expression, he appeared to notice for the first time that there were others present. "Nice to meet you," he said, dipping his chin in greeting. "But I can't hear myself think over the band. Do you think we could go somewhere quieter?"

That he thought to ask, rather than simply order, impressed her. When Merc had first assumed the mantle of kingship after their father, the sudden elevation to power had gone to his head in a big way. He'd taken to ordering even his own family about, until their father had not-so-gently corrected him. Now that he'd been settled in his position as ruler for a few years, he'd gained both experience and wisdom.

And he'd apparently remembered he had to treat his kid sister with respect.

Glancing at her watch, Shayla grinned. "The band should be taking a break at any minute."

No sooner had she spoken those words than the music stopped. As if on cue, the band announced they'd be out for fifteen minutes.

"There you go." Shayla waved her hand. "No loud band. What's going on, brother mine?"

"That's king to you," Merc shot back. She laughed; he tried to, but came up short. Eyeing him, she waited for him to tell her what was wrong.

Finally, after glancing around him with a look of clear discomfort, he sighed. "Look, I'm not really comfortable talking about this in a bar or in front of your friends. Especially since they clearly aren't Merfolk."

Not sure how to respond to that, Shayla opened her mouth and then closed it.

"I was just leaving." Shooting Merc a bored look, which Shayla knew to be false, Carmen gracefully got up and sauntered away, no doubt hoping Merc would watch her go. But Carmen didn't know Shayla's brother. When Merc fixated on something, he couldn't be dissuaded. He barely even glanced at the Vampire when she left.

Zach, however, didn't move. Either he hadn't gotten the too-obvious hints or he simply didn't care. Shayla would bet on the latter.

She decided that was fine with her. She liked having Zach close. He could even act as a buffer with her sometimes overpowering brother.

"Ahem." Merc cleared his throat, sending Zach an irritated glance. "Weren't you just leaving, as well?"

"Was I?" Zach glanced at Shayla, one brow raised. She knew he needed her to let him know what she wanted him to do. If she said go, he'd go.

And she realized she definitely didn't want him to go.

"He's staying," she said firmly. "Merc, he's helping me work the Mermaid blood case. Plus, his mother is married to Ion, Nantha's father. So, if that's why you're here, he needs to hear what you have to say."

Expression disgruntled, Merc finally nodded. "Fine. That is why I'm here, as you so astutely guessed. Ion's daughter has been taken into custody."

This surprised her. "Into custody? That was quick."

"We had to move fast because of what she did," Merc said. "You know as well as I do that she broke the law. We can't allow young Mermaids to go around luring humans. Just because this backfired on her doesn't mean she didn't do wrong."

Which, as she knew Merc remembered, had been one of the awful things Shayla had done when she'd been mindless with grief. Her jail time had been a time of learning and reflecting. Hopefully, that would also be the case with Nantha, even though the young Mermaid wasn't a princess.

Turning to eye Zach to see how he was taking this, her breath caught. This was his baby sister after all. But to her relief, he nodded his head in agreement.

Before Merc could speak, Carmen reappeared with Maddie in tow. "We're back," she said, smiling sweetly. "We couldn't just run off on our friends, especially when you all might be discussing business."

Grateful, Shayla nodded. "Good thinking. We were just talking about how Nantha has been taken into custody due to her crime."

Both women nodded, pulling out their chairs and grabbing their drinks as if they'd never left. "I'm not surprised," Carmen commented.

At this, Merc smiled. "Yes, but to our consternation, her father, Ion, protested. Apparently, he feels his little girl should be above the rules. He claimed favoritism on our part."

"Favoritism toward whom?" Shayla asked, though she suspected she might know.

"You." Merc shook his head. "Imagine our shock when he tried to use you as an example."

"Shayla?" Now Zach glanced from brother to sister, his expression confused. "Why would anyone show favoritism toward Shayla?"

"Exactly," she drawled. "I did my time."

Merc grinned back. "Yes, you did. But that doesn't seem to matter to him. He was practically rabid, demanding you be held accountable for your past sins while also insisting his daughter should be let go. He's so inconsistent, he seems unhinged."

Clearing his throat, Zach rapped on the table to get their attention. When they both looked at him, he spoke. "This is my family you're talking about."

"Who is this again?" Merc asked, raising one brow.

"Ion's stepson, Nantha's stepbrother," Shayla said.

"And Shayla's special friend," Maddie interjected, barely hiding her smile.

"Special?" The word distracted him, as Maddie had to have known it would.

"Thanks," Shayla mouthed to her friend, even as she felt that telltale blush heat her face.

But before Merc could question her, Zach redirected him. "Yes, we're friends. But that isn't important right now. I need to know what's going on with Ion and Nantha."

Merc turned his attention to Zach, considering his request. Finally, he dipped his shaggy head in acknowledgment. "Ion is part of a small, but very vocal group who still, despite the years that have now passed, say they believe Shayla murdered her fiancé. They have no proof, and most of us believe their stance is politically motivated."

"You saw how he was," Shayla interrupted. "Your stepfather says he believes I was involved in a crime."

"Which she was," Merc continued smoothly. "But not of murder. In her grief at losing Richard, she attempted to enact vengeance against the hapless humans who killed him."

"Did you?" Zach asked, leaning forward and fixing her with an intent look.

"No." She supposed she didn't blame him for asking, but it hurt. "I did commit a crime, similar to the one Nantha committed. I sang to them, lured them to the rocks. I'm lucky there weren't any deaths."

"And she was caught and punished," Merc added. "Exactly the same way your sister will be."

Zach took a deep breath and then nodded. "How long?"

"Six months."

He winced, turning to Shayla. "Were you imprisoned for six months, too?"

"Yes." She smiled, hoping to soften the blow. "But undersea prisons aren't like human ones. They're actually pretty comfortable. The punishment is the isolation."

"Nantha is very sociable. I worry she'd lose her mind if she has to be isolated that long."

"She won't," Shayla reassured him. "There is lots to do. Reading and learning, classes in everything from knitting to painting to cooking to teaching. I broadened my education while there. And most importantly, I came to terms with my grief."

"At least until you got out," Merc added, only partly teasing. "Then you decided you wanted nothing more to do with your own city or your own people. I guess we should be glad you didn't disown your family, as well."

Deciding to ignore her brother, she continued to focus on Zach. Maddie and Carmen listened, their rapt expressions attesting to their fascination with learning all of this about their very private friend.

"I needed my space," she continued. "And I don't think anyone could blame me. Though I knew I needed to be near the sea, I still wanted to live on land. So I moved here to Galveston Island. I'd been dabbling for years in selling artifacts I'd found on the ocean floor, so I had plenty of money saved up. I bought a house right on the water."

"I see." Zach watched her, his gaze so intent that even Merc took notice. "And then you were fine?"

"Relatively," she allowed. "I continued to grieve, but I went to a grief support group similar to the one I attended while in prison. I lived my life, developed my business and made friends." She included Maddie and Carmen in her smile. And finally, I was well enough to be able to visit my friends and family again."

"Though not often enough," Merc put in. "She rarely stops by the palace now since Dad retired and I became king."

"You healed, but some people, like Ion, continue to hold a grudge?" Clearly Zach still struggled with the idea of his stepfather believing such things about her."

Nodding, she eyed Zach, hoping he'd understand what she meant. "As always in life, there was gossip and rumors. Some kind and some…not so much. Apparently, there remains a determined camp who still believe I did horrible, unspeakable things to the man I was to marry. The fact that I went after the fishermen instead doesn't seem to register. I'm lucky I pulled myself back in time, or I might have been guilty of murder."

Saying this out loud shocked her brother. His quick intake of breath told her he'd never considered such a possibility.

"I can understand that," Zach said softly, surprising her. "You're a very passionate woman."

Her face heated at the compliment. Meanwhile, her brother snorted. "Cool it, you two lovebirds. While I think all of this is cute, I've come here because I need your help. I'm trying to keep Father from involving Poseidon."

"You're the king." Shayla protested, taken aback at his immediate assumption that she and Zach were lovers. "Can't you simply forbid it?"

Her brother stared at her as if she'd grown two heads. "Who are you and what have you done with my sister? You know as well as I do that no one forbids Father anything. Though he's no longer the ruler, he was king long before I was even a gleam in his eye. If he wants to talk to his friend Poseidon, then that's exactly what he's going to do."

"Poseidon?" Maddie exclaimed. "This entire conversation is beyond interesting."

Even Carmen appeared absorbed. She tilted her head, interest gleaming in her eyes. "Why would one of the ancient gods care what mortals or Merfolk do?"

"Merfolk are his creatures," Merc explained. "He has always protected us. It won't be good if he learns a small group of humans are capturing Mermaids and using them for nefarious purposes."

"Nefarious," Maddie repeated dreamily. "Nice choice of word."

One thing about her brother, he knew how to charm the ladies without even trying.

"Why would this be a bad thing?" Carmen asked.

"Since he's so powerful, wouldn't that make it easier on everyone? He could get the captive ones back and shut down the entire operation."

"Except he doesn't do things in half measures," Merc said.

"Poseidon's not known for his rational behavior when something angers him," Shayla explained, for all of their benefits. "Think tsunamis and cyclones. He has a terrible temper and tends to act before applying logical thinking."

"To say the least," Merc added, with a mock shudder. "He could wipe out entire cities with one sweep of his hand and not even blink."

"So what you're saying is we need to find these guys and shut them down before Poseidon gets involved?" Zach asked.

Merc glanced at him before bringing his gaze back to Shayla. "Can you do that?"

"Can we?" Shayla shook her head. "I don't know. We just recovered Nantha. We know where the other guys were operating, but they've long since vacated that place."

"Then you need to search for them," Merc insisted.

"We already are," Shayla shot back. "We've put the word out among our various supernatural groups, and we were just beginning to work on formulating a plan when you showed up. Having you sitting around issuing kingly orders isn't helping, you know."

Merc glared at her. Carmen and Maddie simply watched, wide-eyed. And Zach… Zach laughed.

Chapter 13

Both Shayla and her brother eyed him as if they thought he might have lost his mind. "What?" Shayla asked, when he'd stopped guffawing long enough to be able to hear her.

"It's good to know sibling relationships are the same whether you're Shifter or Merfolk," he said, still chuckling. "Listening to you two bicker reminds me of me and my stepsister. We occasionally argued like that."

Nantha. Though he didn't say her name, they all knew who he meant. This had a marked sobering effect, especially on Merc.

"I'm sorry," he said, meeting Zach's gaze. "I promise she's being treated fairly."

"Do you have any idea what's going to happen to her?" Zach asked, putting the question directly to Merc. "I mean, I know you said she'd be going to prison. Is there a process similar to the way it is among humans?"

"Definitely. She'll have a trial. Since she's already been

charged, she'll be imprisoned until the trial. I'm sure counsel has already been assigned to assist her."

"Counsel? Like a lawyer?"

When Merc nodded, Zach's expression appeared to war between being impressed and feeling worried. "Just like the humans. I never would have guessed it."

"Why not?" Merc regarded him sternly. "Just because we have fish tails and use gills to breathe underwater doesn't make us a bunch of savages."

Instead of scrambling to explain his comment, Zach laughed again. "Point made," he said. "And don't look now, but I think a couple of the ladies over at the bar just bought you a drink."

Of course both Maddie and Carmen immediately swiveled around to stare, making Zach laugh and Merc frown.

"Or maybe it's for you, Zach," Shayla interjected. While her brother certainly was handsome, he couldn't hold a candle to Zach. She'd noticed earlier the women at the bar checking both men out, their gazes lingering on Zach. They'd also eyed her, clearly trying to figure out if she had a claim to either of the men.

Grinning, Merc shook his head. "I was about to leave. But now I have to see who the drink is for."

A moment later, the waiter appeared with two beers. One for Zach and one for Merc. Shayla clapped, delighted. "They're after both of you," she said. "Maybe we ladies should just take off and leave you guys at it."

"Don't." Zach grabbed her arm. "I'd much rather be with you than any other woman in this bar."

Whoa. Shayla sucked in her breath, stunned. Helpless to react as she wanted to with everyone watching, she looked down instead. Every part of her body buzzed with the connection.

"Okay, that's it." Throwing up his hands in defeat, Merc

stood. "I'll leave you two alone. Or as alone as you can be with a Vampire and a Shifter sitting with you. All this sizzling crap is making me feel ansty." He took a deep drink of his beer. "Plus I've got two ladies over there waiting to talk to me."

They both watched as Merc made his way to the bar, the way he sauntered speaking volumes about his confidence. Several other feminine heads swiveled to watch him.

"Your brother is really something," Maddie breathed. Carmen nodded, as if to second that statement.

"Sorry," Shayla said. "He's always been pretty confident, even before he was crowned king."

"How does that work, exactly?" Zach asked. "Since your dad's still alive, I mean."

She knew what he meant. "Well in the human world, one is a king until death. We're a bit different since our lives are so much longer. Kings—and queens, too—can retire. My father had ruled for 116 years. He said he was tired, so he passed on the crown to Merc. I think it was a good decision. Now he fishes a lot. Mom teaches cooking classes and cooks."

Both Carmen and Maddie had swiveled in their chairs, not bothering to hide the fact that they were watching Merc chat with the women at the bar. Merc had taken a bar stool in between both women and they were all laughing, no doubt at something he'd said.

"He's a charmer," Shayla said. "He always did have a way with the ladies."

When she looked back at Zach, their gazes locked.

"Did you mean what you said a minute ago?" she blurted, lowering her voice so that Maddie and Carmen hopefully wouldn't hear.

His gaze never wavered. "Yes. With one addendum."

Heart skipping a beat, she waited.

"I'd rather be with you somewhere else. Want to get out of here?"

She didn't ask where he wanted to go, or what he had planned, if anything. She simply tossed back the last bit of her wine and nodded. He stood, helping pull back her chair before taking her arm. She felt his touch all the way down to her core.

"We're leaving," she said, touching Maddie's shoulder. Her two friends nodded, barely able to tear their gazes away from her brother.

Zach grinned and took her hand. Without a backward glance, fingers intertwined, they left the bar.

Zach couldn't believe they were holding hands. Shayla's small hand fit perfectly in his larger one, and the connection made his blood heat. The tension had been building in him ever since meeting the beautiful Mermaid. Certainly, at first her beauty played a large part in his attraction to her. But the more he'd been around her, the more he admired her steadfast devotion to her friends, her family and her newfound passion for private investigative work. Though he knew she felt the same pull of attraction to him that he did her, she played none of the coy games other women played. She made it clear that what he saw was what she was, and her refusal to pretend to be something more or less intrigued him. Her confidence and unabashed sexuality drew him in.

He burned for her, though he'd held himself in check until his sister had been found. It felt like he'd been waiting forever. Far too long. Now, though… He needed to tell her the truth. The fact that he hadn't would probably make things worse.

As she pushed through the front door ahead of him, he was right on her heels, still holding her hand. Outside, in the deserted alley, she turned to him. Surprised, he gazed down at her, waiting to hear what she wanted to say.

Instead, she pulled him down and kissed him.

There was no hesitation in the sensual movement of her lips on his. The first touch ignited a fire. He tugged her close, body to body, and kissed her back.

Emotions—desire, certainly, but something stronger—flared. He lost track of time, forgot where they were, because everything about her filled up his entire world. He wanted to push her up against the wall and make love to her right then, right there.

When they finally broke apart, each was breathing hard.

"I want you," she said, her forehead resting against his chest.

"I want you, too," he replied. Only one thing held him back. The little matter of his arranged engagement to one of her subjects. The fact that he hadn't yet met his Mermaid fiancée didn't matter. He'd agreed several months ago, as a favor to Ion. It was a tangled mess he'd need to unravel before he could go any further with Shayla.

Starting with telling her the truth.

When she moved closer to him, Zach put his hands on her arms to keep her back.

"What's wrong?" she asked, bewilderment plain on her face.

Stomach twisting, he took a deep breath. "There's something I need to tell you. There's no easy way to say it, so here goes. I'm engaged."

She froze, then jumped back. The look she gave him told him that he might as well have slapped her. "And you're just now telling me this?" Her icy tone matched the shock in her gaze.

"I… Yes. It's complicated. To be honest, the engagement has never seemed real. It definitely doesn't now. I didn't know I'd start to care for you."

Arms crossed, she shook her head. "Please don't give me that line about how you don't care for your fiancée. Because at some point, you had to propose."

"Actually, I've never met her. Ion asked me to do it as a favor to him. When he explained how much the alliance would help Nantha, how could I say no? I wasn't involved with anyone."

Her frown deepened. "Help Nantha how?"

"I'm not sure. Something about family connections. As in if Nantha was related to her family by marriage, her status would improve."

And to be fair, in the photo Ion had shown him, the Mermaid had been beautiful, the kind of heart-stopping gorgeousness that seemed to be common with Mermaids. Though she couldn't hold a candle to Shayla.

"You're telling me she's *Mer*?" Disbelief mingled with hurt in Shayla's voice. "One of my own people?"

Bracing himself, he nodded.

For a moment, she turned away from him, her shoulders rigid as if she was gathering herself back together. Meanwhile, he felt like he was still shattered in pieces from the force of his desire for her.

"I think you need to go," she told him. "Before I do or say something I'm going to regret."

"Wait." He grabbed her arm.

She shook him off. "Don't touch me."

"I'm going to break off the engagement," he continued, meaning it. "Ion will understand as that was one of my conditions to the arrangement. I promise you, I agreed for Ion's sake, not mine. And it was long before I met you. Let's be honest here. After what Nantha has done, I'm pretty sure there's no alliance on earth that could help her out."

At that, she spun around to face him. Clearly, all her composure had returned. "I'm not sure what to think, Zach. I don't like cheaters."

Ouch. "That's why I told you before we went any further. That's a situation I need to resolve before we can continue to explore our relationship."

To his relief, she didn't immediately dismiss his words. Which meant there was still hope.

"From what I've come to know of you," she finally said, "you've been honest and straightforward. I can't see why that would change. I don't appreciate you not telling me this up front, before all the flirting and stuff. But I'm glad you told me now."

He nodded. "I promise you, as soon as I see Ion again, I'm breaking it off."

"I think you should wait," she said, shocking him. "I'm very curious as to what Ion is up to. Who is this woman?"

"Her name is Teredia," he said, shrugging. "Beyond that, I don't know much about her. Ion said he'd arrange a meeting between the two of us, but so far he hasn't ever gotten around to it. I'll admit, I haven't pressed him either."

"Teredia." She mulled over the name. "I can't say I recognize the name. But if a marriage to her would form an alliance, she has to be from a powerful family. Do you have a photo of her?"

"I do." Not sure whether he should be embarrassed to admit he'd placed the folded-up picture Ion had given him in his wallet, he simply dug it out and handed it over. "Honestly, I haven't thought much about it since I agreed. I figured once we met, it'd be easier to decide if this was a good match."

She looked up from studying the picture, frowning. "If

you agree to an arranged marriage, anything after that is a moot point."

"One can always change their mind," he said firmly. "I made that clear with Ion up front. He was cool with it."

"Maybe so, but I'm willing to bet he wasn't being truthful. You can change your mind, but not without bringing disgrace down on your parents. Or in this case, on your stepfather. While your fiancée is beautiful, I don't recognize her face. I have to wonder what Ion hopes to gain by arranging the marriage."

"I wondered why she—or her parents—even sought this type of marriage. There must be something in it for them, as well."

"I'm going to find out." She had that determined tilt to her chin that he was coming to recognize. "I know he's your stepfather, but I can't help but feel he's up to no good."

She started to hand the photograph back, but paused. "I'm going to ask Merc. He'll hate me interrupting him, but this could be important."

She spun around and went back to the Broken Chains door. Intrigued, he followed her.

After the requisite series of knocks, they were inside. Merc still sat at the bar with his two feminine companions. They were now falling all over each other, still laughing at something, though he wondered how they could hear over the death metal sounds coming from the band. Though Zach didn't care for this kind of music, lots of others did, judging from the head bobbing of many in the crowd.

Shayla pushed her way up to Merc, earning a furious look from one of the women with him.

"Chill out," Shayla said. "He's my brother."

Merc, too, appeared less than pleased. "What's up?" he asked, not bothering to hide the annoyance in his voice. "It better be something important for you to interrupt my fun."

"It is." Shayla handed over the picture. "Do you know her? She's Mer."

Lazily, Merc studied the image. "Pretty," he finally said, handing it back. "But, no, I have no idea who that is. Why?"

One of the women leaned in, pouting. "We're kind of busy here," she informed Shayla. "Maybe you can save the rest of this for a phone call?"

Both Zach and Merc stiffened. Shayla's mouth tightened. Slowly, she swung her head around, fixing her gaze on the still clueless woman. "Excuse me?" Though her voice dripped politeness, the undertone contained a clear warning. Zach didn't know if the other woman was drunk, stupid or both, but she didn't back down. Her aura revealed her to be a Shifter.

"Yes, honey," she purred. "This man and I are in the middle of arranging a very interesting evening. Now why don't you run along and leave us to our fun?"

Merc's eyes widened. He jumped down from his bar stool and took Shayla's arm. "Come on, sis," he said. "Let's go outside and talk. No need to start a fight."

With her jaw locked into place, at first it appeared that Shayla wasn't going to go along. But finally, she let out her breath and jerked her chin in a quick nod.

With Merc holding on to one arm and Zach the other, they moved through the crowd toward the door.

Back in the alley, they waited as a small group of Vampires glided down the alley and to the entrance to Broken Chains. Once they'd been admitted and disappeared inside, Merc turned to face his sister.

"Okay, what's going on? Who is the Mermaid and why was this so important you felt you had to interrupt me on one of my rare nights on land?"

"It has to do with Ion," Shayla began. "And with Merc." Succinctly, she filled him in on what little details they had.

When she'd finished, Merc eyed Zach. "You're engaged, then?"

Feeling sheepish and a bit angry, Zach nodded. "I've changed my mind, though," he said. "I'm no longer willing to go through with the arranged marriage. I'm not sure why I even agreed in the first place, other than to help Ion."

Brow raised, Merc looked from Zach to Shayla and back again. Zach braced himself for the next comment, because it certainly would be true. His life had begun to change since meeting Shayla. He was no longer willing to simply continue to coast along the path of least resistance.

Surprisingly, Merc appeared willing to let that particular aspect of his sister's life remain private. He simply nodded. "Sometimes the sacrifices we're willing to make for our loved ones turn out to be too great." He turned his attention back to Shayla. "Thank you for bringing this to my attention."

"What do you think it means?" she asked, frowning.

"Who knows?" Merc shrugged. "It could be something or it could be nothing. One thing I've learned is that there's always some sort of intrigue going on at court. Dad used to hate it and I can see why." He sighed, dragging a hand through his golden hair. "I'll talk to Ion when I return. Once I learn the identity of this Teredia, your fiancée, I'll know more."

Zach nodded. "Let Ion know I need to speak with him, will you?"

"Of course." Glancing at the Broken Chains sign, he grimaced. "I'm going to have to take a pass on the no doubt exceptionally vigorous activities those two women had planned for me tonight and head home."

"I'm sorry," Shayla said, sounding anything but.

"No, you're not." Merc ruffled her hair, making her grin. "But you were right to bring this to my attention. It might be nothing, but in case it's not, I'm going to get right on it."

After giving his sister a quick hug, he shook Zach's hand and took off.

Leaving the two of them standing in almost the exact same spot as they'd been when they'd kissed.

"I'll walk you out," Zach said.

After a second, Shayla nodded. "Okay. I always feel better with some Shifter protection. That's why Maddie often goes with me."

They walked a few blocks in silence. "Do you usually catch a cab?" he finally asked, aware after one more block it would be much easier to wave one down.

She shot him an arch look. "Yes. There's no way I'm walking all the way to the other side of the island."

Things weren't right between them. He understood, he didn't blame her, but that didn't mean this new remoteness didn't hurt. It pained him to think he might have managed to ruin a relationship that had so much potential. Not if he could help it. He'd fix things. Starting with contacting Ion and calling off the arranged marriage. Once that had been done, there no longer would be anything coming between him and Shayla.

Once they'd reached Broadway, they hailed a passing cab. As it pulled up, Shayla glanced back at him before she yanked open the door. "Thanks for the company," she said, her tone impersonal. "You've given me a lot to think about."

It sounded like a goodbye. A forever goodbye.

As she climbed into the back seat, he acted on impulse, something he rarely did, and jumped in after her. "I'm going with you," he said, hoping she wouldn't say no.

Though she shook her head, she gave the cabbie her address and they were off. There were a hundred things he wanted to say, but not in the back seat of a cab and not without weighing his words. This was far too important to blow. So he held his silence and let his gaze wander over her while she looked out the window.

Beautiful, perfect and his, he thought, the fierce need to possess her as strong as an animal instinct. His. Meant to be, preordained, an agreement reached between them in another realm, between two souls. How had he not seen this, how could she not realize they'd be happiest together? Apart, they'd be nothing. United, they'd be complete.

This realization stunned him, at first. But as the knowledge settled in him, he knew it was true. Conscious of every breath she took, every move, the rustle of her clothing, the graceful way she pushed back her hair from her face, he marveled, drinking in the sight of her.

His.

And now it would be up to him to help her feel the same way.

Talk about uncomfortable. Shayla wasn't sure what to think, how to act, what to say. She really didn't even want to look at Zach and didn't understand why he'd decided, at the last minute, to come with her. It wasn't like she'd welcome him into her home. Not now, anyway.

Engaged. A tiny little detail he might have mentioned a lot sooner. And even worse, engaged to another Mermaid, someone from her hometown. Despite the fact that they'd never met, according to him, she couldn't help but feel a twinge or two of jealousy for the other woman.

Except Zach claimed he intended to break off the engagement. She had to wonder about that. Maybe it was different among Shape-shifters, but for Merfolk, an agreement to an arranged marriage was considered binding. For all she knew, Zach might end up married to this other Mermaid. And then where would they be?

The thought brought a stab of pain. She and Zach shared a strong connection. So much potential for a future that might be...or could have been. Thinking about losing out on that made her despondent.

The entire taxi ride felt endless. Despite the fact that they didn't speak, she couldn't help but be overly aware of the big man sitting next to her.

He belonged to another woman. Another Mermaid.

The news of his engagement had shocked her. Still did. But now, with some distance between her mouth and his, she shored up her resolve. The news might have actually come at the right time and was probably for the best. If only it didn't hurt so much.

Truthfully, she didn't need involvement. Even with the passing of time, she hadn't gotten over losing Richard. She wasn't sure she ever would. It wouldn't be fair to lead any other man on. She felt guilty that what she felt for Zach seemed stronger, deeper and more passionate that anything she'd ever shared with Richard. Until now, she'd always believed maybe everyone only got one chance, one love in their life, and when it was gone, it was gone. But then she'd met Zach. Would loving him be a betrayal of her memory of Richard?

Now she'd worked herself into a state of depression. Anger might have been better. At least that would be more useful in helping her resist such a handsome and sexy man as Zach.

She should have known he was too good to be true.

When the cab glided to a stop in front of her house, she went to pay the fair, but Zach beat her to it. "I'd like a moment of your time," he said gravely. "I promise, I won't take too long."

Though initially, her first impulse was to decline, she finally gave in and nodded. As the cab drove away, she turned and began climbing the steps, a wave of her hand his invitation to follow.

She unlocked her front door and went in. Inside, once she'd turned on the lights, she offered him a drink. Coffee or water, because that's all she had. He went with water. She got them both a bottle of water, and motioned him to take a seat. Instead of the couch, he chose her chair, which made her feel both relieved and disappointed. Still, she had to admit to being curious to hear what he had to say. In a detached, remote way, of course.

"About the fiancée," he began.

"Teredia," she interjected. "She has a name."

"Yes, you're right." He looked suitably dejected. "If I'd had one inkling that I'd be meeting someone like you, I never would have agreed to Ion's request."

She nodded. "You do realize that none of this is her fault." Though they both knew it might be.

"To be honest, this all might be something Ion's cooking up. I don't even know if Teredia is aware of our engagement," Zach continued. "After I agreed to marry her, I never heard anything. She didn't request a meeting or anything. But then again, neither did I." He scratched the back of his head. "I kind of put it to the back of my mind. It was a maybe someday thing, and it never seemed real to me."

Men. Shayla rolled her eyes. "It's okay, Zach. We're in a business relationship. There's no reason you'd think you'd need to tell me about her."

Proud of herself, feeling strong in her ability to remain aloof, she lifted her chin.

At this, he leaned forward. "Maybe we started as a business relationship. But you know as well as I do that there's huge potential for something more. I know you feel that spark between us."

Whales help her, but she found his quiet confidence sexy as hell. This man was trouble. She'd known that from the moment she first laid eyes on him.

Chapter 14

"Don't lie," he ordered, his gaze warm and insolent.
"And don't even try to scurry back behind that wall you've
built around your emotions."

What? Shayla blinked. On the verge of denying it, she
gave up. Because he was right. Only recently had she allowed herself to even consider unlocking her heart.

And look where that had gotten her.

"Shayla?" he prompted.

"I do feel that spark," she finally admitted, shoring up
her rapidly crumbling defenses yet again. "But that's all it
can be. I can't be involved in a relationship. Not with you,
not with anyone. I'm still not over losing my Richard."

Zach's eyes narrowed, and his sensual lips tightened.
Watching him, she felt a sudden, swift longing for him to
do something completely out of character and yank her up
and against him and cover her mouth with his. She wished
he'd kiss her deep and slow and persuasive, kiss her until
she couldn't think, or move. Until she could only feel.

He shifted his weight, almost as if he knew her thoughts, but he didn't get up from his chair. "I can do casual, if that's what you want."

For the first time, she felt a surge of hope. Maybe, just maybe, if they had a fling, she'd get him out of her system and return to normal. "Interesting," she replied, striving to sound cool even though she was breathless to hear what he'd say next.

Now he did push up to his feet, crossing the small space that separated them. He towered over her, which she found she liked, and she couldn't help but stare longingly up at him. He crouched before her, the intensity in his gaze making her shiver inside. Then, just when she thought she might do something foolish, like launch herself at him and cover his mouth with hers, he touched her face, the gentle trace of his fingers down her cheek sending a shiver of awareness up her spine.

Right now, she thought helplessly, her body aching and thrumming, she wished he'd push her back on the floor and have his way with her instead of talking.

"How about we just agree to a no-strings-attached, friends-with-benefits type of thing?"

She caught her breath, ordering herself to focus. Once upon a time, earlier in her life, if anyone had ever asked her to do such a thing, she would have laughed at them. She'd always had a serious nature, especially for a freedom-loving species like Mermaids. Just as Zach had, she'd been contracted to be married to a man she'd never met. Once she had, and Richard had come into her life, she hadn't seen anything wrong with that. Merfolk looked at arranged marriages as natural. Something Zach clearly didn't understand.

"You're engaged," she reminded him, even as her body

continued to burn with desire. "I don't think we should even be talking about anything like this."

Her prim tone made his mouth curve in a dangerous smile. Her heart stuttered in her chest as she stared. Emotion flooded her, more than lust and therefore dangerous. He could make her want him, crave him, need him, but she couldn't allow him to get close to her heart. She nearly hadn't survived it before. To her, love had been like a blaze of fire, a lightning strike inside a whirlwind. Full force and then gone forever.

Love and loss, light and dark, opposite sides of the same coin. She knew she was a better person for having loved Richard, and she wouldn't give that brief period of happiness up, even to spare herself the pain of losing him.

Aware there was no timeline on grief, she'd always known she'd be mourning for years. Now, with Zach, she felt herself slowly coming back to life. The color and texture had returned to her world. She'd begun living again.

Horrified, she wondered if that meant she was beginning to forget Richard? If she allowed Zach close, would Richard's handsome face slowly fade from her memory? Even as she panicked, she knew it wouldn't. She wasn't built that way. And her heart was big enough to allow herself to try and love again.

The thought paralyzed her. Love again? Love? What the hell was she thinking? She knew better. She knew all too well what would happen to her when it ended, as it surely would. Nothing lasts forever. She'd never survive it. No. She simply couldn't set herself up for that kind of pain ever again.

"No strings attached," he repeated. "If either of us wants out, it's a done deal."

Her mouth went dry. Mermaids were by nature sensual creatures, and she'd denied her body's needs for far too long. Plus, she wanted him. Oh, how she wanted him. Damn him for knowing this.

Zach, leaning close and tasting the skin at the base of her neck with his mouth, brought every forgotten need and craving back to the surface full force. "We can make love. Hang out. Eat. Have fun. No commitment."

This time, her walls didn't just crack; they crumbled to dust. "I don't know," she managed, her voice sounding more breathless than she wanted.

He kissed her then, long and deep and oh-so-hot. She melted into him, yet still a part of her held back. Could she do this? Was she capable of allowing herself the pleasure of him without letting him destroy her?

As he deepened the kiss, he slid his hand down the curve of her side, making her shiver. And she decided she could do this, would do this. As long as they both stuck to their agreement, she could already tell they'd be perfect together.

Except he was still engaged.

The thought was like a dash of ice water. She pulled away, got up and put as much distance as she could between them. "You need to go."

Though he stared at her in disbelief, he finally nodded. "You're right. I'm sorry."

As he got up to leave, regret flooded her. She dug her fingernails into her palms to keep from going after him and begging him to stay.

At the door, he turned. "I'm not married," he said, his gaze dark. "And not really engaged, as in I don't even know this woman. I understand that you want to wait until I've broken it off, and I get that."

All she could do was nod.

"But know this. I want you. And only you. I want to

bury myself inside you until we're both senseless with pleasure."

So help her, her knees almost gave out. Zach sure did have a way with words all of a sudden.

When she didn't respond, he nodded and turned to go. And then, as if desire had set her brain on fire, she went after him. Shoved herself between him and the door and grabbed hold of him, pulling him down for another kiss.

Rationality and speech vanished. Consumed by desire, by need, they shed their clothes standing. At least he had the momentary bit of clarity to grab a condom from his wallet and put it on. Once he'd taken care of this, he shoved her up against the wall and entered her with one swift move. Urging him on, the guttural sounds escaping her throat made him wild. With swift and deep strokes of his rock-hard body, he claimed her, and brought her to the brink and beyond. Oh, so far beyond.

When she shuddered, convulsing around him, every pulse of her body echoed the pounding of her heart. He groaned, and then cried out; his body spasms brought her even more pleasure.

He supported her as she sagged against him, her body as slick with perspiration as his. "I didn't mean for our first time to be like this," he said, barely able to catch his breath enough to get the words out. "I'd planned for a little more finesse. You know, with a mattress and sheets and maybe candlelight. Less…savage."

His rueful comment made her smile. "I like savage. And next time, we can try it in my bed."

Which they did, a few hours later. She fell asleep in his arms, startled when she woke and realized he was still there, sleeping beside her.

Outside, thunder boomed and lightning flashed. Rain drummed on the roof and windows, and the wind drove the sea in white-capped waves. Her kind of weather. She especially loved slipping under the water during a storm, leaving the destructive surface energy for the serene calmness below. Part of her longed to run out there now, letting the storm buffet her, while the rest of her wanted to slide back under the covers and nestle up with Zach.

Zach. Who even managed to look ruggedly sexy with his eyes closed. She sighed, and then told herself to get a grip. Using her best drill sergeant voice, she called his name. "Zach." She shook him. "Wake up. It's morning. You have to go."

He opened one eye and smiled, the pure sexiness of him making her body twinge. "Why?"

Though sorely tempted, she stuck to her resolve. "Casual, remember? We both have a lot to do today."

When he stretched, hands over his head with a sexy move that made her mouth go dry, she had to take a step back. "You need to get ahold of Ion and cancel your engagement," she reminded him. "And I've got some detective work to do." Though all she really wanted to do was stay in bed with him.

"Gotcha." He pushed up off the bed, and walked into her bathroom, completely and gloriously naked. It took every ounce of self-control she possessed not to follow him there.

While he showered, she went to the kitchen and slugged back coffee, waiting nervously for him to finish and go. Somehow she'd foolishly believed once they'd made love, she would have gotten him out of her system. Instead, it appeared she only wanted more.

Finally, he sauntered into the kitchen, fully clothed, with his hair still damp. "I thought I smelled coffee."

Dropping a casual kiss on her cheek, he poured himself a cup. Sipping it, he eyed her. "What's wrong with you?

You're an awful lot on edge after someone who spent most of the night—"

"I'm stressed," she said, cutting him off. "I really didn't intend for things to go as far as they did. Especially with you still being engaged. I'd really like you to go now. I'll talk to you again once you've broken off your arranged marriage." She hoped her no-nonsense tone showed him she meant what she said.

Apparently, it did. His smile disappeared as he set the half-empty coffee mug on the counter near the sink. He eyed her, clearly on the verge of saying something, but when she shook her head in warning, he didn't.

"Gotcha."

She followed him to the door, pressing her lips together to keep from saying anything she might regret later.

One hand on the doorknob, he turned. "I'll be back," he promised. "And we'll pick up exactly where we left off."

And then he took off jogging in the pouring rain.

After showering and dressing, Shayla eyed the weather. The storm appeared to be moving out to sea, which was good since she and Maddie had agreed to meet for lunch.

They'd chosen Joe's Crab Shack on Pier 21. It was a short drive from Shayla's house as long as she avoided the seawall area with its tourist traffic.

Maddie had already been seated at a table. She smiled and waved when Shayla walked in. Today she'd pulled her wild red hair into a bun, though a few strands had already escaped, framing her face.

Though bursting with her news, Shayla ordered an iced tea. They both agreed to split an order of oysters on the half shell. Though the ones she got on land were never as tasty as those harvested fresh under the sea, Shayla's mouth watered.

As soon as the waitress left, Maddie tilted her head,

studying Shayla. "What have you done different? Is it your makeup, your hair? I can't quite put my finger on it, but something's changed. You're positively glowing."

"Am I?" Pleased, Shayla leaned forward and told her friend what she'd been doing since the previous day.

"You did what?" Maddie's mouth fell open. "Are you kidding me?"

"No." If Shayla would have been a cat Shifter, she would have purred. "Not kidding." She stretched, her body pleasantly sore in all the right places. "It was amazing, let me tell you."

"I'm so happy for you, but..." Maddie held up her hand. "I confess I'm a little worried about mixing business with pleasure. Maybe you should wait. I get that he's sexy as sin, but he's our client."

"Not anymore. His case was solved, and he's settled his account. There's no conflict of interest." Aware of how smug she sounded, Shayla shook her head. "I'm sorry. There is one complication, though. Turns out, he's engaged."

"What?" Since she'd just taken a sip of her iced tea, Maddie nearly sprayed it. "Engaged? To another woman?"

"A Mermaid, actually. It was an arranged marriage." She explained what Zach had told her.

Maddie's frown deepened. "That sounds like a line," she said bluntly. "I'm surprised you fell for it. Look, I care about you, Shayla. While Zach seems like a nice guy, I don't want to see you get hurt."

The waitress brought Shayla's tea and their oysters. They went ahead and ordered their lunch, shrimp po'boys. Then they got down to the business of slurping raw oysters.

Only when they'd emptied every half shell did Shayla answer her friend. "I appreciate that, Maddie. And I won't be hurt. He knows I don't want a relationship. We talked about that. Once his engagement is off, we're going to have a very casual relationship. Friends with benefits, he called it. He doesn't want strings any more than I do."

Head tilted, Maddie eyed her, lips pursed. "I'm not convinced."

"Why not?" Shayla asked, genuinely curious.

Exhaling, Maddie looked down. When she raised her face again and met Shayla's gaze, her expression was troubled. "It's just that…"

Shayla waited.

"It's just that he's a Shifter," Maddie finally blurted. "We don't do casual very well."

"What?" Shayla blinked. "You can't make a blanket statement like that. Not all Shifters are exactly the same. That's like saying all Mermaids are sex-addicts."

Maddie didn't even crack a smile. "Well, aren't they?"

The notion made Shayla laugh. "Hardly." The thought sobered her up. "Are you trying to tell me you think Shifters aren't capable of casual flings?"

"Sort of. But I'm thinking of Pack, since that's what I know best. Wolves tend to mate once and only once, forever."

"But you told me about events where a bunch of people would go shape-shift together and pair off for casual sex after they changed back to human."

Twin spots of color bloomed on Maddie's cheeks. "True, but what you're talking about is different. It's not a one-time, chance encounter."

This entire train of thought confused Shayla. "For all we know, Zach could be another kind of Shifter. We don't know for sure that he's Pack and becomes a Wolf. There are lots of other kinds of beasts, aren't there? He could be a Bear or a Lion."

Now Maddie crossed her arms. "Not only did he confirm it when I originally asked him if he checked with the Pack Protectors, but you know as well as I do that most of the Shifters around here are Pack. Bears are almost as rare as Dragons. I think it's safe to say that there's a ninety percent chance Zach's a Wolf."

"I have to agree. But why would he even suggest something like this if it wasn't what he wanted?"

When Maddie started to speak, Shayla held up one finger. "Before you say anything, consider how long it's been since I've…indulged in sexual relations."

Carmen appeared at their table. "I heard that," she said, grinning. "So the ice princess finally hooked up?"

"With Zach," Maddie interjected glumly. "What are you doing here? I thought you said you couldn't make it."

"My plans changed." Pulling up a chair, Carmen glanced from one to the other. "What the heck is going on? Shayla, you're practically glowing. I'm happy for you. But you, Maddie, you look like you're about to cry."

"Not even close," Maddie huffed. "I'm just trying to make sure no one gets hurt."

"By taking away all her fun?" Carmen guessed. "Maddie, I don't know about you, but Princes Shayla here hasn't been involved with a man since…"

Luckily, Carmen checked herself before saying it. Both of Shayla's friends knew from past experience that even the mere mention of Richard's death was enough to send Shayla into a tailspin.

Except this time, it wouldn't have rattled her. What did bother her was Maddie's disapproval. "Maddie, come on," Shayla said. "What exactly is the problem? And don't give me any baloney about being worried about Zach."

"Fine." Maddie sighed. "If you must know, I'm concerned about you. You say you can do casual and freewheeling, but you forget. I know you."

"There's no need to be." Shayla reached out and touched the back of her friend's hand. "I promise you, I'll be okay."

"Will you be?" Maddie held her gaze. "Richard's death broke you, honey. I know it better than anyone."

Their sandwiches arrived, interrupting the conversation. Carmen waved away the waitress, claiming she'd already eaten. Since Vampires didn't partake in anything other than blood, that may or may not have been true.

"I appreciate your worry," Shayla said once they were alone again. "But I promise, you'll be the first to know if I think I'm in trouble. For now, I plan to enjoy being spontaneous."

"And enjoy your lunch," Carmen said, smiling. She waited until both Shayla and Maddie had taken a bite before asking her question. "Why are you making him break off his engagement if you plan to keep things super casual? Let the man have his fling with you before he goes off and becomes someone else's husband."

The pang of jealousy that sliced through her, shocked her. "Because she's a Mermaid," she said. "How do you think she'd feel to know her fiancé cheated on her with her princess?"

Carmen nodded. "Good point. Not to change the subject, but I've got some news about those creeps who kidnapped Nantha."

Shayla dropped her po'boy on her plate. Maddie did too, mid-bite. "You could have led off with that, you know."

"Sorry." Carmen shrugged. "Watching you two with all the drama was so entertaining that I almost forgot. I've been talking to some of my Vamp friends that hang out down by where the fishing boats come in. They were telling me of a couple of guys—humans—who were dealing with a Merman to procure innocent Mermaids."

Shayla gasped. "Did they get any names? Or a location?"

"No names. But they said the guys were holing up in a boarded-up old house taken out by Hurricane Ike. You know, one of those ones that were abandoned and never repaired?"

Heart pounding, Shayla nodded. "Can you narrow it down to neighborhood? You knew there are quite a few all over the island."

"They weren't sure about that. But you can bet it will be someplace where there either aren't a lot of close neighbors, or where people don't care. At least we have a starting point. We can split up and search."

"One of us needs to stay with Shayla," Maddie put in. "It's too dangerous for her to be wandering around the seedier parts of the island without backup."

"Agreed." Carmen flashed a smile, taking care to keep her fangs hidden. "As a matter of fact, I think you two should search together. You know me. I work better alone."

Though Shayla was getting tired of the other two treating her as if she was fragile, she knew, compared to them, she sort of was. Maddie could change into a menacing Wolf if needed, while Carmen had Vampiric speed and strength. All Shayla could do was breathe underwater and change her legs for a Mermaid tail.

"I'm also interested in getting more information about this Merman who's making deals to procure innocent Mermaids," Shayla said. "I need to have more information to pass on to my brother."

"I'll see what I can find out." Rising gracefully, Carmen eyed their plate, her pert nose wrinkling in revulsion. "I'll leave you two to your meal. I need to rest up before tonight." She winked. "I've got some hunting to do. You'd be surprised how much they talk if you ask them at the right moment."

After Carmen left, Shayla and Maddie scarfed down

the rest of their lunch in silence. When the check arrived, Shayla paid, waving away Maddie's attempt to give her money.

"Where do you want to check first?" Maddie asked. "I know there are several in the vicinity of Avenue L."

"Let's start there," Shayla agreed. "We can take my car." That way Maddie wouldn't have to worry about paying for gas.

After leaving Shayla's house, instead of going home to Texas City, Zach drove to his mother's. He really hoped Ion would be there, because he needed to end this farce of an engagement so he could get on with his life.

Making love with Shayla had been…earth-shattering. While he'd known it would be amazing, he marveled at the way he still craved her, just hours after they'd last touched. And while he wasn't good at being casual, he'd give her the space she needed until the day came she was ready for more. No matter how long it took.

When he got to his mom's house, June wasn't home. Nor was Ion. Just in case he got lucky, Zach dialed Ion's number. When his stepfather answered, Zach was shocked.

"Glad you called," Ion said, his tone businesslike. "I need to talk to you, in private. How about lunch? We can do Gaido's, if you want."

The popular restaurant was always crowded, but Ion knew Zach loved it.

Zach wasn't sure what to make of this request, but it suited him fine, so he agreed. He wondered if Ion somehow knew Zach wanted out of the agreement. He definitely hoped so. That would make things go a lot more smoothly.

Chapter 15

Zach had arrived first and waited on the decorative metal bench out front. When Ion pulled up, the instant he emerged from the Jeep he used whenever he was on land, he seemed different. Off, somehow. He kept running his hand through his longish-grey hair and one eye appeared to have developed a nervous twitch. In addition to losing weight, he practically vibrated with a nervous sort of restlessness. If Zach hadn't known him so well, he would have suspected drugs. Since he knew Ion didn't even indulge in alcohol, it had to be something else. But what?

His stepfather had been acting weird for days. As Ion walked up, he shook Zach's hand. His palms felt sweaty. Instead of meeting Zach's eye, the older man looked away. Odd. Especially since Zach hadn't yet mentioned wanting to break off the engagement to Teredia.

"How are you?" Zach asked, not bothering to hide his concern.

"Good, good," Ion answered, sounding anything but.

Ion's agitated movements continued, even after they were seated. He couldn't seem to stop jiggling his leg, and he drummed his fingers on the tabletop, the same repetitive beat, over and over. Zach pretended to survey the menu, even though he always had the same thing when he ate here. He considered asking Ion what was wrong, but figured the older man would tell him in his own time. After all, he'd requested this private meeting.

The waitress asked about their drink orders. Zach ordered iced tea and Ion his usual sparkling water, a particular affectation of his.

When she left, Zach waited for Ion to fill him in on the reason he'd wanted to meet, but Ion didn't speak.

The menu sat untouched in front of Ion, who alternated between scanning the interior of the restaurant and glancing out the window at the parking lot.

"Expecting someone?" Zach finally asked. His question made the man jump, as if he'd been so lost in thought he'd forgotten he wasn't alone.

"No." Ion scowled. "At least, I hope not." He looked down at his still tapping fingers and shook his head before raising his chin to meet Zach's gaze. "I think I'm being followed," he said, lowering his voice. "Not so much on land, but at home."

"Why?" Zach asked. "Does this have something to do with Nantha?"

"What? No."

The waitress brought their drinks. Zach ordered his favorite, the shrimp po'boy. To his surprise, Ion claimed he wasn't hungry.

Once the waitress left again, Zach leaned across the table. "Ion, what the hell is going on? You're as jumpy as a cat on coals."

To Zach's surprise, the mere fact of his noticing seemed to calm his stepfather down a little. Exhaling loudly, Ion relaxed his shoulders before jerking his chin in a decisive nod. "I'm just worried," he said. "It's probably nothing."

"But I'm guessing you want to talk about it, since you asked me to meet you for lunch."

Again a quick nod. "I need your help," Ion said.

This surprised Zach, as there wasn't a lot he could do under the ocean. "Go on. I'm not really sure how I can be of assistance, but I'll do the best I can."

Ion grimaced. "Actually, the best way you can assist me is to help me get Princess Shayla on my side."

"What?" Unable to believe his own ears, Zach stared. "You filed a complaint against her and now you expect her to want to help you?"

"I know, I know." At least Ion had the grace to sound sheepish. "But I'm desperate. I need her backing. It would do a lot to, er, clarify my situation."

"What did you do?" Zach couldn't imagine what could be so terrible that...wait a minute. "Are you somehow involved with those men who are kidnapping Mermaids and using their blood?"

"Of course not," Ion scoffed. "Anyone who'd help those idiots deserves to be shot. No, I haven't broken any laws—human or Mer—yet, but I really cannot tell you. Honestly, the less you know, the better."

"Yet? Ion, you're scaring me. What the hell is going on?"

"Again, it's not anything you need to know about."

This stung. "Yet you plan to involve Shayla?"

"This already involves her." Ion's instant response worried Zach. "Or she will be, before all of this finishes playing out. I know she doesn't go home much, and I need to learn what exactly her views are."

"About what?"

Ion waved his hand, as if the answer was inconsequential.

Zach's sandwich arrived just then. Not sure whether to be glad of the distraction or not, Zach dug in. Ion watched him eat as if he regretted skipping the meal. Finally, Zach offered him half his sandwich.

Surprisingly, Ion declined. He waited until Zach had polished off everything on his plate before speaking. "Will you help me?"

"I'm afraid not," Zach answered. "I'm going to need a lot more information before I'll even consider involving Shayla."

Ion's expression darkened. "Seriously? You're my son. You know I'm facing extreme difficulties, and yet you still refuse to help?"

"I don't know what you're facing," Zach gently pointed out. "Because you won't tell me." He took a deep breath, aware that what he had to say next might be a bit like pouring salt on a wound. "However, I do have something I need to tell you."

And then he proceeded to let Ion know he was breaking off the arranged engagement.

When he finished, Ion appeared as if he was about to blow a gasket. His face had turned the color of one of his pet lobsters. "I don't need this right now."

"I'm sorry." Zach spread his hands. "I have no choice."

"No choice? Wrong. You can't break that off. The contracts have already been signed."

"Really? By whom?" Because Zach knew damn good and well he hadn't signed anything.

"I acted as your proxy." Ion spoke through clenched teeth. "This is a done deal. You have no idea how much this marriage matters. Without it…" He covered his face with his hands for a moment. When he removed them, he met Zach's gaze, his own hard. "It's a done deal."

"No. It's not. I want out. I haven't signed a contract, and you can't act as my proxy unless I've designated you to, which I haven't. It was a mistake, one that I'm going to rectify now. Ion, I'm sorry. I won't be marrying a woman I've never met."

Expression calculating, Ion eyed him. "You know what? I didn't think it was possible for things to get any worse, but…" He narrowed his eyes. "Does this have anything to do with the princess?"

Though impressed with Ion's insight, Zach feigned disbelief. "Why would it? She and I have only worked together on a case, not dated. We're friends."

"Uh-huh." Ion didn't appear convinced. "Well, now that you're calling off your marriage—one that you agreed to, by the way—you owe me a favor. Set up a meeting with me and your friend the princess. There still might be a way to salvage all this. I need to talk to her. The sooner, the better."

"Giving me orders now?" Zach asked. He'd never liked this. Though he'd been young when his mother had married Ion, the Merman had learned through trial and error what wouldn't work discipline-wise with his Shifter stepson. Apparently, he'd managed to forget. Or had become so desperate he no longer cared.

Zach wasn't sure which hurt worse.

"Contact me as soon as it's arranged." Pushing to his feet, Ion tossed a twenty on the table. "Lunch is on me." And he took off, moving quickly with constant glances over his shoulder, as if he still thought someone might be following him.

Zach remained seated, staring after the man his mother loved, the only man he'd ever considered a father. He wasn't sure what to think about what had just happened. Needing a distraction, he dug out his phone and called Shayla.

"Hey," Shayla answered. "How are you?" The warmth in her voice meant she was glad to hear from him.

"Where are you?" he asked, hoping she'd be at home so he could run by there.

"Maddie and I are exploring abandoned houses," she said. "We just checked one out on M Street. Carmen got some intel that said Nantha's kidnappers might have set up in an abandoned house on the island."

"That sounds dangerous. Do you want some help?"

"Nope." She sounded cheerful. "We've got this under control. But I'll call you if we find anything."

"You do that. Listen, I just had lunch with Ion." He detailed their conversation, including the fact that he'd told his stepfather he wanted out of the arranged marriage.

"He signed the contract for you?" she asked, her shocked tone making him smile. "He can't do that."

"I know. I told him so."

"Oh, that's terrible. That poor woman and her family are going to be crushed. With a signed contract, the marriage is universally regarded as a done deal."

Which were the exact same words Ion had used. Instead of passing along Ion's request on the phone, he decided he'd rather do it in person. Maybe she'd have some insights as to what his stepfather might be planning.

"Are you busy tonight?" he asked. "Do you want to meet up at Broken Chains? We can grab a drink and then maybe go have dinner. What do you think?"

She went silent for the space of a few heartbeats. "Zach, are you asking me out on a date?"

After she'd asked the question, he clearly heard Maddie squeal in the background, which made him grin.

"I think I am," he allowed. "Now that I'm no longer engaged. Are you up for it?"

He swore he could hear the smile in her voice when she answered. "Yes. Yes, I am."

They made arrangements to meet at Broken Chains at seven. Then she wanted to get back to checking out potential locations. While he…found himself at loose ends. He might as well do some investigating himself. Since Shayla and Maddie were tackling residential areas, he figured he'd check out some of the abandoned warehouses close to Broken Chains. To him, it made more sense using a warehouse rather than a home as a base for whatever nefarious purposes those guys were up to.

He parked in the Pier 21 parking lot and walked. Though it was broad daylight, he knew he'd have to be careful. There might be someone who'd take exception to him prowling around their empty warehouse.

The first one he came across had boarded-up windows and doors and no clear way to gain access. Nevertheless, he prowled the perimeter, careful to remain aware of his surroundings.

Despite this, when a tall man wearing a hoody materialized in front of him, he was startled. Biting back a curse, Zach debated pretending to be a lost tourist. But, as he eyed the man, he realized all he could see in the hoody were glowing red eyes. A Vampire, then. Or maybe a Wraith. His inner Wolf growled, hackles raised to signal danger. Zach tried to appear relaxed, though every instinct had sharpened, ready for danger.

"Are you a friend of Carmen?" he asked, figuring it couldn't hurt.

"Yes. And I know who you're looking for. They haven't been here," the stranger said, an odd inflection coloring his voice. "This is my territory. I prowl it constantly. There have been no men with white coats or Mermaids here. I've told Carmen I would watch for them."

"Thank you." Zach inclined his head in a gesture of respect. "We appreciate your help."

"You may leave now," the other man said. Not quite an order, but clearly a given. "I promise if I come across them, they will pay dearly for their crimes."

Zach nodded, turning carefully, his slow, deliberate actions intended to show the Vampire he wasn't a threat. Some Vamps had heightened predatory natures. He suspected it wouldn't take much of a wrong move to make this one attack.

When he reached his car, he got in and drove out to his mother's house. He wondered if Ion had gone there or back to the sea.

"No, he hasn't been here," June answered in response to his question. "Why?"

Zach outlined the events of earlier at lunch. June listened, swallowing hard. "I wish I'd have known you two were meeting," she said, clearly hurt. "I'd have joined you."

"I think Ion wanted this meeting to be private, Mom." Zach hugged her. "I'm just wondering why he's acting so weird. Do you have any idea what he's up to?"

"No." She shook her head slowly. "He's pretty much completely shut me out. I've been worried." Her mouth twisted. "I think he wants to end our marriage."

Shocked, Zach wasn't sure what to say. Going by instinct, he offered reassurance. "I doubt that, Mom. You know he loves you. He's just going through some hard times. Even though we don't know what's happened, he won't break ties with those who love and respect him. Don't let yourself think such horrible thoughts."

Blinking back tears, she nodded. "Thanks, son. It's difficult, but you're right. I'll try to stay positive."

He still had a few hours before he was due to meet Shayla. "How about we make a pot of coffee and drink some out on the back porch?"

The simple act of having something to do seemed to snap her out of her mood. He watched her as she bustled about in the kitchen, measuring coffee grounds, getting out mugs, even arranging some homemade cookies on a plate. So help Ion, he'd better not hurt her.

After checking out five boarded-up houses, Shayla and Maddie called it a day. Maddie didn't tease her, for which Shayla was grateful as she hurried home to get ready for her date.

Her date. Say that three times fast. She hadn't been on a date in years, not since before her engagement to Richard.

Shocked, she realized she'd been humming as she got ready for her shower. Quite honestly, even thinking about Richard hadn't dimmed her mood. This didn't mean she'd forgotten him—she never would—but it made her realize she might have finally healed. At least enough to go forward with the next phase of her life.

Allowing herself to relax and have fun with someone who would make no demands, giving her the time and space she needed right now.

Normally when she met her friends at the bar, Shayla wore jeans and a T-shirt. Since Galveston was at heart a beach town, people tended to dress more casually. But for tonight, in honor of her first real date in forever, she chose to wear a formfitting little black dress and strappy heels. Under it, she chose red, lacy lingerie. As she spun in front of her mirror, she imagined Zach peeling the dress off her and flushed.

She took special care with her makeup as well, going with a smoky look for her eyes. Though initially she considered wearing her hair up, in the end she left it down and flowing. She chose dangly earrings, several bangle bracelets and a couple of her favorite rings.

Finished, she decided to head out. Even if she was a bit early, she could drink a glass of wine to calm her nerves.

She'd barely walked into Broken Chains and chosen a table when Zach arrived. He grinned when he saw her, the heat blazing from his gaze making her smile back.

They decided to have a drink while they debated where to eat. Finally, they settled on Italian, a little hole-in-the-wall off Broadway favored by the locals.

Leaving Broken Chains with a man was a new experience for Shayla, and one she found she relished. Walking through the crowded bar with his arm around her waist, she noted the way other women eyed him, as if he were a piece of candy they wanted to eat up.

Exactly the way Zach looked at her.

Warmth suffused her as she considered this. It had been a long time since a man had looked at her like that. Too long. One look from Zach made her entire body come alive. A single touch and she felt like she might go up in flames. Her knees felt weak as she contemplated whether or not they'd make love again tonight. Hopefully, they would. The sooner the better, as far as she was concerned.

The stars shone bright in the velvet canopy of the night sky. As they exited the alleyway, she paused to inhale the slightly salty tang carried on the southern breeze from the ocean. This, the way the sea always felt close no matter how far inland she was on the island, was one of the reasons she'd chosen to make this place her home.

A perfect night. A perfect man. She was happy. Happier than she'd been in a long time.

"Are you hungry?" Zach smiled down at her, the warmth

in his gaze intoxicating. Suddenly, she realized she didn't care about eating dinner or food. All she wanted was him.

"For you," she murmured. "How about we skip the restaurant and go to my place? We can always eat later, once we've worked up an appetite." She'd spoken impulsively, but once said, she knew it felt right.

Appearing startled, he eyed her. "Are you sure?"

"More than I've ever been." She let her desire show in her gaze. "Unless you're starving and need nourishment." Worried, she realized she wasn't sure how it worked with Shifters, but she knew how Maddie could be. When Maddie got hungry, she became irritable until she ate. Something about her Wolf needing food.

"I can wait on the meal." He took her hand, his large fingers completely engulfing hers. She liked the way this made her feel safe and protected. "But I can't wait for you."

Yes! Suppressing the urge to high-five, she tugged him forward. "Then let's hurry up and go. I can't wait to show you what's on under this dress."

As they'd done before, they headed up toward The Strand, where all the tourists would be. Cabs would be plentiful there.

When they passed a boarded-up building with signs explaining it was under renovation, a man came out from the doorway, nearly walking into them.

"Oh. Sorry," he said, his pleasant voice only mildly annoyed. "I didn't see you two. My apologies."

"It's okay," Shayla began, right as he grabbed her arm. She felt the pain first, searing and strong, as if he'd branded her with a red-hot poker. Then, as she stared at her arm numbly, still in shock, she saw the blood running out in rivulets, crimson drops staining the concrete sidewalks. She realized she'd been stabbed.

"What the...?" Dizzy, she stumbled and nearly fell.

Zach caught her, his shout of outrage making her turn her head. The man, her assailant, took off running, blending into the crowd of tourists.

"Here." Zach yanked off his shirt, using it as a make-shift tourniquet to try and stem the bleeding. She let him help her to the ground, while someone dialed 911 on their cell. A small crowd of onlookers formed a circle around them.

"Any special healing abilities?" Zach's voice rumbled in her ear, the gentleness bringing tears to her eyes.

"No," she answered, attempting to shake her head. Even this small movement made everything start spinning. "Why?" she croaked. "Why would someone do something like that?" Tears stung her eyes.

"The world is full of crazy people," a woman answered from the spectators.

"Is anyone here a doctor?" Zach asked. No one came forward.

Her arm throbbed, the pain and loss of blood turning her vertigo into light-headedness. She hoped the knife hadn't been coated with anything, poison or chemicals or cells carrying disease.

The next few moments passed in a blur. Sirens and flashing lights, paramedics speaking to her and placing her on a stretcher. The ambulance, an IV and machines.

"I'm okay," she tried to protest, though she knew she wasn't, not really.

Then she saw Zach, his handsome face a buoy in a sea of confusion.

"I'm here," he said, taking a seat next to her. "I'm with you, don't worry."

"Your husband's going to ride to UTMB with us," one of the EMTs said. At first, this confused her, but then she realized Zach must have told the paramedics they were married, so they wouldn't refuse his request to stay with her.

For that, she was glad. Briefly, she wondered if her dress could be salvaged, but given the amount of blood that had soaked it, she doubted that. Too bad. It was one of her favorite dresses.

Just for a second, she closed her eyes. Tired, so tired.

When she opened them next, she was in a small hospital room, lying on a bed with rails and hooked up to an IV and a couple of machines. True to his word, Zach had pulled up a chair at her side. Her arm no longer throbbed. In fact, she realized with a sense of wonder that it no longer hurt at all.

"Hey," he said softly. "You're in the ER. I, uh, located your insurance card in your wallet and gave it to them. They've given you some pain meds and cleaned you up. A doctor will be in here soon to stitch you up."

"Then I can go home?" She thought of the evening she'd envisioned earlier and winced. "This night isn't going like I'd planned at all."

"Me neither." His rueful grin made her smile. "The police are supposed to come up and take your statement, too. Right now, they seem to think this was just a random attack."

She nodded. "I agree. It was crazy, though. That guy came out of nowhere. He even seemed very pleasant. I have no idea why he stabbed me."

"That's what worries me." Zach leaned close. "With all the craziness going on, I have to wonder if he wasn't sent by those guys who had Nantha."

"What's your logic?" she asked, aware he wouldn't make such a statement without something to back it up.

"Remember how Nantha said those men were after Mer blood? When that guy knifed you, he cut a little chunk out of your arm. And I saw some kind of glass rectangle, like a slide. I think he might have gotten some of your blood."

"Wow." She considered this. "But unless he'd seen me before, he wouldn't have known I was Mer. Which means he might have been one of the men we met with to exchange Nantha. At least now the attack makes some sort of sense." If they were still hunting virgin blood, they'd be disappointed with hers, though she kept this to herself.

"Yeah. Except we still don't know why they want Mermaid blood or what they're doing with it."

She realized he was wearing a T-shirt. The last thing she remembered was him removing his shirt to use it to stop her wound from bleeding. "Where'd you get that?" she asked, motioning toward his chest.

"Hospital lost and found. They felt bad for me when they learned I no longer had anything to wear." He flashed a grin that sent a tingle all the way to her toes. "Plus one of the nurses said my bare chest was too distracting."

Shayla could imagine. Right now, she found him way too distracting, even fully clothed.

The doctor arrived right then. After inspecting Shayla's arm, he got her stitched right up. Once he'd finished, while the nurse bandaged her, he gave her a prescription for some antibiotics and pain medicine. Though she nodded and thanked him, she knew she'd be tearing up the pain medication one. Mermaids and opiates didn't mix well. In fact, she wondered what kind of pain med they'd given her earlier. Her entire body felt flushed, her skin super sensitive to the rasp of the material on her body.

Once the doctor finished, he gave her discharge instructions and told her she was free to go.

"Let's get you home," Zach said. "Do you need any help getting dressed?"

Startled, she looked down to see she was wearing one of

those white, flowery hospital gowns that tied in the back. Underneath that, except for her thong, she was naked. And with every breath she took, the slightest movement of the cotton gown felt like fingernails raking her skin.

Yet in some odd way, she found it pleasurable. Which meant they'd probably given her some narcotics. Narcotics of any kind acted like a potent aphrodisiac on Merfolk.

Chapter 16

Great. Just great. Shayla knew she needed to warn Zach. But she couldn't make her mouth form the words.

Even though she still seemed capable of rational thought, her body continued to ride the wave of the drugs.

"Shayla?" Zach asked. "Did you hear me? Do you need my help?"

His voice seemed to be coming from a distance. Pleasure and pain. Pleasure.

"Help me?" she repeated. The thought of Zach's hands on her skin made her shudder. Desire and need had her body clenching, hovering on the verge of an explosion.

From this? She could only imagine what would happen if he actually touched her.

"Here," he said. "Let me help."

Damn. "No." She scooted back, away from him. This simple movement so distracted her, she had to fight to keep herself from convulsing, bucking, riding the wave of pleasure.

"What?" He cocked his head. "You're acting weird. Are you sure you're all right? Should I go get the doctor?"

She pulled herself together. "I'm fine. I can dress myself. Why don't you wait in the hall and I'll be there in a minute."

"But your arm…"

"It's bandaged. I can manage. Please." She managed to infuse a note of desperation into the last word.

Zach nodded. "Your clothes are right here. I'll be right outside the curtain." After he got up, he pulled a light blue curtain closed. She hadn't even noticed it before.

He'd placed her clothing in a neat little pile on the bed. Both her dress and undergarments were stained with blood. Even her bra had a few rust-colored spots on the pretty red lace.

Since there was nothing she could do about that, she managed to get her bra and panties on. Gingerly, she swung her legs off the side of the bed and worked the dress over her head, tugging it down over her hips.

Shimmying to make sure it covered her, she nearly lost control of her body twice. Only by grimly focusing on the task at hand did she manage to keep herself on track.

Her shoes. Where were her shoes? Finally, she located them, tucked under the hospital bed. She slipped her feet into them, wondering if she'd be able to walk a straight line.

Finally fully clothed, she stood, holding on to the bed rail just in case. No dizziness. Good. She took a step toward the curtain, meaning to pull it back.

"I got it." Zach was there before her, drawing it back. "You look better," he commented. "Now your face has some color."

She nodded, even as she swayed toward him. She wanted to climb up on him, rub herself against him like a cat in heat. Because that was how she felt, as if nothing else would do.

Despite knowing her reaction was due to narcotics in her system, part of her relished the freedom from having to make a choice. All along, she'd been hanging back, afraid to make the first move, while her desire for him simmered deep inside her. Now, egged on by the meds, that need had built to explosive heights. Once they were finally alone, she'd have no qualms about taking what she wanted.

"Let me help you walk," Zach said, taking her arm.

"No, wait." A nurse bustled in, pushing a wheelchair. "Please sit down in this and let me take you out. Hospital procedure."

Grateful for the distraction, Shayla let herself drop into the wheelchair. She couldn't help but notice the nurse fluttering her lashes at Zach, who seemed oblivious.

When they reached the front door, Zach pointed at a waiting cab. "I called them," he said, motioning to the driver, who got out and opened the back door.

"All right, then." Zach held out his arm. "Are you ready to go?" he asked.

Shayla nodded. She took his arm and used it to help pull herself up. Somehow, she managed to keep herself from sliding her body up against his as she got into the back of the cab.

He slid in next to her. Even sound was amplified, she thought, noting the way his jeans grated against the cheap vinyl seat.

With a detached air, she gave the cab driver her address and they were off. While she noted the way Zach continued to shoot worried glances her way, she was too busy trying to keep her errant body under control.

All Merfolk knew to avoid pain meds. If she'd been conscious when it had been administered, she would have claimed to be allergic. As it was, as long as the drug remained in her system, it would act like an erotic stimulant. Some people used it this way in small doses to enhance their sexual pleasure. Small doses were manageable. Too much, and one lost all control.

She suspected she'd been given a lot. If so, she was glad Zach was with her. There was no one else she'd want to experience this with.

Still, she thought she'd better warn him. As soon as they were alone. Right before she ripped off her clothes and jumped him.

Even picturing what she'd do to him brought a swell of arousal. She gasped, ruthlessly pushing it back down. Doing so was getting more difficult. Soon, she wouldn't be capable of anything but giving in to her raw desire.

After what felt like eternity, they pulled up in front of her house. She climbed out, still moving unsteadily, and waited while Zach paid the cabbie.

He took her arm as they walked up the stairs, and this time she allowed herself to lean into him with a sigh. At her front door, she handed him the key. Once he'd unlocked the door, she stumbled inside.

Moving swiftly, Zach caught her, preventing her from falling. At his nearness, a sensual haze settled over her. She inhaled, searching for the right words to let him know what had happened.

Instead, she pulled his face down to hers and kissed him. To her relief, he kissed her back. And then, without her being able to deliver a warning, she lost all control.

Barely remembering her wounded arm, she pushed him back on the sofa. Still fully clothed, she went after him. Kissing, caressing, she could barely breathe. She couldn't get enough.

"Shayla?" he choked out her name, not in protest but

in question. His fully aroused body only inflamed her more. "Your wound," he said, his voice raspy. "You really need to rest."

Damn. He was right but also so, so wrong. She pushed herself up off him, until she was standing. Then, with her gaze locked on his, she yanked her dress over her head. Her bandaged arm was a bit of a distraction, but she managed. "There," she gasped, triumphant. "Zach, I have to have you." And she told him what pain meds did to her kind.

Staring at her, his eyes widened, his pupils darkening to nearly black. "Are you sure?" he rasped. "I don't want to hurt you."

"If you don't touch me soon, you're going to cause me a thousand times more pain than you can imagine," she promised. "I wore this lingerie for you. Now take off those clothes. Please." She added the last word out of desperation.

He needed no second urging.

Clad in nothing but her bra and panties, she watched as he tugged off his borrowed T-shirt. Her mouth went dry and her woman parts moistened as he stood and slid his belt through the buckle. Despite the size of his arousal, he managed to unzip his jeans and get them off. He pulled a condom from his pocket and, gaze locked with hers, pulled it on.

"Are you sure you should be doing this?" Zach asked. "You just were stabbed."

"Believe me, I'm sure," she managed, closing her eyes against a fresh wave of desire. "I need fast and hard and furious. The way it was before."

His devilish grin warned her. "Come here."

Not only did she go to him, when she reached him she put her hands on his chest and tried to push him down on the couch so she could straddle him. But he was having none of that.

Laughing, he caught her wrists and held them tight. "None of that. We're doing this my way."

As she opened her mouth to protest, he kissed her. Ahh, finally. She felt as if she'd been starved for skin to skin contact. Sinuously, she wound herself around him, well aware of ways to use her body to coax him into doing exactly what he might not think he wanted to do.

His arousal jumped against her belly. She practically purred.

"Hold still," he ordered, holding himself rigid. Then, as she contemplated whether or not to comply, he eased her down on the couch, still holding her wrists tightly. He climbed over her, keeping his body far enough above hers that her wiggling and shimmying had no effect.

"Now," he murmured. "We're going to do this the way we should have the first time. Taking our time. Slow and easy."

"But," she started to say, but he effectively cut off her voice when he used his tongue to taste the skin at the base of her neck. He went from there to her breasts. When he suckled her, she gasped, arching her back and begging him—begging him—to take her right then and now.

He only smiled and continued what he was doing. She could see his swollen arousal, aching to lick the beads of moisture from the head. Again she wiggled, trying to work herself down enough to where she'd be in the perfect position to do exactly that. He shook his head. "Not yet, my Shayla. Not yet."

And then, as if he had all the time in the world, as if she wasn't throbbing with need, he entered her, but only partly.

She bucked again, drawing him so deep inside her, that

she cried out. And when he withdrew, he pulled himself out completely.

"Stop," she ordered, half crying, half laughing. "I know you want this as much as I do."

He did, she could tell. His concentrated expression showed the strain of holding himself back. He shook his head and entered her again, filling her completely. Afraid to move, she somehow forced herself to hold still, letting him dictate the pace.

He began to move. Each slow, deliberate stroke a pleasurable form of torture. Tension built and built, and just when she thought she might explode, he captured her mouth and kissed her deeply. As their tongues mated, she shattered, her body pulsing around him for what felt like eternity.

While she began to come back down, he cried out and let go. Wild, no longer deliberate. Hard and deep and fast, exactly as she'd wanted in the beginning. To her stunned disbelief, the tension began building in her again. A second climax ripped through her, making her scream. His release came almost instantaneously.

They held each other, clutched each other close, until the shudders and tremors and ripples died away. He stroked her hair, she touched his face. Emotions, those pesky feelings she sought to keep at bay, threatened to overwhelm her. Normally, such a thing would have concerned her, but she knew the pain medication still coursed through her body. That had to be the reason. Of course.

Feeling no pressure to get up and do anything else right away, they lay on the couch. He snuggled in behind her and she turned so he could spoon her. It felt both fantastic and odd to allow herself to relax this way. She couldn't remember a time when she'd felt so protected, safe and content.

With this thought, she drifted into a doze.

* * *

Zach was in trouble. He'd suspected all along, but had convinced himself he could keep his feelings under control. But this, the raw passion again, the way Shayla clearly let down her guard, had filled his heart so full he thought it might burst.

He loved her. Though she could never know, at least not anytime soon. Such sentiment would send her into a panic, giving her a reason and an excuse to run.

As she relaxed in his arms, her breathing evened, letting him know she'd fallen asleep. What could he do but hold on to her, wishing he never had to let her go. When she woke, they'd go get that dinner, but he'd wait until she was ready.

His cell phone rang, startling her awake. He checked Caller ID, saw his mom's phone number and let the call go to voice mail. He'd check in with her later.

After a few seconds, she texted him. Urgent. Please call me as soon as you can.

By now, Shayla had pushed herself up into a sitting position. She frowned when she read the text. "I hope everything is okay."

"Me, too," he said, punching in his mother's number.

"Thank goodness you called. I don't know what to do. Something's wrong with Ion." His mother's voice sounded frantic. "He's here, but he doesn't seem like himself."

"He was acting weird when I met him for lunch earlier," Zach said. "But he flat-out refused to tell me what's going on."

"He won't talk to me either. He's angry. In a rage. I've never seen him like this. I'm—" she paused, and then lowered her voice "—frightened."

"Of Ion?" Stunned, Zach tried to process her words. His

stepfather could be gruff, sometimes moody, but he'd never been a violent man. "Mom, what exactly is going on?"

Next to him, Shayla froze. Absently, he reached out and squeezed her shoulder.

"Not of him, but for him. Please come home," June said. "And if you can, please bring Shayla with you. Ion keeps repeating that he needs to talk to her."

After she ended the call, Zach pushed himself up and out of bed. He told Shayla what his mother had said, including her request to bring Shayla with him.

"I'm not sure what to make of that," Zach concluded. "Ion seems to think you'd be willing to assist him somehow. I'm not sure what's going on with him, but he's acting more and more unbalanced. I plan to ask my mom to try and talk him into getting a thorough medical checkup."

"That's a good idea. Because I can't get past you saying that he needs my help," she said, sounding incredulous. "I wonder what for?"

"Come on, let's get cleaned up and dressed. Then I guess you'll find out for yourself."

When they pulled up to his mother's house, every light was on. "Great," he muttered, turning to Shayla. "Whatever happens, I don't want you to be alone with Ion."

She studied him. "I appreciate your concern," she said. "But he's one of my people. I'm his princess. If he needs help and it's something I or my family can realistically do, I'm going to talk to him."

"I understand. But he's been acting strange. My mother said she was frightened, though she did clarify not of him, but for him."

"Do you believe her?"

He considered for a moment. "Yes. I don't see that I have a choice. And she and I have always had a code—811.

If she were truly in danger, she would have texted that to me, or said it in the phone call."

"Then I'll be fine." She opened the door and got out of his car. He hurried to catch her, taking her arm as they went up the steps.

His mother flung open the door before they reached the top. "Oh, thank hounds you're here," she exclaimed. She hugged Shayla first, and then Zach. "Ion's on the back porch, glowering at the sea."

They went through the house, heading for the kitchen and the French doors. Outside, several solar lights and a wall light illuminated the porch. Ion jumped up when he saw Zach and Shayla. "Thank you, son." He pumped Zach's hand. "Princess, I'm glad you agreed to meet with me."

"Are you?" Her tone cool, Shayla eyed him. "I need to ask something first. Did you ask to see me so you could insult me the way you did the last time we met?"

Ion's eyes widened before his expression hardened. "Again, my apologies. In my zeal to do what I believed to be right, I've made too many mistakes to count." He took a deep breath. "May we speak in private?"

Zach inhaled sharply, waiting to hear how Shayla would respond. She glanced at him, a slight smile hovering on her lips, before returning her attention to Ion.

"Anything you want to say to me, you can say in front of them," she said. "I understand not wanting to appear weak in front of your wife and son, but I feel this is necessary."

At her words, Ion blanched. "June," he ordered. "Go inside."

June didn't move. "No. I want to hear this. Maybe whatever it is will make me feel better about the way you've been acting since Nantha disappeared."

At the sound of his daughter's name, Ion swallowed. "I'm not sure I can do this," he admitted.

"Then don't." Shayla shrugged, turning away. "Come on, Zach. I think we might have just wasted our time. I don't know about you, but I'm hungry. Let's go get something to eat."

Careful not to show his surprise, Zach took her arm. They'd barely gone a few steps before Ion called after them. "Wait."

Slowly, Shayla turned. Crossing her arms, she eyed his stepfather.

"Everyone, please, sit down." Ion indicated the empty chairs surrounding the fire pit. He patted the seat next to him. "June, please sit here."

Once everyone had settled, he exhaled. "I'm in trouble," he began. "And partly responsible for what happened to Nantha."

"What?" June jumped to her feet.

"Please. Let me finish." Expression tortured, Ion waited until his wife had retaken her seat. "I fell in with some people who were advocating for change under the sea." He gave Shayla an apologetic grimace. "I arranged the marriage for Zach to strengthen my connection to them. His intended is the daughter of one of the leader's cousins."

"Now, that's over," Zach interjected. "Right?"

Ion sighed. "I haven't actually attempted breaking the contract yet. The king—" he eyed Shayla "—your brother got wind of our groups and decided to put an end to it. He's been rounding up our supporters."

Judging by Shayla's frown, her hope to see the best in Ion had rapidly slipped away. "The only reason Merc would do such a thing would be if your group posed a threat to the throne. Is that the case?"

Ion held her gaze. "Our group believes our people

should become a democracy rather than a monarchy. As such, yes. I'd say we are a threat to the entire royal family."

"I don't understand." June glanced from her husband to Shayla. "What does any of this have to do with Nantha?"

"We needed to raise a lot of money fast." Defeat deepened Ion's tone. "For quite a while there's been a human scientist obsessed with Mermaid blood. He believed he could make something with it as an ingredient and use this concoction to force others to do his bidding."

Both June and Shayla gasped. "You didn't…" June said, her voice breaking. "You sold your own daughter?"

"No. Of course not. Nantha's been working closely with him, of her own free will." He swallowed. "But we have been supplying him with Mermaids to use for testing. Volunteers all. He always returned them to us after a few days. They were a bit weak, but a lot richer. See, we let them keep a cut of the proceeds as payment for their services."

"And then they went rogue?" Zach guessed.

"Yes. I feared they had her when Nantha disappeared. They'd taken to posing as fishermen hoping to lure Mermaids to them. And they've cut off all contact with me and our group. They're no longer returning any of the women they took. And money no longer changes hands."

Everyone sat in stunned silence, attempting to digest Ion's words.

"This is where you come in," Ion continued, addressing Shayla. "I need to meet with the king, confess my part in this, and see if he and his army can help us stop this before anyone dies."

"Someone already has," Shayla pointed out. "According to what Nantha said, they've bled a Mermaid out."

Ion's composure crumbled. "I was afraid of that," he muttered. "There's more. Some in our group learned I intend to go to the king. They've been following me. I think they want me dead."

Zach figured things couldn't get any worse. Judging from his mother's horrified expression, she felt the same way.

He glanced at Shayla. He could only imagine how she must feel.

"Please," Ion implored. "Princess Shayla, you're my last hope. Could you get me a meeting with your brother, preferably here on land?"

"How do I know you don't want to harm him?" Her level tone revealed her resolve. "I refuse to put my brother, our kingdom, in danger because of your foolish actions. However, these scientists or whatever they are must be stopped. And those Mermaids still being held captive must be freed."

As she neared the end of her impassioned speech, Shayla's cell phone chimed. And chimed again. She pulled it out of her purse and checked it. "Oh, no," she exclaimed, her voice both panicked and furious. "Dad's contacted Poseidon. There's going to be hell to pay now."

"Poseidon?" Ion leaped up so quickly, he knocked back his chair. It fell to the wood deck with a clatter. Ion barely noticed. "Why on earth would your father involve the God of the Sea?"

Instead of answering, she only regarded him sternly. "I take it you know what this means."

"Oh, I do. Believe me. I'm a dead man."

As if saying the god's name out loud summoned him, the wind picked up, kicking the waves into whitecaps, spraying foam over the beach and the boat dock. Shayla shivered, hoping Poseidon wasn't really near and trying to figure out the best way to diffuse the situation if he was.

Face pinched and miserable, Ion cast an imploring look her way. "If that's him, will you at least help me?"

"As best as I can," she answered. "You know as well as I do once Poseidon gets riled up, there's no stopping him."

"Ancient Greek gods," June marveled, clearly not comprehending the gravity of the situation.

From the tense set of Zach's jaw, he did.

Shayla reached out and touched Ion's shoulder, making him jump. "The only way to rectify this is to tell us where we can find those men. We need to shut down their operation, bring them into custody and save whatever captive Mermaids remain."

"That's just it," Ion said. "I don't know where they are. They always had me do the exchanges on the Pleasure Pier."

Like they had with Nantha.

Chapter 17

"I don't know if they'd fall for the decoy thing again," Shayla mused, turning the idea over in her mind. "But I'm willing to see if we can set something up."

"There's more," Ion interjected. "I've recently gotten word there's to be a transfer of four volunteer Mermaids tomorrow night. This will take place at the Pleasure Pier. One of the men from my group is arranging the entire thing."

"I see." Shayla actually smiled. "Finally, a lead we can use." She raised her voice, just in case Poseidon was there and listening. "We'll need to contact my brother, King Merc, and let him take charge of this investigation."

"What will happen to my husband?" June asked, worry carving fresh lines in her face.

"Ion's fate isn't up to me," Shayla explained. "That will be for Merc to decide. But I can tell you one thing. Things will go better for him if he gives up the names of all the Merpeople in this ring."

Ion nodded. His conflicted expression told her how much he hated the idea of turning on his friends. But he also knew as well as she did that the penalty for such crimes was severe. His only hope was to throw himself on the king's mercy and offer to make restitution. And pray Poseidon chose not to become too involved. Hurricanes had been created over less.

"Did Poseidon get involved when your fiancé was poisoned?" Zach asked. Ion perked up at that, reminding her that he was among the group of Merfolk who'd refused to believe she hadn't been involved in Richard's death.

"No," she answered quietly. "I refused to let his killer cause any other loss of life. Though we never found out who killed Richard, or why, the general consensus was poison in something he drank. He loved his sea ale."

"Really? Because I don't know how many barkeeps, under the sea or on land, spike their ale with poison. I'm going to say none of them."

At his words, the sea seemed to shudder. The wind howled, pushing up water so high it sprayed them on the porch.

Shayla stared at him. "You ask for my help and then you again accuse me or murder. Your behavior is...unstable to say the least."

For a moment, confusion filled Ion's eyes. "I don't..."

June squeezed his arm. "Ion's agreed to have a complete physical by the best physician in Coral," she said.

Again, the wind howled, spattering them with sea foam.

"Maybe we should go inside," June said, twisting her fingers nervously. "I don't see any reason to continue to tempt...fate."

"You go on," Shayla said, flashing Zach's mother what she hoped was a reassuring smile. "And you, too, Zach.

If Poseidon does show himself, it'd be best if we Merfolk are here to greet him."

Ion swallowed, his nerves showing. But he straightened, putting on a brave face for his wife, which made Shayla respect him. "I'll be fine, June. Go on into the house. I'll join you in a few minutes."

"Okay." With a nod, June moved toward the back door. "Are you coming, Zach?"

"I'm going to stay here," Zach answered. "Just in case these two need any help. Go on, Mom. Everything will be fine."

Shayla admired the conviction in his voice, even though she knew everything being fine was far from certain.

Once June had gone inside, closing the French door behind her, Shayla walked to the railing. She eyed the churning sea and took a deep breath. Though she'd always been terrified of the God of the Sea, she knew she had to at least try to intervene. "Great Lord Poseidon," she said, pitching her voice to carry. Please give us a chance to make this right, to bring the evildoers in for justice, and to reclaim the Mermaids being held prisoner."

From the waves, a huge squid appeared, riding one cresting wave and landing on June's boat dock. When the water receded, the squid remained. Since Shayla wasn't sure what Poseidon wanted her to do, she didn't move. Keeping her gaze locked on the monstrous symbol of the ancient god's wrath, she pulled out her cell phone and texted her brother. Urgent. Please come immediately. West Beach, Galveston Island. Near the underwater rock.

Once she hit Send, she slowly returned the phone to her back pocket.

The huge beast didn't move. She wasn't sure what she expected it to do—begin speaking in a theatrically booming voice? Produce a handwritten directive? While she wouldn't put it past Poseidon to do any or all of those things, after a moment the squid flipped itself around and disappeared beneath the sea.

Once it was gone, the waves quieted and the wind died down.

"What the…" Zach asked.

"The ancient gods are like that," Shayla said. "Cryptic. They like to express themselves using symbolism. Just a second."

She dug her phone back out and did an internet search for what an octopus or squid symbolized. "Bingo," she said. "There's a lot, but these are the ones that are probably the most relevant. An octopus symbolizes strong will, focus and reason. Illusion, mystery and defense."

"Which means?" Ion asked.

"I think maybe that was Poseidon's way of saying he has faith in us and pointing out the tools we'll need to use to stop this ring of Mermaid kidnappers and killers. I've contacted my brother and asked him to come. I'm sure he's on his way even as we speak."

Too nervous to sit still, Ion paced. His restless energy made even Shayla feel unsettled. She was tempted to go for a quick swim to burn off some of her own jumpiness. But she didn't want to leave Zach and Ion, especially with the very real possibility the Merman might decide to flee. It wouldn't be the first time a Merfolk had decided to bolt before being convicted of their crimes. The vastness of the oceans made it certain those that ran would never be found.

Of course Ion had plenty of reasons not to leave. His loving wife. His daughter. And his stepson, Zach.

Merc arrived in under one hour, which meant he'd been swimming fast. Eyes flashing, he radiated fury. He rose out of the sea like an avenging warrior, exchanging his tail for his legs in an instantaneous move. Shayla envied him for that, while it made her smile. Her older brother had always worked hard to be such a show-off.

"Where is he?" Merc snarled. When he glanced past Shayla and caught sight of Ion standing silently by the chairs, his lip curled. "Are you prepared to pay for your crimes?"

When Ion started to speak, Shayla interrupted. "Not yet, Your Highness. We need his help to catch the humans responsible for kidnapping and murdering Mermaids. Not to mention the fact that he's agreed to provide the names of the Merfolk who are in the ring of conspirators."

"Have you?" the king demanded, eyeing Ion the way a whale eyed a jellyfish.

Ion swallowed hard. "Yes," he croaked. "In hopes that you will be lenient in my punishment, I will—"

"Betray your friends and colleagues in order to save your own neck. I see." Merc's voice dripped with disgust. "Just so you know, my security council has been monitoring those people's activities all along. We know who all is involved. And not to make you feel awkward, but I've never regarded that group or any other as a threat to me or my family. So I'm not sure how much any intel you give on them will help you alleviate your just and due punishment."

Someone gasped, making them all turn to look. June had stepped back onto the porch, unnoticed. Hand over her mouth, she looked at Merc with eyes brimming with tears. "My Ion is a good man," she said, advancing on Merc. "And if you're Lord Poseidon and truly a god, then you would already know this."

Clearly startled, Merc glanced over his shoulder as if half convinced Poseidon stood behind him. When he realized June actually assumed *he* was the God of the Sea, some of his tension vanished. He chuckled. "Allow me to introduce myself," he said. "I'm King Merc of the Merfolk."

"Shayla's brother," Zach put in helpfully.

June blinked, but her determined expression didn't waver at all. "Well, you still have power," she said, crossing to stand between him and her husband. "I beg you, please consider all the good this man has done when you get ready to pass judgment on him. He's been a wonderful husband to me and father to my son and stepdaughter." She sighed, and turned to face her husband. "I truly believe there may be some underlying medical issue affecting you. I pray it's nothing serious."

Though Ion's mouth tightened, he only nodded.

Merc slid his gaze past June to Shayla. The way one corner of his mouth quirked told her how hard he was trying not to laugh. The idea that he might actually be Poseidon continued to amuse him. She shrugged, caught Zach's eye and shrugged again. Zach crossed over to stand beside her.

"I'll add my voice to those who support him," Zach said. "Ion has been a good stepfather to me over the years. He's a loving father to his daughter and a great husband to my mother."

"I'll keep that under consideration," Merc said, allowing a brief smile before turning to Shayla. "Get me up to speed as quickly as possible."

She told him everything Ion had revealed, saving the worst news of all for last. "And Poseidon was here. Dad must have contacted him."

Her brother's eyes widened. "Are you sure? Did he speak to you?"

"After putting on a show with wind and waves and current, he appeared as a giant squid. I remembered how symbolism was big with his kind, so I looked up the meaning.

I'm guessing he was trying to tell us what qualities we'll need in order to shut the human group down."

"Maybe. At least he didn't give you a deadline."

Ion cleared his throat. "I'm afraid there actually *is* a deadline," he said. "They're meeting to take possession of four more Mermaids tomorrow night. Though occasionally they're volunteers, most times they're actually not. The girls will either be drugged into a stupor, or convinced they're meeting these men for some other reason."

"Like the way we pretended they were movie producers," Shayla said.

"Right," Ion continued. "Anyway, this batch of Mermaids is important. They've implied this group will be their last. And they've hinted that they are really close to developing whatever they were making with the Merblood. If we don't find them and stop them, I fear they'll soon unleash their creation upon the world."

June served them all hot tea and cookies while they gathered around the outdoor table and plotted. Zach took the seat next to Shayla, his knee bumping hers. She curled her hands around her mug to keep herself from squeezing his leg under the table.

Merc was in full-on King of The Merpeople mode. He interrupted their discussion by standing and slamming both of his hands down on the wooden table. "Here is what will happen," he said, his steely tone leaving no room for argument. "I am activating the Pod Enforcers. They will form an unbroken chain around the Pleasure Pier underwater."

Shayla nodded. "Sounds great, but what about on land? For all you know, these Mermaids are already out of the water. Having an army of Enforcers is an impressive show of force, but it won't do anything to stop the exchange if it takes place above the surface."

"I'm aware of that." Merc's stare let her know he didn't appreciate her statement. "Which is why the head of the Pod Enforcers is contacting the head of the Pack Protectors. We'll have them completely surrounded, both on land and sea."

"Sounds like a plan," Zach said. "And since my stepfather and sister were involved, I intend to be there, as well."

Zach hadn't had to argue at all with Merc about his intention to be there when the ring was rounded up and shut down. Shayla, however, did. With the tension thick enough to cut with a knife, Zach put a quick stop to that. "She's coming with me," he said, daring Merc to disagree.

The Mer-King clearly had too much on his mind. He back down right away, muttering something about tending to final arrangements. He and Shayla wanted to go back to her house, but Merc didn't want to let Ion out of his sight since he should have already been in custody, so they all decided to stay at June's house.

Ion seemed subdued. Zach didn't blame him. He made several attempts to catch his stepfather alone, but with June clinging to her husband's side, a private conversation seemed impossible.

Merc and Shayla bunked down in the living room, the king claiming the couch and Shayla taking the love seat. While Zach fervently hoped Shayla would join him in his bedroom after everyone else fell asleep, he had an idea her brother would be watching her like a hawk.

Early the next morning, Merc went into the sea to make sure his troops were in place and ready. Since Zach was Shifter, he'd been given the duty of being the point of contact with the Pack Protectors. Shayla had called Maddie the night before, and she'd passed along Zach's cell phone info to Maddie's brother. He'd be one of the Protectors fanning out to make a perimeter on the Pleasure Pier.

The operation had a high potential for success, but Zach knew failure might still be a possibility. The crowds of tourists were smaller than they'd be if it was summer, but there'd still be a lot of people who could inadvertently get in the way and be subject to being hurt. Especially if gunfire was involved. He hoped it wouldn't be, but given what had happened when he and Shayla met up with these guys, guns were a definite possibility.

At the house, June and Ion stayed shut up in the bedroom. June emerged mid-morning to grab a couple of donuts and two mugs of coffee, smiling sadly at her son before disappearing behind closed doors again. Since Ion would soon be going to prison, Zach figured they were saying their goodbyes the only way they could. He felt terrible for his mother, but Ion had brought this on himself.

Even worse, Zach had a sneaking suspicion there might be more that his stepfather had not yet told them. It would all come out in the end, no doubt.

Merc reappeared in the late afternoon. He brimmed with confidence, telling them his Enforcers were assembled and clearing the sea around the Pleasure Pier. There wouldn't be any dolphin shows for the humans to ooh and aah at this sunset.

The Pack Protectors were assembling near Moody Gardens. From there, they'd fan out, making their way to the Pleasure Pier in small groups of two, three and four. The decision had been made to allow no single stragglers.

Since the kidnappers had seen Zach and Shayla, Merc made one last attempt to get them to agree to stay home.

"No," Shayla said flatly. "We'll wear baseball caps and sunglasses. With so many people on the pier, there's no way they'll recognize us."

"Fine." With too much on his mind, Merc shrugged. "Do whatever you want. Just don't get in the way. We'll rendezvous at Murdoch's Souvenir Shop at the end of the pier. See you soon." With that, he strode away.

Zach decided they'd stroll Seawall Boulevard, arriving at the pier as if they were average tourists, taking in all the sights.

The pier at dusk was a beautiful place. The amusement park turned the neon lights on for their rides, the garish colors somehow blending with the rose-and-purple sky. Quite a few of the tourists had drifted away to find food.

Zach and Shayla strolled arm in arm. They both wore baseball caps, and she'd tucked her long hair up inside hers. The sunglasses weren't really necessary with the dimming light, so Zach removed his and tucked them in his shirt pocket. Shayla kept hers on.

Pretending to be tourists, they examined everything, exclaiming over gaudy souvenirs, clocks made of seashells and garish, poorly made tote bags. Though Zach continually scanned the crowd, he saw nothing suspicious. No men with several tipsy teenagers. But then, he also couldn't spot the Pack Protectors. Merc and his men waited under the water, which was probably a good thing, since due to his sheer size and massive amount of confidence, Merc tended to stand out in any size crowd.

Some kind of commotion seemed to be going on by the Ferris wheel. Exchanging a quick glance, Zach and Shayla jogged on over, joining the circle of people that had begun to form. They managed to work their way to the front, just in time to see a scuffle. Four young girls—Mermaids in human form—huddled together near a wooden building, wide-eyed and shaking, clearly terrified.

One man wearing a Galveston Police officer uniform and whose aura revealed him to be Shifter, had started questioning a young man with bright yellow dreadlocks, his pale skin and aura marking him as Mer. He shook his head, braids whipping around his face, clearly not wanting to answer whatever question the Protector had asked him. In fact, he began backing away, his furtive glances around revealing his cohorts. Two men, older, human, took off running. Several other Protectors, who'd been hanging back on the fringes of the crowd, went after them.

Taking advantage of the distraction, the young Merman ran for the edge of the pier. The crowd gasped in unison as he jumped, hitting the sea twenty some feet below.

Though many of the humans believed he'd killed himself, Zach knew better. Merc and his crew of Pod Enforcers would be there to foil his attempt at escape.

Meanwhile, several other Pack Protectors formed a protective ring around the terrified young Mermaids.

"I've got to go talk to them," Shayla said. "But I'm also concerned that they didn't catch the doctors or scientists or whatever they are. That young Merman clearly was the courier, trying to make the trade. I'm afraid they might have moved in too early, and the real bad guys got away."

"You don't know that," Zach reassured her. "By the time we got here, they might have already apprehended the others."

"I hope so." Taking Zach's arm, Shayla tugged him toward the girls. Two Mermen had already moved in, talking to the teens quietly. When Shayla reached them, they stepped aside. Catching sight of her face, the girls gave a collective gasp.

"Your Highness!"

"Shhhh." With a wave at the crowd, Shayla silenced them. "Are you all right? Were you drugged?"

"I don't think so." The youngest of the four, a petite raven-haired girl who appeared to be thirteen or fourteen, stepped forward. "Gresh—the guy who jumped into the water—he's our friend. He told us he'd met a guy who owned a modeling agency and wanted to take our pictures."

A slim blonde girl nodded. "It sounded harmless enough, and fun besides. What girl doesn't dream of being discovered and made into a supermodel?"

Shayla's lips tightened, but she didn't address this comment. Instead, she fixed each girl individually with a royal glare. "Do your parents know you're here?"

Four young heads went down in unison.

"I thought not." Shayla gestured at the two Mermen. "Have them all checked out to make sure they haven't been given anything. I'm sure their king will want to have a word with them, as well."

At the mention of the king, the girls groaned. Shayla shook her finger at them. "Believe me, you won't be in half as much trouble with the king as you will be once your parents find out what almost happened to you."

With that, she swept away. Grinning, Zach went after her. "Way to leave them stressing," he said.

"They deserve it. They have no idea what almost happened to them." When she raised her face to his, he was stunned to realize she was blinking back tears. "It's also horrible that a friend betrayed them. I sure hope Merc caught that kid."

Zach pulled her close, wrapping his arms around her tightly, offering comfort while all the while wishing he could kiss her, even though he knew this wasn't the time or the place.

"Thank you," she said, stepping out of his arms and smiling up at him. "You have no idea how badly I needed that hug."

Which only made him want to hold her again. Instead, he

knew they needed to get moving. The Pod Enforcers were shepherding the teens down the pier toward Murdoch's.

"Let's go rendezvous," he told her. "And find out if they got all the bastards."

As they neared the gift shop, Shayla saw their group. Merc's golden head stood tall above the rest. She hurried over to him, staying to the side while he spoke to the over-awed teenagers. Finally, the girls were escorted down the beach, presumably to find a secluded enough spot where they could disappear into the ocean so they could go home.

Silently, she and Merc watched them go. Zach continued to stay close by as well, which made her happy. "Did you manage to grab that kid who jumped off the pier?" she asked, keeping her voice low.

"Yes." Jaw set, Merc grimaced. "Those girls were his friends. They're all in the same class in school. Someone offered him the opportunity to make money, so he decided to sell out his so-called friends. He'll face charges."

"What about the others?"

"All the humans have been rounded up and are even now being interrogated by the Pack Protectors," Merc said. "Including the purported mastermind. He's revealed the location of his laboratory, and I've sent men there to retrieve his captives. They're there now."

Again, inexplicably, she felt like crying. Mustering every ounce of self-control she possessed, she managed to only nod.

"I've got several medical personnel checking out the young Mermaids. The ones who were to be traded. They appear to be all right, and so far, there are no indications they were drugged. And the captives..." He shuddered. "My men tell me they appear near death. Their blood has been taken so many times, their arms are a jagged mess of scars."

Her sharp intake of breath felt painful. When Zach put his arm around her, offering his support, she took it. Merc eyed them both, but didn't comment, for which she was grateful. Zach had no idea how much his physical presence comforted her. She hoped to show him, slowly and thoroughly, later.

For now, though, she needed closure. At least she knew this entire crazy underground bunch of lowlifes would pay for what they'd done. And even better, they wouldn't have the opportunity to do it again.

"No more deaths?" she asked, needing to know.

"No." He swallowed hard. "I'm hoping everyone pulls through."

One of the Pack Protectors motioned to Zach that he wanted to have a word with him. Releasing her, he stepped away.

"Can I go see them?" Shayla asked, her heart aching. She couldn't imagine what those women had gone through.

"Not yet. Maybe later. I want them thoroughly examined, given IVs and whatever else needs to be done to help them heal."

Zach returned, shaking his head. "I was just talking to one of the Pack Protectors. The leader of the group turned out to be Mer, not human," he said. "I'm guessing he wasn't there when Shayla and I were prisoners or we would have known. When they rounded him up, he was wearing a white coat and trying to blend in with the humans, but you know that pesky thing about auras. Can't hide."

Merc snarled. "Mer? Then he belongs to me. Where is he?"

Zach pointed to a group of Pod Enforcers who'd formed a circle around someone. "They're talking to him now."

Merc strode over, Shayla right behind him. Halfway there, someone grabbed Merc's arm and drew him aside, speaking urgently, leaving Shayla to continue on without him. Zach remained at her side. The circle of Pod Enforcers moved apart, clearing a path for their royal princess.

In the center of the group, a tall, extremely thin, bald Merman stood, his hands behind his back. His patrician features were notable only in their ordinariness. Jolted, Shayla realized she'd seen him before.

"You." Stunned, Shayla stared at the handcuffed man. Still defiant, he raised his head and stared back.

"Do you know him?" Zach asked, glancing from one to the other.

"We've met." Shayla swallowed hard. "Though I'm not sure I ever knew his name. He was part of Richard's protection detail. I believe he was there when Richard was killed."

The man said nothing, though a challenge flashed in his cold eyes. A challenge to what, Shayla wondered, feeling sick. Surely, this man hadn't been involved in murdering the very man he'd been charged with protecting.

Merc strode up just then, doing his own double take when he saw the man the Pod had captured. Then, clearly putting two and two together in a way that Shayla had been afraid to, he narrowed his gaze. "Treason is a crime punishable by death," he declared. "And so is murder."

Shayla gasped. "Are you saying you think he…?"

"You have no proof," the captive stated, lifting his chin even higher, the curve of his mouth mocking them.

"Actually, we do." Merc turned to Shayla, taking her hand. "That's what my guard just took me aside to tell me. One of Richard's former protection detail has come clean, in exchange for leniency. He's already provided us with the names of those involved with poisoning Richard."

The captive paled. "I didn't poison him," he said. "I swear."

"But you looked the other way when someone did." Arms crossed, Merc shook his head. "Aiding and abetting a murder. Added to your newest crime, treason against your king, and I think your days are numbered."

"I want a deal," the man said, desperation coloring his voice. "Like the other guy got. Life imprisonment instead of death. Give me that, and I'll tell you everything."

Chapter 18

Holding her breath, Shayla waited to see what her brother would do. Beside her, Zach put his arm around her, pulling her close. Though tempted to rest her head on his shoulder, she didn't. Better to stand tall and straight when given news that might feel like a savage blow. Zach would be her cushion, helping her to absorb and understand.

"Before we come to any agreement," Merc finally answered. "I need to know what you were doing with all the blood you stole."

"Stole?" The man appeared honestly surprised. "I was told all the Mermaids who participated in the experiment were willing participants."

"Seriously." Shayla spit the word. "What about the ones who died?"

Her question seemed to bewilder him even more. "I don't have any idea what you mean by that. No one died. This was all handled very professionally by my employees. I have a lab, and the volunteers came in and donated blood. They left after that. No one died."

Shayla and Merc exchanged a long look. If this man spoke truth—and clearly he believed what he said—then someone else had been responsible for keeping innocent Mermaids captive, starving them and taking so much blood they died.

Not mincing words, Merc outlined all this to him.

As he listened, all the color leached from the man's face. "I had no idea," he said. "I swear. I keep meticulous records, and I'll be more than happy to share them with you." He swallowed. "That is, once you grant me a deal."

Merc considered again. "Any deal will only be valid as long as you tell the truth. If I learn that you've lied—about anything—the deal is off."

Slowly, the man nodded.

"One more question," Merc asked. "What did you do with the blood?"

For the first time since he'd been taken captive, the man brightened. "Perfume," he said. "I've perfected a formula. With just the right amount—very little, actually—of Mermaid blood, any female human wearing this can become irresistible to men. I was just about to start scheduling meetings with various perfume manufacturers. I'll take the highest bidder. This should make me a fortune on the black market."

"On the backs of dead women," Shayla pointed out.

The other man's animated expression fell. "Sorry. Truly, I didn't know. I'm actually convinced there must be a misunderstanding. No one possibly could have died. My men would have told me." Shaking his head, he kicked at the wooden pier. "I would never allow this to happen. Not only would someone dying be a crime, but blood taken from a dead Mermaid would taint that entire batch of perfume, rendering it unusable. Since noting like that happened, I have to believe you're wrong."

"I wish we were." Merc's grim voice didn't reveal whether he believed the other man or not. "But even if you didn't know, you were still responsible when all's said and done." He narrowed his eyes. "Now tell me what you know about Prince Richard's death."

"Not without an agreement." His quick response showed none of this fazed him. "You're the king. I need your protection. I have too much to offer the world to be put to death."

Modest little guy, wasn't he? Shayla had a sudden, fierce urge to slap him. Of course, she reined this in, keeping quiet and waiting to see what her brother, the king, would do.

"Agreed," he finally said, raising his voice so all could hear. "I, King Merc of the Atlantic Ocean, swear that this man's crimes shall be punishable by life imprisonment rather than death, as long as he fulfills his part of our agreement and provides me verifiable information about the death of Prince Richard of Gill. Let my words be written down."

The leader of the Pod Enforcers nodded, carefully transcribing the words into some sort of electronic device that looked exactly like a computer tablet.

For the first time since he'd been arrested, the captive appeared to relax. "Thank you, my king." He bowed low. Once he stood straight again, he met Shayla's gaze.

"I know you loved Richard and he loved you, but there was another woman," he began.

"I know," Shayla interrupted. "He broke it off with her before the engagement."

"True. But she refused to accept that it was over."

* * *

Zach held Shayla while the piece of Merman excrement spewed garbage about her dead fiancé. Judging from the tight line of Merc's jaw, the king appeared to be regretting granting the criminal leniency. The horrible part of it all was that immediately there was no way to verify whether or not the man's words were true.

After initially going rigid in his arms, Shayla listened intently, not asking a single question. Zach couldn't tell if she believed all the nonsense the other man said, but he knew hearing it hurt her. Pain radiated from her, and he longed to take it inside himself and destroy it for her, but he couldn't.

In a nutshell, the story boiled down to this. Prince Richard had taken a lover, the sister of one of his royal guards. When he accepted the arranged marriage to Shayla, he'd done the honorable thing and ended the affair. But the other woman, who claimed to love him, refused to accept it and convinced her brother that the prince had taken her by force. For that, she'd said, Prince Richard needed to die.

"What was her name?" Shayla finally spoke, the question uttered in a voice dripping with ice.

The man sputtered, clearly startled. "Teredia Shiles."

Zach and Shayla exchanged a stunned glance. The very same woman Ion had wanted Zach to marry.

And now Zach knew beyond a shadow of a doubt that in fact, his stepfather hadn't told him everything.

Speaking of Ion, had the older man come down to the pier or remained at June's house? Zach casually scanned the area, actually beginning to wonder if Ion would try to escape his punishment. If Ion went on the run, that meant he'd never see his wife, Nantha and Zach again.

About to dig out his phone and call his mother to see if Ion was still there, Zach located him. Ion stood, hands in his pockets, in a corner engaged in what appeared to be an earnest discussion with a Pod Enforcer. Eyeing him, Zach could feel a muscle working in his jaw.

Teredia. The woman Ion had wanted him to marry had been Richard's lover and had him murdered. Had Ion known?

"If that son of a gun tried to involve me in some murderous plot, so help me…" He didn't realize he'd actually spoken out loud until Shayla squeezed his arm. When he looked back at the captive, he saw the other man not only understood what he meant, but knew the answer.

"You'd better tell me," Zach said, forcing the words out past clenched teeth. "Was this Teredia involved in a plot to overthrow the royal family?"

The man blanched, which for Zach seemed answer enough. Apparently, for Merc as well, because he took a threatening step toward the captive, making the other man flinch.

Looking from one to another, Shayla cursed. "What a tangled web they weave. Now it all begins to make sense."

"Are you all right?" Zach asked, watching Shayla closely. It had to be difficult, finally knowing what she'd suspected all along. Her fiancé had been murdered.

"I think I am," Shayla answered, bemusement and wonder in her voice. "It almost feels like a relief, to finally get some closure." She took a deep breath. "However, this Teredia has stolen enough from me. I want to meet her and see her punished for what's she's done."

"Oh, she will be," Merc interjected. "She's been apprehended by law enforcement in her own kingdom. I have men on the way to take custody of her now. But what I want to know is who is this Teredia, and why do you both seem familiar with her name?"

"Ion signed a marriage contract binding me with her,"

Zach explained. "I had him break it off when Shayla and I got involved, but clearly there was much more to it than I imagined."

Merc frowned. "Ion," he bellowed, causing the entire group to go silent. "Come here."

Several humans passing by turned and stared. Shayla shot her brother a warning glance. "Maybe we'd better go somewhere else to have this talk."

Merc nodded. "Not Broken Chains. As much as I love that place, not only can I not hear myself talk over the music, but women won't leave me alone in there."

Unable to help himself, Zach muttered, "Braggart." This earned him a grin from Shayla and a raised brow from Merc. Clearly, they'd both heard him. He shrugged.

"Zach?" Shayla asked. "Do you think your mom would mind if we went to her house? We could go to mine, but hers is a lot closer. Plus—" she lowered her voice "—I haven't had time to clean my place up. It's a wreck."

He couldn't help but laugh. "Only you," he told her, kissing her on the cheek, "would worry about something like that right now. But to answer your question, I'm sure my mother wouldn't mind if we all adjourn to her place. In fact, she's probably waiting for us."

"She is," Ion said. "She wasn't happy when I insisted on coming out here."

"Then let's go." Merc signaled his men, and one of the Pod Enforcers hurried over, nodding as Merc gave instructions.

Zach turned to find the Pack Protector he'd been speaking to, Maddie's brother, and found him waiting with a cluster of other Shifters. Zach told him what was going on.

"Are we still needed?" the other man asked. "Since there are no other Shifters involved…"

Overhearing, Merc shook his head. "I think we can

take this from here," he said. "My men have custody of the offenders."

"What about the humans?" the Pack Protector asked. He motioned to the Shifter who wore the Galveston PD uniform. "They'll need to be booked here locally. We've ascertained that they don't know anything damaging. What they do know sounds more like a drug-induced fantasy than truth. I doubt they'd be taken seriously if they start rambling about Mermaid blood."

"Good point." Merc motioned to his men, ordering they release the humans to the local police officer who happened to be a Shifter. The offenders who were Merfolk went with the Pod Enforcers, who would take them under the sea and book them into jail.

As they all headed toward their various vehicles, Merc fell in with Zach and Shayla. "What's going on with you two?" he asked, his voice casual, though the look in his eyes warned Zach he'd better not hurt his sister.

Zach opened his mouth to answer and then thought better of it. He'd let Shayla take this one.

"None of your business," she told her brother, smiling.

Merc shrugged. "You're happy, that's all that matters anyway. Just be careful, okay?"

To Zach's surprise, Shayla linked her arm with his and laughed. "We always are. Right, Zach?"

Zach nodded. Ion walked past them, head down, hands jammed in his pockets.

"Should maybe someone ride with him?" Zach asked, unable to keep from wondering about the wisdom of letting his stepfather take his own car anywhere alone. "While I appreciate you holding off from taking him in custody for my mother's sake, his irrational behavior might lead him to do something crazy."

"Good point," Merc said, splitting off from them and

hurrying after Ion. "Plus, I'm sure you two want your privacy."

Did they? Zach always would, but he wasn't sure about Shayla. Once her brother disappeared, her lighthearted mood fell off her. Clearly, she'd been putting on a brave face. She'd received a lot of upsetting news.

While he was grateful that she didn't feel the need to be fake with him, he also couldn't stop worrying about her. "Are you all right?" he asked, as they got into his car and buckled up.

Instead of answering, she tilted her head as if carefully considering his words. "You know, I think I am." The sense of wonder in her voice made him believe her. "I never understood *why* Richard died. Knowing he might have been murdered made it a thousand times worse. I went over a hundred different scenarios, things I could have done to change things."

She gave a heavy sigh. "Knowing the truth doesn't make his death easier, but I finally have some closure." With a rueful shake of the head, she grimaced. "Overused word, *closure*. But it's the right one."

"I'm glad," he said, starting the car. "I confess, I'm dreading hearing how all of this is connected. Ion arranging to marry me off to your fiancé's murderer? Why? What would be the benefit there for him?"

"I don't know." She touched his shoulder. "But get ready. I have a feeling we're about to find out."

When they pulled up to June's house, Ion and Merc had already arrived and were just getting out of the car. They stopped and waited while Zach parked.

As Zach and Shayla joined them, Ion met Zach's gaze. "I'm sorry," he said.

And then they all went inside.

* * *

Shayla wasn't sure what she expected to hear. Nothing Ion could say could shock her more than learning Richard had truly been murdered and why. Another woman. The old love triangle. Oddly enough, by some mutual form of tacit agreement, she and Richard had never discussed their previous love lives. It had been enough, Richard said, to know they would be each other's last. He didn't need to know about what had come before.

She'd always found that sweet, believing it proof that Richard was a good man. Now she had to wonder if maybe he just hadn't wanted her to know. Since he'd been with Teredia, who from all indications had long been part of a plot to overthrow the throne, what did that say about him? Of course, he'd broken things off, but she had no way to know what his beliefs were. And now that he was dead, she couldn't even ask him.

While also a royal prince, his home was far from hers, in the North Sea. Had it been possible Richard had ambitions to expand his family's kingdom?

Maybe Ion would know. If not, she imagined this Teredia, once she'd been interrogated, would be able to shed more light on things.

Zach's mother ran to greet her husband, throwing her arms around him and holding on tight. He held her too, his composed facial expression at odds with the anguish in his eyes.

Merc cleared his throat. "Ion, I believe you haven't told us everything." He outlined what the ringleader had said. With every word the king spoke, Ion appeared to shrink.

Finally, he pushed out of his wife's embrace and walked to stare out the window. "I know you've given a couple of others a deal," he began.

"Let me guess." Mockery filled Merc's tone. "You want a deal too, before you'll talk?"

"No." Jamming his hands into his pockets, Ion turned to face them. "I don't deserve a deal. I almost caused my own daughter's death, I plotted to overthrow the crown and a Mermaid died because of me. I've been involved in all of it, working as hard as I could to disrupt everything good about the only life I've ever known."

"No." June rushed toward him. "You are lying. Ion, I know you're a good man. You helped me raise my son. I see how you are with your daughter. You're a good, loving father and kind and gentle husband. I refuse to believe you would do this—any of this—without a really good reason."

Zach stepped forward, standing at his mother's side. "I agree. So Ion, before you start confessing, if you really did do all these awful things, why don't you start with telling us the reason why?"

The older man stared at his stepson, shock and sorrow warring in his eyes. "I can't."

"You do realize it will all come out in the end," Merc said, taking no pity on him.

"Not if I die first." Ion's chin came up and defiance flashed in his eyes.

June cried out. "Don't even talk like that. Think of me, your daughter and Zach. Your death would destroy us."

"Better me than…" Ion didn't finish.

"Falling on your sword, so to speak?" Merc shook his head. "Dying to protect someone else will only ensure that person gets away with their crime and will be free to commit the same thing again. Others will be hurt. Is that what you want?"

Shayla had a sudden flash of insight. "I think I know who you're trying to protect. It's Nantha, isn't it?"

For a split second, alarm flashed across Ion's face. But that was enough. Everyone saw it.

"No." His denial, though strong, came too late. He realized this from the looks on everyone's faces. "Please. She's just a young girl."

"Who is already in a whale's worth of trouble," Merc said sternly. "You might as well tell us the rest of it."

But Ion kept his mouth closed.

"Ion, listen." Zach spoke up. "If Nantha has done something even worse than what we already know about, she needs help. When I talked to her, she seemed strangely unrepentant about her actions. If there's more, allowing yourself to be punished for her crimes will not help her. Think about it."

Ion slowly nodded. "You're right," he finally said. "Nantha got involved with the wrong people. I did what I had to do in order to save her."

June gasped. Zach frowned. Shayla's heart ached, both for the woman about to lose her husband to either prison or death, and the man she loved who clearly struggled to come to terms with what his impetuous sister might have done.

Wait, what? Loved? Filing that info away to examine in detail later, Shayla focused on the topic at hand. "Hold on," she said, drawing everyone's attention. "In getting all these bits and pieces of information, I don't see how all this is tied together. The Merman making perfume from Mermaid's blood, the other men who worked for him torturing young Mermaids and letting them die, Nantha running off and getting captured by these same men, you—Ion—arranging a marriage between Zach and a woman who killed my fiancé. Not to mention Ion stating that this perfume could be used to influence others. What is the common thread tying all this together? Can you explain that to me first?"

Merc gave her a look, full of respect. "She has a point," he said. "And we need to know what exactly Nantha has done."

Ion began to talk. "Nantha has always been brilliant, but she has little common sense or empathy for others. She was the one to come up with the idea of making a perfume from Mermaid pheromones and selling it to the highest bidder." He sighed, dragging a hand through his silver hair. "And she was the one who actually discovered the blood was more powerful if it came from a virgin."

"How do you know this?" Zach asked, his expression telling Shayla he was hoping against hope that none of what Ion said would be true.

"I caught her experimenting with two of her friends. She was collecting their blood. When I walked in, she lied and told me it was for a science project."

"And you talked to the teacher," June put in, with a mother's understanding.

"Yes. When I confronted my daughter, Nantha told me everything. By then she'd revised her plan. Instead of selling the formula off to the highest bidder, she wanted to use the perfume herself on a much larger scale. Domination. Think about what can be done if a scent can make any man, all men, fall madly in love with you. She even had a name for it. Sirens' Song."

So far, Merc hadn't interrupted. "That's an awful lot of planning for a seventeen-year-old," he said.

Ion shrugged. "I thought so, too, but like I said, she's brilliant. Before she had this idea, she was the head of her class with a bright future. But this project consumed her, causing her schoolwork and social life to suffer. Which of course came to my attention."

"I remember that." June went to him, slipping her hand into his. "You were so worried about her. You even thought she might have gotten involved in drugs."

"What?" Zach looked from one parent to the other. "Why didn't you say something to me? I would have talked to her."

"Because I didn't want to speak badly of your sister with only suspicions. And then, when I knew for sure what was going on, the web had spread so far and become so entangled, I feared for her life."

It turned out Nantha had decided she needed help. One of her friends' parents was actively involved in the group trying to overthrow the crown, and when Nantha found out her own father was as well, she'd decided this would fit right in with her plans. Insinuating herself into the group, she engineered everything, using people like chess pieces being moved across a board. Until after a period of merely months, she'd managed to become one of the movement's leaders.

"They'd come up with a plan," Ion continued. "And when Nantha told me all this, I realized my daughter was likely a sociopath. Nantha left no stone unturned. I'm sorry, Zach." Ion's expression crumpled. "I should have told you the truth."

"What about you, Ion?" Shayla asked. "From your erratic behavior, I think you're leaving out your part in all this."

Ion grimaced. "I will take her punishment gladly," he finally said. "But she needs to be locked up, so she can't hurt anyone else."

Zach's mouth worked, but no sound came out. Shayla wanted to cry for him, for all of them. Zach and June had clearly no idea about Nantha. They'd believed her mischievous, but innocent. This had to hurt them on a visceral level.

"What about the men who were holding young Mermaids hostage?" Merc asked. "Wasn't Nantha one of their captives for a while, too?"

"So help me, if you lied about that, too..." Zach said, the harsh rasp in his voice revealing his pain.

"I didn't." Ion met his stepson's gaze. "Believe me. Everything I said was true. She and her friends were singing to fishermen, after which they tried out the latest batch of her perfume. She's the one who came up with the idea of pretending to be held hostage, asking for the virgin Mermaids in exchange. She must have been having difficulty finding enough willing participants in her bloodletting scheme. But I didn't know any of this. She played me, just like she played all of you." He covered his face with his hands and quietly wept, his shoulders shaking.

June wrapped her arms around him tightly, holding on as if she never intended to let go.

Shayla's throat ached. "What will happen now?" she asked her brother. "To Ion, and to Nantha? And Teredia, as well as all the others who were involved in this?"

"The Pod Enforcers are rounding them all up now. They'll be interrogated, of course. There will be hearings and trials, and each one will be dealt their punishment."

She thought about asking to speak with Teredia before the other woman was sentenced, and then decided against it. That part of her life was over. She'd gotten closure and had finally learned the truth about what had happened to Richard. The time had come to put all that behind her. After all, the future beckoned.

When Zach took her hand, she glanced up at him, letting her heart show in her eyes. His gaze locked on hers, and after a moment, some of the pain left his expression.

Merc looked from one to the other. "I'll keep you informed," he promised. "As soon as things settle down, I'll be in touch."

"Thank you," Zach said. "I appreciate that."

June sniffled, signaling how hard she was trying to hold back tears.

"Come," Merc said, gesturing at Ion. "It's time to return home and face justice."

Face resolute, Ion nodded. He turned and kissed June one more time before leaving her to go with his king.

Everyone followed them outside, Zach still holding tightly on to Shayla's hand. Side by side, they watched as Merc and Ion walked into the ocean, eventually disappearing. Shayla waded out, waiting until their human clothing floated to the surface, collecting each sodden article and bringing it back to shore. Avoiding looking at anyone, she spread everything out on the patio table, knowing the sea breeze and the sun would dry it.

Behind her, Zach conversed with his mother in low tones, offering words of comfort. When June requested to be left alone, Shayla understood. Each person had their own methods of dealing with grief.

Chapter 19

Taking a deep breath, Shayla went over and said her good-byes. To her surprise, June offered her a hug. "Take care of my son tonight," she whispered in Shayla's ear. "He'll be hurting, too."

Shayla nodded. "I will." To prove it, she once again slipped her fingers in Zach's. Hand in hand, they walked to his car and drove away.

During the drive to her house on the other side of the island, Zach didn't speak, and Shayla didn't try to fill the silence with meaningless words. When they pulled up in her driveway, Zach didn't kill the engine or make any move to get out of the car.

"Don't you want to come in?" she asked.

"I'm sorry, but I don't. I need a distraction. I think I'm going to head over to Broken Chains and have a beer."

"I'll go with you," she said instantly. "That sounds a lot better than sitting around my house." She knew she had to be careful not to let him suspect she was afraid to leave him alone.

He shrugged. "Suit yourself." Putting the car in Reverse, he backed out of her driveway and headed toward Harbor Shore Drive.

Broken Chains was packed, and the band—country swing this time—was going full force. Hand in hand, they twisted their way through the crowd, looking for a table. Of course, there weren't any on the main floor, so they headed for the stairs.

The top floor was nearly as full. Someone near the back stood up and waved. Maddie. And Carmen. Shayla pointed them out to Zach, standing up on tiptoe to put her mouth closer to his ear as she asked him if he wanted to join them. After a moment of hesitation, he nodded.

They made their way to the table. Right when they pulled out chairs, the waitress appeared, bringing Shayla's white wine and Zach's beer. When they thanked her, she grinned and waved before walking off to take someone else's order.

"I heard from my brother," Maddie said, bouncing in her chair from excitement. "He told me what happened, or at least as much as he knew."

Shayla filled them in on the rest, still holding tight to Zach's hand. He sipped his beer, listening without commenting.

When she finally wound down, even Carmen appeared stunned. "Wow. I can't believe a seventeen-year-old could do all that."

Zach grimaced. "Me, either. Part of me doesn't want to believe it. The other part knows it's true. When I spoke to her right after we saved her from the kidnappers, she had zero remorse for her actions. And she played me well, since all along she wasn't really being held prisoner." After speaking, he immediately looked stricken.

"Are you going to be okay?" Maddie asked.

"I'll be fine." Zach's immediate and curt response told Shayla that he wasn't. At least not right now.

Getting through the next few days was tough. If Nantha and Ion's betrayal had ripped him apart, Zach could only imagine how his mother must feel. She'd firmly refused his offer to stay with her, telling him he needed to get on with his life as she intended to get on with hers.

Then she'd packed everything up and gone to visit her sister in Denver. With Ion imprisoned, she'd told Zach she needed space between her and the sea.

Part of him could relate to this need to put distance between the old, familiar life where even the sight of the ocean would make her think of Ion. She hadn't said how long she'd be gone, and he hadn't pressed her.

Shayla stayed close, as if she understood how alone he felt. He wondered how she could, when he didn't understand it himself.

"You still have a family, you know," she told him.

He shook his head. "Do I? Sure, I have my mom. But Ion was like a father to me, and Nantha..." He couldn't even finish. The person his baby sister had become hurt too much to think about.

"The love is still there, no matter what." She hugged him. "That will never change, no matter the circumstances."

Though he nodded as if he agreed, inside he felt hollow. "You don't know what I'd give to be able to turn into a Merman and go under the water and visit them. I hate not knowing what's going on."

"Me, too," she agreed. "Three days have passed with no word from my brother. I haven't wanted to bug him and call, but if we don't hear anything by tomorrow, I will."

"I appreciate that." He put his arm around her, loving the way she leaned into him. Though they'd both agreed that their relationship should have no strings attached, that was no longer enough for him. He knew he had to tell her, even if doing so risked losing her for good. As June had so succinctly put it, time to get on with his life.

Yet every time he opened his mouth to tell her how he felt, he couldn't force the words past the lump in his throat. He decided he'd show her instead.

"I'd like to cook dinner for you tonight," he said. "At my place."

Her lovely eyes widened. "Your place?" Her mischievous smile made him smile back. "Since I haven't ever been there, I was beginning to wonder if you even had one."

"You've got me there," he replied ruefully. "I don't live on the island, so it's not as convenient as your house or my mother's. And it's an apartment. But if you don't mind coming up to Texas City, I'm a pretty decent cook."

Studying him, she nodded. "I'd be honored. You're full of surprises, aren't you?"

She had no idea how much he planned to surprise her.

Carefully nonchalant, he shrugged. "I try."

"You don't have to cook for me," she said, her expression earnest. "We can just go somewhere and grab a bite if you want."

Leaning in, he kissed her cheek. "Indulge me. I need to feel grounded."

Of course she let it go then, as he'd suspected she would. He told her he'd pick her up at six and then left to hit up the grocery store.

When he stepped into his small apartment, grocery bags in hand, he saw the place through a stranger's eyes. He liked his home neat and in order, but for the first time he realized the apartment appeared a bit austere, more like a hotel room than a home.

Since there wasn't much he could do about that right now, he decided to ignore it. Unpacking his bags, he assembled all the fixings for his favorite meal: homemade lasagna with garlic bread and a side salad. Humming under his breath, he got busy.

By the time he needed to leave to go pick Shayla up, the lasagna was assembled and ready to put into the oven. He'd also mixed up a nice salad, which was chilling, and the bottle of his favorite red wine blend would complement everything perfectly.

He only hoped she liked Italian food. Despite the way they fit together, despite the heat and the passion and the fact that they just plain enjoyed each other's company, there was a lot he didn't know about her and vice-versa. More than anything, he hoped they could change that.

His buoyant mood felt great; even the underlying hint of nervousness simmering below the surface didn't faze him. He'd bought her a bouquet of grocery-store flowers, figuring she'd like the simplicity of the unarranged blooms. Driving to her house, he felt confident she'd make the same choice he had to take their relationship to the next level.

After parking in front of her house, he hopped out of the car and started for the front door. She opened it before he got there, wearing a long sundress that showcased her lithe figure.

Suddenly tongue-tied, he smiled and handed her the flowers. Her face lit up.

"Thank you," she said. "Come in. I'll just need to put these in water."

He waited while she did, his heart racing as he tried to find something casual to say. Alone with Shayla, the last thing he wanted to do was talk. He had a sudden image of his hands tangled in her long black hair, her face up-turned, gaze eager, and her lips parted to receive his kiss.

His entire body reacted. She was beautiful and sexy, true. But with her, it was much more than that. She had a way of looking at him as if she truly knew him. And she seemed to genuinely like him, as if she actually considered him a friend despite the sizzling electricity that seemed to be constant when they were around each other.

If he gave into his desire now, things would remain the same as they were. Too casual. He thought of the meal he'd prepared and the evening he'd planned and resolved not to touch her. Not yet. Not until he knew they both wanted to be more than just friends who hooked up.

And if not? Then what? Did he possess the strength to simply walk away?

When she returned, her warm smile made him smile back.

"Are you ready?" he asked.

"I am."

When they pulled up in front of his apartment, he tried to see it through her eyes. "Sorry, it's kind of boring," he said. "Brick and wood, all the same. And no ocean view."

Still smiling, she shook her head. "I can't wait to see where you live. You can tell a lot about a person from their home space."

He thought of his bland apartment and winced. "Not me. I never really took the time to fix the place up."

Unlocking his front door, he stepped aside for her to enter. He closed and locked the door behind her. As he'd planned, the delicious aroma of his lasagna baking filled the room.

"That smells amazing," she commented, prowling around the room. He watched her closely, ready for her expressive face to reveal disappointment, but her thoughtful expression never changed.

She stopped in front of a framed print of a wolf that hung above his sofa. "This is beautiful," she said. "Who took this photo?"

"My father took it," he said, going to stand beside her. Close, but not touching. "Not Ion, but my birth father. He died in an oil well fire when I was two. That's my mother in her Wolf form. She gifted me this print when I graduated from college. She'd been keeping it up in the attic, all wrapped up because she couldn't bear to look at it."

"So you'd never seen it before?" she asked softly, slipping her hand into his.

Again the wild, fierce yearning to pull her close and claim her mouth in a kiss. Instead, he closed his fingers around hers and nodded. "Exactly. It's been with me ever since."

A timer went off in the kitchen, and he reluctantly released her hand so he could check on the meal. Time to pull out the lasagna and let it cool while he heated the loaf of garlic bread and opened the wine.

Shayla stayed in the other room, still studying the portrait. "Do you look like her when you're a Wolf?" she asked, eyeing him over her shoulder.

He brought her a glass of wine. "Not really. Females are a bit smaller. My coat is darker, too. More like my father's."

"Thank you." Accepting the glass, she took a small sip. "I'd like to see that someday. You changing into your Wolf form. Would you mind if I did?"

His heart stuttered, even though he told himself she didn't know what asking such a question meant. Except for other Pack members, Wolf Shape-shifters only allowed their one true mate to see them in their other form. By Shayla asking to do this, she was asking to be his mate.

Which is what he wanted more than anything. In his heart, she already was.

"Maybe." Deliberately keeping his answer noncommittal, he returned to the kitchen. She followed, her eyes widening as she saw the lasagna.

"You made this yourself?"

The shock in her voice made him chuckle. "Yes. I invited you for a home-cooked meal. What'd you think that would be?"

"I don't know." She shrugged. "I thought you'd probably buy takeout or something. Or maybe grill some steaks."

"I didn't think you liked beef." Taking the salad from the fridge, he placed it on the table. "And almost everyone loves Italian food, so I figured it'd be a safe thing to make. This is my grandfather's recipe. My father's dad. He used to make it all the time for family get-togethers."

"Wow. Handsome, sexy and a cook, too." She grinned at him as if she knew the effect her words had on his libido. "You're quite the package."

Though restraining himself from touching her had become increasingly difficult, he kept his hands busy with the food. After removing the loaf of garlic bread from the oven, he sliced it and placed it on the table next to the salad.

"Have a seat," he told her, taking his own. "We'll have salad and bread while the lasagna cools a little."

The wine—something about which he wasn't the slightest bit knowledgeable—turned out to be a perfect match. Silently he thanked the blind luck that had prompted him to choose this bottle.

They ate and talked and laughed. He loved the way she devoured her meal without the faintest pretense of nibbling at her food the way some of the other women he'd dated had. Of course, he'd never cooked for anyone else either.

Finally she pushed her plate away. "That was amazing," she said, her eyes sparkling. "I'm stuffed. I couldn't eat another bite."

"Too bad," he teased. "Because I have the most amazing tiramisu."

"You baked?"

He had to laugh at her shock. "No. There's a limit to what I can do. I picked some up at the store. Believe it or not, their bakery is top-notch."

"Maybe later," she said. "After some of this food settles."

As he gathered up their plates, she jumped up to help. He waved her away. "This will just take a few minutes. Have another glass of wine and relax. I'll join you when I'm done."

"I want to help," she insisted.

"I don't have a dishwasher," he warned her. "But if you really want to help, would you rather wash or dry?"

To his surprise, she wanted to wash. Working side by side, he marveled at how domestic the scene felt. As if they were already a committed couple. She hummed while she washed, which made him think she might feel the same.

Once the chore was done, they went back to the living room. Again, he tried to rehearse what he wanted to say. And just like before, he couldn't come up with much. Best to talk from his heart, he thought.

"There's something I've been meaning to talk to you about," he began. She'd taken a seat on his couch, clearly expecting him to sit with her. Instead, he paced.

"What's wrong?" she asked, sounding alarmed. "You seem agitated. And to be honest, that 'we need to talk' statement makes me think you're about to show me the door and tell me you don't want to see me again."

Stunned, he stared. "*That's* the conclusion you came to? After the meal and the invite to my apartment?"

Though she had the grace to look a bit sheepish, she lifted her chin. "If that's not what you want to discuss with me, then what is?"

"I want a commitment." Damn. He hadn't meant to blurt out the words like that, but he didn't want her getting any other wrong ideas.

"You what?" And then she smiled, a brilliant, dazzling smile that left no doubt she not only understood what he'd said, but that she liked it.

"I want a commitment," he repeated. "You and me. I don't want to be just friends who make love. I want more."

"Like what?" she asked calmly, though her eyes sparkled. Was she actually enjoying this?

He hoped so. Because from what he already knew about her, if she didn't like the idea of them being committed, she would have clearly and plainly said so.

"Mates." Emboldened, he said the word without thinking, before realizing she might not know what that meant to a Shifter. "Exclusive," he added. "You and me."

She considered for a moment, just long enough to make his heart stutter in his chest. Then she pushed herself up off the couch and launched herself at him, catching him so unprepared he almost didn't catch her.

But he did. He always would. And as she wrapped herself around him, he knew he had his answer.

He kissed her then, and as she opened her mouth to him he realized he wanted no misunderstandings. "Wait." Raising his head, he struggled to control his breathing. "I need an answer."

"I just gave you one," she murmured, wiggling suggestively against his obvious arousal. "But I'm guessing you want to hear it in words. So, yes, I'd love to be your mate. And yes, I do understand what the word *mate* means."

Staring down at her upturned face, at the mischief lurking in her gorgeous eyes, his chest ached. "Well, then, I might as well take this one step further. I love you, Shayla."

When she started to speak, he held up his hand. "You don't have to say it back. I mean it. And I wanted you to know."

"Zach." She smacked him in the arm, shaking her head slowly. "You know me. I'd never say words like that unless I meant them."

"Good." Struggling to hide the crushing disappointment he felt, he swallowed. "I don't ever want you to pretend something you don't feel."

"Oh, I won't." Her arch look and airy smile confused him. "Because I love you, too. If you weren't so busy trying to convince yourself otherwise, you'd have realized that a long time ago."

They kissed then, and one thing became another until they both completely forgot about the tiramisu.

One month later

Shayla had never been happier. Though she would never forget her earlier relationship with Richard, loving Zach was like a lasting and all-consuming blaze. They were each other's missing puzzle piece, and she could no longer imagine life without him. She had no doubt that she and Zach were meant to be together forever.

A few days after they'd agreed to commit to each other, she'd taken a swim back to Coral and checked with her brother. Ion, Nantha and Teredia were all in prison awaiting trial, along with others who'd been part of the group to overthrow the crown.

Despite Merc's offering, Shayla had declined to visit Teredia. She told her brother she needed to put that part of her life behind her and move forward, and then had shown him the ring Zach had given her.

She'd also shown her parents, who claimed not to be surprised. Her mother had wept, and Shayla could have sworn even her father's eyes got shiny.

"We were worried you'd never find happiness again," her mother cried. The two of them had wrapped Shayla up in a group hug, their love and joy for her palpable.

Once the shock of the news had settled in, Blythe had wanted to talk weddings, but Shayla promised her she'd discuss that with her later. She only wanted a small, intimate ceremony, close friends and family. Though clearly disappointed, her mother had agreed.

When she left her parents' house, instead of heading home to Galveston, Shayla paid a visit to Ion, aware both Zach and June would want to know how he was doing. The underwater prison where he was being held was luxurious, more like a resort hotel than a human prison, though Ion couldn't leave. The guards bowed to her, which made her feel funny, but quickly buzzed her in.

Ion appeared rested, the stress lines gone from his face and his posture relaxed. When she entered his cell, he'd jumped from his bunk, brows raised in surprise. He told her that his lawyer was working on getting him released on bail, though he wanted Shayla to tell June he wouldn't be allowed to visit her until he'd been acquitted. She decided not to break the news to him that June had left town, aware it wasn't her story to tell.

After she'd told him about her and Zach's engagement, at first Ion had no reaction and then, in keeping with his bizarre behavior, he'd laughed out loud, acting pleased. He'd hugged her and offered his congratulations, expressing sorrow that he wouldn't be out in time to attend the wedding. She told him they'd miss him and promised to send a video of the ceremony. Medical tests had been ordered, but the results weren't back yet.

When she got back home, she immediately phoned Zach. He'd hurried over, arriving at her front door less than thirty minutes after her call. Zach had gone back to work, so they didn't get to see each other as much as they liked. He'd finally agreed to give up his apartment and move into her beach house with her, but not until after they were married. Which he hoped would be sooner rather than later, since his lease was up at the end of the month.

His reasoning had made her grin.

Zach had been both relieved and saddened when she'd passed Ion's words along to him. He'd promised to let his mother know, since she was going to try and fly home to attend their wedding ceremony. They'd decided not to wait, both certain and aware they shouldn't waste any time. Life was far too short and unpredictable.

They'd talked it out, both agreeing they wanted something small. She wanted to wed on her pier, an idea he loved. Together, they'd chosen a date, made a guest list, hired a local florist and purchased their wedding finery.

This wedding would be exactly the way she'd always dreamt of. Not some pompous formal ceremony in Coral, but something reflective of both their personalities. They'd decided on a simple wedding, to be held at her home on the pier as the sun had begun to set. Dusk would enable their Vampire friends to attend.

And now the day had come. The wedding would be in a few short hours. Behind them, the florist and her staff worked feverishly to handle the decorations. Shayla refused to get involved, telling the decorator she had confidence in however she chose to decorate.

Instead, she and Zach sat outside, at the very end of her pier, right where they'd be married. Zach exhaled, his contentment obvious in his relaxed posture and calm expression. The sun made his dark blond hair golden, lighting up his skin and turning his light blue eyes the rich color of her sea. His hip bumped hers, making her smile. The tide was in, which meant they could sit on the end of her dock and their feet could dangle below the surface of the water. She felt...satisfied. More than that. Happy. Aware that she was exactly where she was supposed to be, and with whom. The vows would only be a formality, because in their hearts, she and Zach were already committed.

Inside the house, June had started baking, insisting she could make a cake as beautiful as any bakery. Shayla had shrugged and let her, because one less detail to worry about was a good thing. She and Zach had picked up June at the airport that morning and now they had a little time before the other guests arrived. Zach's coworkers and friends would be here in a little over an hour, giving her family plenty of time to make their appearance. Once they showed up, Shayla would go up to her room and get dressed.

"Any time now," Zach muttered, glancing at his watch. Shayla kissed the side of his neck, loving the way this made him shiver.

As if on cue, Merc appeared, rising out of the water in the dramatic fashion he'd perfected when they were teens. "I brought someone to see you," he said, smiling.

A woman appeared, her heart-shaped face and long-lashed eyes glistening with seawater.

"Shayla, meet Lanessa," Merc announced. "She and I are now betrothed."

"What?" Shayla scrambled up, smiling. "When did this happen? Congratulations! Welcome to the family."

Zach echoed her sentiment.

"Thank you both." The beautiful Mermaid turned her large eyes on him before looking back at Shayla. "I'm sorry, I don't mean to stare. I've never met a Shape-shifter before."

"You need to get my brother to bring you to Broken Chains," Shayla told her. "It's a paranormal bar here in Galveston. You can meet Shape-shifters and even Vampires there, plus dance to live music."

She turned her gaze on Merc. "Will you take me later?"

"Of course," he agreed. "Maybe after the reception."

"Um…" Shayla smiled. "The reception is at Broken Chains. That's where we met. Where else would we hold it?"

"Perfect." Magnificent as always, her brother flipped the end of his glistening fish tail. "Can you hand me a towel or a pair of shorts, please?" He glanced at his companion. "And Lanessa will need something, as well."

Because they'd been waiting for her family, Shayla was prepared. She reached into a basket behind her, retrieving two beach towels, a swimsuit cover-up for Lanessa that she'd been going to give her mom and a pair of men's swim trunks for her brother. Luckily, she'd brought extras, since she wasn't sure what other relatives her parents might bring.

Then she took off for her room, where her dress hung in a plastic bag. She slipped it on, loving the way the lacy sheath hugged her curves. She'd decided to wear her hair long, with one large white flower as her only ornament. She'd carry a bouquet of similar flowers.

Maddie and Carmen arrived together, hurrying up to her room and squealing as they caught sight of Shayla in her white minidress. "You know it's bad luck for the groom to see the bride before the ceremony," Maddie whispered. "So stay up here and don't let Zach see you."

Shayla only shrugged. "We're different. We've already

spent the day together. We didn't see the logic in making one of us hide out until we're married."

"I concur," the ever-practical Carmen agreed. "Makes everything go much more smoothly."

Pursing her lips, Maddie shook her head. "At least he hasn't seen you in this dress, right?"

Slowly, Shayla nodded. "I wanted to surprise him."

"Perfect!" Maddie smoothed her dress down, glancing at Carmen and frowning a little. "It's weird how two women can wear the exact same dress and look totally different."

For her two bridesmaids, Shayla had chosen dresses that appeared to be made of sea foam. The simple, classic design flattered both her friends.

"I look like a slutty nurse," Maddie muttered, "while she manages to somehow look classy."

Both Shayla and Carmen laughed. "You look beautiful," Shayla hurried to reassure her.

Her mom and dad arrived shortly after that, both beaming with happiness. Her mother only poked her head into Shayla's room, oohing over her dress, before hurrying outside to join her husband. Shayla and Zach had set up some folding chairs on the pier, the florist had decorated them, and once Zach's coworkers arrived, everyone took their seats.

The officiant, a friend of Carmen who appeared to be a Vampire, swept past everyone in a long robe that might have been a replica or might have been several centuries old. She scanned the crowd before nodding to signal she was ready.

Shayla watched from her window. A soft tap on her door meant her father had arrived to walk her down the aisle.

Seeing her, he beamed. "You look stunning. Every bit a royal princess."

She took his arm, aware he meant well. "Thanks, Dad."

The music started to play. They'd decided to go old school and use the typical wedding march. As Shayla stepped outside, she focused on Zach waiting next to the officiant, his powerful, muscular body standing tall and straight and handsome as sin. When he saw her, his rugged expression softened. The blaze of warmth in his eyes let her know he found her beautiful. She was glad. She'd chosen her dress with only him in mind.

With her arm in her father's she made her way to the end of the pier. Even the stern-faced officiant smiled as her father released her arm. There'd be no giving away in this ceremony. Shayla had been adamant on that. She gave herself to Zach quite freely and joyfully, with her heart full.

The officiant cleared her throat. Shayla and Zach took up their positions on either side of her. As they did, the wind gusted, sending up a spray of seawater on them, though the moisture barely touched her dress.

"Look," Maddie said from her other side, pointing. Shayla turned to see. Out in the open ocean, a large waterspout spun, purple and gray and green. It swirled and dipped, coming closer and putting on a show before disappearing back out to sea.

As soon as it vanished, the wind died down, and the sea became calm and smooth as glass.

"Poseidon," Merc said, making everyone who wasn't Merfolk laugh, thinking Merc made a joke. The Merfolk knew better. Shayla's father appeared especially pleased, making her wonder if he'd invited Poseidon to her wedding.

And he'd come. Wide-eyed, Shayla dipped her chin in homage. She felt honored that the Sea God had blessed her wedding. She caught Zach's eye and smiled, her heart full of love and joy.

And then, with the sun setting orange and red over the water, she and Zach spoke their vows.

Maddie caught the bouquet, a feat that clearly surprised her. Then they all piled into the bus Zach had rented and made their way to Broken Chains, to wind down the celebration in the place where it had all begun.

* * * * *

*Be sure to check out Karen Whiddon's
next exciting shifter romance
FINDING THE TEXAS WOLF,
available in June 2018 from Harlequin Nocturne!*

*And for more stories of the Pack,
try these otherworldly tales:*

*HER GUARDIAN SHIFTER
TEMPTING THE DRAGON
BILLIONAIRE WOLF*

*Available now wherever
Harlequin books and ebooks are sold!*

Get 2 Free Books,

HARLEQUIN
ROMANTIC suspense

Plus 2 Free Gifts—
just for trying the
Reader Service!

Get 2 Free Books,
Plus 2 Free Gifts—
just for trying the Reader Service!

Get 2 Free Books,
Plus 2 Free Gifts—
ust for trying the Reader Service!